For my Spaceman, who believed even when I didn't.

SEDITION

E. M. Wright

PROLOGUE

At first, she was aware only of the heat: pleasant, wonderfully warm, like being cradled in the arms of her mother. But then it grew hotter, blistering her skin, searing the backs of her legs, her neck. She shrieked, but the sound was smothered by the smoke, choked by the absence of oxygen in the air. She arched her back, trying to get away from the heat, but something pressed upon her chest, keeping her tiny, heaving body pinned.

Images returned to her, flashes of memory, ugly glimpses of the events that had led up to this moment. Mother and Father screaming at one another. The oil lamp getting knocked to the floor. Fire, bright orange, crackling, devouring everything in sight. Shrieks. Darkness. And now, this. This searing pain, the pressure on her chest, the smoke filling her eyes and lungs and throat. She lifted her head enough to glimpse the charred beam that lay across her chest, weighing her down. She moved her hands, trying to make it budge, only to realize her left hand would not move at all. She could not even feel her fingers.

She glanced to her left and froze, staring. Her stomach

lurched into her throat. Where her left arm should have been, there was just a bloody stump. She couldn't remember losing the limb, couldn't feel any pain, but her stomach roiled at the sight of the blood. The little girl turned her head away from the horrible sight and wretched.

A whimper rose in her throat, despite the sting of the smoke. Where were Mother and Father? Why didn't they come for her?

She understood a moment later, as more flashes of ugly memory returned. Mother's skirt catching fire. Father batting at the flames, his waistcoat catching... The knowledge weighed on her young heart: Mother and Father had died in the blaze. They were not coming. She was trapped. Alone. And *no one* would ever come for her.

The little girl coughed weakly, her tiny body expending what little energy it had left to expel the smoke from her lungs. The air was so dense with soot that her next breath was just as noxious as the last.

"Hello?" A voice broke through the sounds of crumbling wood and crackling flames: low, unfamiliar, and wary.

Her eyes widened. There was someone out there! *Mother? Father?* No, the voice was more sophisticated than any she knew. She opened her mouth to cry out, to exclaim, "Yes! I am here! Help me!" But only a weak croak emerged from a throat too parched to call for help. She was beginning to see black spots dancing at the edges of her vision, their darting movements distracting her from the urgency of answering whomever had called out.

Her eyes had nearly drifted shut when the man appeared, kneeling beside her. He had auburn, curly hair and copper stubble across his chin. His kind, forest green eyes crinkled at the corners. "Hello, little one," he said gently. Strong hands lifted the charred beam from where it lay across her chest, relieving the pressure. A rush of air surged from her lips, emerging as a half-cry, half-sob.

"Shh," he soothed her, placing one gentle hand against her forehead. "Hush, my child. Lie still. Everything shall be all right."

She stared at him, small eyes wide and wondering. Beneath the soot on her cheeks, her face was pale with the pain.

Gently, he lifted her into his arms, pausing whenever she whimpered to make sure he was not hurting her. Finally, he rose, cradling the tiny, damaged girl in his arms like a baby, and carried her from the burned wreckage of her home.

CHAPTER ONE

The students of Grafton's School of Mechanicks followed their guide deeper into the newly opened London Museum of Bioclockwork. The building was huge, regal in a bare industrial sort of way. Their footsteps clattered across a stone floor inlaid with metal gilding: copper cogs elevated from functional to beautiful.

The students crowded together in their crisp school uniforms, daunted by the imposing glory of the soaring building. The group consisted of boys and young men, all bright-eyed, eagerly soaking up the information presented before them, and looking forward to the bright future they would have as clockmakers or mechanicks. Or, if they were very fortunate, as biomechanicks. But near the back of the group, the crinkle of crinoline and the sweep of a bustled skirt could be heard. A fierce-looking girl with a shock of bright red hair pulled into a tangled braid stood, her arms crossed, one hand covered with a black satin glove. Her expression was stony, somewhere between blank and cross. Beside her, a boy with unkempt dirty blond hair and a face that appeared to smile too much bounced from foot to foot, trying to see over the heads of the other students.

"Bioclockwork was first introduced to the field of mechanicks in the early 1820s, when a man named Vincentio Dolltevi created a clockwork hand for himself after losing his own in a factory accident. Little did Mr. Dolltevi know that his innovation would lead to the creation of a race who would become the labourers of the British Empire—"

"Slaves," the red-haired girl muttered to her friend. He glared and elbowed her teasingly.

"Shh, Taryn!" he whispered.

"If you will follow me this way..." The guide directed them into a hallway filled with glass cases. Huge glass windows on both sides of the hall let in plenty of light, and immense chandeliers dripping with candles illuminated any shadowy places that remained. "Look around, gentlemen, and you will see just a sampling of some of the most detailed biomechanicks available today," the guide intoned, his voice echoing in the space.

The tight-knit group scattered across the polished floor to various glass cases, murmuring and marveling at the objects they found inside. The red-haired girl held back, her face seemingly set in stone. Had anyone been watching closely, he might have noticed she was struggling not to display any emotion in her countenance. Her friend eagerly moved toward the nearest glass case, one free-standing on the floor with a pedestal inside. The girl followed him after only a few moments of hesitation, as though they were bound together by an invisible rope and it had pulled taut, dragging her along.

Within the glass case, on the pedestal, stood an intricate clockwork leg built from the knee down. The metal plating had been removed on one side, revealing the intricate mechanickal workings within. The girl stared not at the clockwork on display, but rather at the metal exterior plating of the prosthetic. It was scratched and scuffed, dented and worn. This was not something built for display. This was a true prosthetic. It had been worn by someone at some point before finding its way into this case. The girl paled, ever so slightly, and lifted her gloved left hand to her chest as if to cradle it.

The boys scattered throughout the museum soon congregated in front of a large glass case at the far end of the hall. They murmured amongst themselves, the sound hushed and awed. The red-haired girl and her friend were drawn along with the crowd, unable to resist their own curiosity.

They shoved their way to the front, ignoring the indignant taunts of their classmates. When they reached the front of the crowd, both students froze in their tracks. The red-haired girl's hand went to her mouth, the colour draining from her face. She looked as though she might swoon.

Behind the glass lay a boy, strapped to a wooden board like a dead beetle, his arms splayed, his head tilted back, jaw hanging slightly ajar. The boy's chest had been cut open, displaying a mess of gears and flesh. It was abundantly clear that the boy was dead, but for the first moment or two of observation, he appeared to still be breathing.

The red-haired girl turned, shoved through the crowd, and fled from the hall. Her hand was still pressed to her mouth.

Taryn leaned over the washbasin in the ladies' powder room, waiting for her stomach to settle. She knew she was missing the tour, but at this point she did not care. She couldn't get that biomaton boy in the glass case out of her head. Every time she thought of him, she felt more ill. Had he been vivisected there for the museum, or had he died without ever knowing what his fate would be? She hoped it was the latter.

Cognitively, Taryn understood the plight of the biomaton.

They were slaves, humans who needed clockwork parts in order to survive. Their modified bodies somehow made them less than human, and *that* was the part she did not understand. Why *weren't* they human? What did losing a limb and having it replaced have to do with one's humanity?

With trembling fingers, Taryn ran her right hand over its gloved fellow. The limb felt real enough, if colder and harder than one made of flesh and blood. But she knew it was not real. It was intricate clockwork, a biomaton's limb. Perhaps that was why she did not understand how they could treat the biomatons the way they did. Perhaps *she* was just as different as any of the slaves. But she couldn't quite accept that explanation. Since she was pulled off the streets by Royal (and, more accurately, by Lord Stokker, his father), no one had suspected her of being anything but human. Every so often, someone would ask her what she was hiding beneath that black satin glove, but she always answered them with a story about a scar. It was mostly true, too. She had lost her arm in a house fire when she was six years old. And she would have lost her life as well, had not some biomechanick happened by and saved her life with clockwork. At times she wasn't sure whether she was more grateful or resentful of him for that. Either way, it did not matter all that much. She did not remember him, and he had abandoned her to the streets, alone and frightened. She remembered the fire, and she remembered living on the streets, but between the two, a great expanse of memory was blank. She did not know what she had done or who she had been in those six years.

Taryn forced herself to breathe deeply, realizing why she had been so disturbed by the sight of the boy in the first place. It could just as easily have been her behind that glass, torn open to be gawked at by schoolboys and rich men. She took another deep breath. She was not a slave. No one would discover what she was. She was careful; she was safe at

Grafton's—safe with Lord Stokker and his son, Royal. There was no reason to panic like this.

Taryn drew one more deep breath and straightened up, forcing herself to banish the trepidation from her mind. She exited the powder room, finding herself back in the vast foyer of the museum. She had no desire to go back into that great maze, even to attempt to find her classmates. Who knew what other horrors awaited her in the curated depths of that place? So instead, she left the building and settled on the damp steps of the museum, plucking at the heavy, navy blue wool skirt of her Grafton's school uniform.

A few minutes passed, and then Taryn heard the door behind her swing open. Someone padded down the steps and sat to her right. "There you are, Tiger! I was afraid you were not coming back."

Taryn glanced at Royal, forcing a smile. Royal was one of her few friends in the world; the only reason she was here at all was because of Royal's kindness and his father's generosity. Still, even he did not know what she was, and she could not bear to imagine what would happen if he learned her secret. "I am sorry I disappeared," she answered him quietly. "I was disturbed by the displays."

"But you missed the most incredible displays of bioclockwork!" he exclaimed. His expressive brown eyes lit up with excitement.

She shook her head. Wisps of copper hair blew across her cheeks in the misty breeze. "I have seen slaves before. Are you finished?"

He glanced back at the doors of the museum.

Have you drunk your fill of blood? Taryn wanted to ask, but the words were too vicious for him, her one true friend, who did not know better than what he had been taught. Biomatons were just property, designed to be bought and sold.

"Aye," he finally sighed. "I have seen enough for this trip.

Shall we go and find ourselves a spot of afternoon tea?" He stood and offered her his hand, which she took with a crooked, forced smile.

"Please," she replied, though she was not actually hungry. But it *was* Saturday, and they had the afternoon to themselves. Afternoon tea would be as good as anything to get her mind off of what she had seen.

Taryn slipped her right hand into the crook of his arm, walking beside her friend. They traveled the worn, familiar streets of London side-by-side, lost in the sort of familiar quiet formed by long-standing friendships. They strolled along the cobblestone streets, dodging brougham cabs and pedestrians headed home with their shopping.

As Royal was the son of a lord, he always had spare pocket money, and he shared it generously. Taryn was thankful; the lean year of living on the streets, begging or stealing what she could and enduring without the rest, was still all too vivid in her mind.

Taryn glanced up as they passed one of the many clockwork foundries in the city, its fat brick smokestacks belching black smoke into the sky. A low-frequency rumble rattled her teeth as a merchant's airship passed overhead. *It is 1864,* she mused silently. *With all our technological advances, one would think we could be civil to each other by now.*

They reached a tea parlour that offered an excellent afternoon tea for fairly cheap, and were seated in a bright room by a young man wearing a tuxedo. Taryn allowed Royal to seat her in a rigid whitewashed chair, examining the heavy curtains that cascaded over the tall windows and the pale, flowered wallpaper. Royal ordered a full afternoon high tea, and the waiter left them alone.

"Have you given any thought to the spring holiday yet?" Royal asked.

"What about it?" she asked, running her finger around the

scalloped rim of the empty china teacup.

"Well, you *are* spending it with us, correct? My father has business in Switzerland, but we may explore the city…" He trailed off, his face clouding over. "Why are you looking at me like that?"

Her face twisted. "Roy, I never feel like I belong when I am with your father. All those high society fetes and long dinners —I do not belong in that kind of life."

"Nonsense! Taryn, you did well at finishing school. You are always the highlight of our Christmas parties."

She shook her head. "Just because I did well does not mean I enjoy it. I am always afraid of making a fool of myself and revealing that even with all my education, I am still just a street urchin. Then everyone will know your father's charity project was worthless, after all."

The great Lord Stokker was famous for his charity projects. He pulled bright children out of orphanages and off the streets, then placed them in high profile schools to "civilise" them. Many of these children grew up to become famous inventors, mechanicks, or doctors. When Royal brought Taryn home, gave her a bath, a clean frock, and a meal, and then introduced her to his father, Lord Stokker had recognized her potential immediately. She was just twelve years old at the time. Lord Stokker sent Taryn to finishing school, then signed her up for the mechanicks program at Grafton's School of Mechanicks when she showed aptitude for clockwork. It was not entirely unheard of for a girl to be educated as a mechanick, and it was even becoming fashionable for upper class families to hire women to work on their biomatons and other mechanickal devices in their homes. Still, Taryn was the first girl to attend Grafton's School of Mechanicks, and she received both praise and scorn for it.

"You are not my father's project," Royal responded sharply. "You are a part of the family. If you do not want to attend any grand parties or suppers, then we do not have to attend. We can explore Switzerland together, and do nothing we do not want to do." He smiled his crooked, disarming smile.

Taryn sighed. "Very well, Royal. You do not give me much of a choice. We shall spend our holiday in Switzerland." She gave him a gentle smile, knowing, despite her reluctance, that she would enjoy the trip. Just as long as Royal's rocky relationship with his father did not get in the way.

"Excellent," Royal grinned. The waiter approached, bearing a tower covered in pastries and dainty tea sandwiches, as well as a shining kettle filled with boiling water for their tea. He set the tower on their table, then poured the boiling water into the teapot, delicately steeping the Earl Grey leaves. The scent billowed up in steaming clouds, rich and heady. Taryn breathed deeply, the floral smell evoking warm memories of Royal's mother before she died. The woman had practically adopted Taryn as her own, even asking that she call her Mother. Her death had devastated the entire family, including Taryn. It had been two and a half years since then, but the scent of Earl Grey always brought back memories of her.

Taryn watched Royal add sugar and milk to both teacups after the waiter left. She lifted a cucumber sandwich from the tower, using only her right hand, as she could not remove the glove hiding her prosthetic and it would be poor manners to use that hand. Besides, she did not want to dirty the glove.

"My father will be glad to hear you will be joining us," Royal said, passing Taryn her teacup. "He loves you. He speaks of you all the time." Royal rolled his eyes. "The best thing I have ever done in his eyes is bring you home."

"That is not true," Taryn replied quietly. "He loves you, in his own way."

Royal scoffed. "Not so much as he loves you. I have received exactly one letter from him since we returned to school, and it was the one telling me we would be spending the holiday in Switzerland, and would I please invite you to come along." His lip twisted in an expression of disgust, and he quickly hid the expression behind his teacup.

"Have you written him? Have you told him anything about your classes, or your end-of-year project? Anything at all?" Taryn questioned gently.

"I gave up years ago," he muttered. "I do not think he ever reads them."

"You must put in an effort if you wish to have a relationship with him," Taryn said quietly, casting her eyes down to her teacup. She felt somewhat hypocritical saying so, as much of the way a family worked was an unfathomable mystery to her, but even so, she knew she was right. Royal's father was rough around the edges, but with effort on both sides she thought they could still be on good terms.

Royal reached for a scone and smeared it with clotted cream and marmalade. Taryn knew him well enough to recognize he was not willing to discuss the subject any further. The scone was pale and fluffy, and looked soft in his large hands and slender, dexterous fingers. He had the hands of a mechanick, the kind of hands she'd been inexplicably drawn to for as long as she could remember. It went all the way back to the blank spot in her memory, before she lived on the streets, before her twelfth year.

"I met a biomechanick today," Royal said casually before taking a huge bite of the scone.

"Did you?" Taryn had to struggle to keep her expression flat. A powerful ire bubbled in her stomach at the mere mention of a man who turned other human beings into slaves. She didn't dare let that anger boil to the surface.

"Mhmm." Royal nodded. "He was in the museum. I did not speak to him for long, as the guide moved our group along too quickly, but Alfred told me he is rather famous."

"Famous? For building biomatons?"

"For building strange, *dangerous* biomatons," Royal replied eagerly. His brown eyes lit up with excitement.

"What do you mean?"

"The biomatons this man builds do not have the dampers required by the Biomaton Safety Act. They are built with their humanity still intact!"

Taryn frowned. "Does that not seem absurd to you? To be required to build biomatons in such a way that they are not even considered human any longer?"

Royal's expression dimmed. "Tar, we have had this conversation before. Biomatons are machines built for work."

"Machines that were once human!" Taryn exclaimed. "Why does that not bother you?"

"Because…" Royal shook his head. "They are given a new chance at life. They are given a place to live and food to eat and clothes to wear. It seems rather a good deal to me."

"So, if I had lost my arm in the fire and had been turned into a biomaton, you would not think I was human, either?"

Royal frowned. "That is different. You would not be Taryn any longer."

"Who would I be?"

"Just…another biomaton."

"And that is a *good* thing?"

"It would be to you and to whomever you worked for."

"Belonged to," Taryn corrected. "Whomever I *belonged* to."

"But that did not happen. You are Taryn. And you are still my best friend, even with your radical views." Royal smiled crookedly at her. "Only, do not let my father hear you going on like that. I do not think he would take it well."

Taryn nodded, subdued for the moment. She tried not to bring up the biomaton issue with Royal, though occasionally it did cause a row between them. Each time they argued about it, Taryn found herself tempted to tug her glove off and display her prosthetic, to shout, "Look, *I am* a biomaton! Am *I* inhuman?" Yet she knew to do so would be tantamount to suicide. She would lose everything, and for what? Just to gain the upper hand in an argument. It was not worth it. Taryn fell quiet, watching the other people in the room converse, knowing that if they were aware of what she was, they would never be so serene.

Grafton's School of Mechanicks was located on the Strand, in an ancient stone building that had once been a private residence for a lesser-known member of the royal family. The building had been acquired and converted by Lord Grafton at the turn of the nineteenth century, the servants' quarters converted to dorms, the vast house turned from luxurious suites to spartan classrooms. The grounds weren't large or remarkable, but the central London location more than made up for it. A great clock had been installed in the school, a piece designed by a former student, and its ticking ruled the students' lives like a massive heart beating at the centre of the community.

Taryn retired to her room early that evening, muttering an excuse about having homework. In reality, there wasn't any pressing schoolwork requiring her attention. She needed to work on her prosthetic. Not for the first time, she was thankful to be the only girl at Grafton's; it meant she did not have to hide from a roommate.

Having had no real maintenance on her clockwork arm since sometime before her twelfth birthday, Taryn had been forced to learn the art of repairing it herself. She had some natural intuition for clockwork, and had studied her arm so many times she knew it intimately. Still, it wasn't in the condition it once had been. The arm was a touch too small and did not match her other hand anymore, try though she might to "grow" it along with the rest of her body. The difference wasn't enough to attract attention, and her go-to answer when she was questioned was that the fire in which her parents had died had left her deformed. The lack of access to decent clockwork on the streets had forced her to make do with broken, rusty pieces; whatever she could find that would work. When Royal had pulled her off the streets, though, she'd suddenly had access to better parts, better clockwork with which to rebuild her prosthetic. It worked well now, though she had to oil it regularly to keep the mismatched pieces from sticking or grinding together.

Tonight, she was having trouble with her ring finger. The joint creaked a little when she moved it, and she needed to oil it to ensure the pieces fit together smoothly in order to stop the sound. She couldn't have her finger creaking at an inopportune moment, revealing her secret. Slowly, Taryn drew the black silk glove from her clockwork hand, checking over her shoulder to reassure herself that the door was still closed and locked. She stared at her arm, still in awe of its intricacies even after all this time. The prosthetic limb was built to seem as human as possible. The frame was made of a fine mesh of gold and bronze filigree, essentially impervious to rust. It had been carefully shaped to mimic muscle and bone structure. Within the frame, the mechanisms that actually allowed her to use the arm as she would a real limb ticked away. If she followed the arm all the way up, it entered her shoulder, slipping through a thick leather pad that kept the metal from chafing or cutting her skin. The clockwork was attached to the tendons, muscles, and ligaments that remained after the fire. As far as she understood, that was how it worked. But the prosthetic was clearly so much more complicated than what she understood. The man who'd turned her into this hybrid was clearly a mechanickal genius.

Her graft had been a part of her for so long, sometimes she felt her fingertips really were sensitive, that her arm retained physical feeling. She knew this was impossible, but sometimes her arm *ghosted,* her brain tricking her into detecting sensation even where there was none. This was happening even as she worked on the joint of her ring finger, her fingers prickling as she bumped them. It aggravated her, but she'd long ago learned that there was nothing to do but wait it out.

Taryn flexed the finger, listening for the telltale squeak of mechanisms misaligned. She was greeted instead with silence, and she smiled, satisfied she'd managed to fix it. Her secret was safe for another day.

Sighing, Taryn sat on the edge of her bed, the image of the biomaton boy in the museum returning, as if it were burned on the back of her eyes. It still bothered her, still made her feel sick, still made her angry. She wondered about the boy—who he had been, who he'd belonged to, what he'd felt when they told him he was going to be a museum display.

She knew they probably hadn't told him anything. The men who owned him did not even believe he was human. They would not have told him what they had planned. Most likely, he had been strapped to a table, chloroformed, and simply never woke up.

She needed to stop thinking about it. It wasn't as though she had never seen a biomaton before. She attended a school for mechanicks, after all. Hundreds of boys from upper class families attended Grafton's with her, and most of them owned biomatons. Even Royal's family owned a few. But simply seeing them serve their families was different than seeing the extent of the cruelty that could be inflicted upon them.

She would not think about it any longer. She reached out and shut off the gas lamp above her bed, taking deep, meditative breaths. Just before she fell asleep, she thought she heard someone moving outside her window.

CHAPTER TWO

"Miss Roft? *Miss Roft,* if you would be so good as to join us back on planet Earth."

Taryn started, lifting her eyes from the place where she'd sketched a biomaton with his chest torn open. She'd been lost in a daydream, and now she had to struggle to regain her place in the class. Two seats ahead of her, a young man glanced back, snickering.

"Would you like to share whatever is so fascinating?" the professor, Dr. Carter, questioned.

Taryn shook her head. "No, sir." Quickly, she crumpled the paper with the drawing on it.

As Dr. Carter returned to his lecture, Royal leaned over in the seat beside her. "Bad time for daydreaming, Tiger," he teased.

Taryn kicked him beneath the desk, giving him a disapproving glare. She settled back in her chair, trying to pay attention to the lecture. It wasn't all that interesting, though, and she found her attention drifting to the drawing crumpled on her desk. Almost without thinking, she'd drawn the boy in the museum. He wouldn't leave her alone. He'd haunted her dreams the night before, and now he followed her during the day. Taryn toyed with the paper, fingering its rigid edges. She wasn't even listening to her professor any longer. What she'd seen had captured her, so arresting and shocking that now it would not let her go.

Taryn barely heard the chimes of the great clock that stood at the heart of the school, but as soon as she became aware of them, she roused herself, gathered her things, and rose to her feet.

"Miss Roft, please remain after class," Dr. Carter said loudly over the noise of the rest of the class preparing to go.

A few murmurs raced around her, boys laughing at her for being asked to stay behind. Royal made a face at her. "What did you do this time, Tar?"

"Nothing!" she hissed.

"Dr. Carter does not think so," Royal grinned. "You have gotten yourself into trouble again."

Taryn jabbed him in the arm with the sharp nib of her fountain pen, giving him a scowl before moving toward the front of the classroom.

"Good luck," Royal called, letting her know he had only been teasing.

Dr. Carter was seated behind his desk, staring disapprovingly at her over his spectacles. His hands were clasped upon the desk. Fine, soft hands. Hands that had never seen a day of work. Hands that had never seen the inside of a grandfather clock. The professors here at Grafton's were all the same: upper class men who had never performed manual labour. A few were true mechanicks, with the rough, scarred hands that came from years of working with sharp clockwork parts. Those men were the teachers Taryn liked best, and for the most part, they liked her in return.

"You asked to see me, sir?" Taryn asked, her school books clutched to her chest.

In response, Dr. Carter raised an assignment. Taryn recognized it as the essay she had turned in the week before. Scrawled across the top in red ink were the words *Abysmal. Rewrite.* Taryn swallowed hard, feeling her heart sink. She worked hard to get high grades and prove to Lord Stokker that he had made a good choice in funding her education. Not only that, though the second reason was never so clear in her mind, but she felt that good grades proved she was *not* anything less than human, even if only to herself.

"I am disappointed in you, Miss Roft. Your work has gotten consistently worse. You should be working harder than this if you truly want to become a mechanick." His eyes narrowed. "Lord Grafton made a special exception for you to attend here, *only* because Lord Stokker *insisted* you were bright enough to compete with the other students. But you must work harder, Miss Roft. Will you ruin the chance for your sisters to attend this school as well?"

Taryn shook her head. "No, sir." She was furious with him for equating her performance with all future opportunities for other girls to attend Grafton's. It was too much pressure for her alone to determine the future of women in mechanicks. And she'd worked hard on that paper. The way he lectured her, it was clear he assumed she hadn't even tried.

"Then work harder." He slid the paper across the desk to her. "I want you to rewrite this essay. I shall not accept this."

Inwardly, Taryn groaned, but she didn't allow herself to show her frustration. She just took the paper, speaking through gritted teeth. "Yes, sir."

"I expect the revisions by Thursday. You may go."

Taryn stalked from the room, hardly aware she was holding her breath. Royal was waiting for her outside in the hall, leaning against the wall, swinging his arms by his sides.

"So tell me, Tiger," he said, grinning, "how much trouble are you in this time?"

Taryn scowled. "He is making me rewrite my essay. He said I do not work hard enough—"

Royal snatched the essay from her hands, flipping through it. "Abysmal? That is not like you."

"Dr. Carter does not like me," Taryn complained. "He always gives me poor marks."

"Then you must prove to him you do not deserve them." Royal handed the essay back to her. "But first, it is supper time." He began to strut down the hall, leaving her to follow, as he knew she would.

"How can you always be so hungry?" Taryn questioned, hurrying to catch up with him. Her brilliant red hair streamed down her back, nearly to her waist. The current fashion was to wear one's hair up in complicated knots, but Taryn chose to wear her own locks down, or in braids. The heels of her pointed shoes clacked against the stone floor, echoing down the hall.

Royal smirked. "I suspect I am hollow inside. The only way to fill the void within myself is to eat."

"I remember that feeling," Taryn said quietly, more to herself than to him. Her mind cast back to her time on the streets, where the few ha'pennies she managed to beg off the passersby were all she had, and most vendors refused to even sell leftovers to her. At that time, she'd never felt full, no matter how much food she bought or dug from the bins behind bakeries and restaurants.

Royal looked back at her, a strange, unidentifiable emotion in his eyes. "Taryn, that is over now. Come on. We are missing supper."

⚙

The dining hall was on the bottom floor of the main building of Grafton's School of Mechanicks. It was a wide stone hall with long wooden tables, which were laden with food delivered by the kitchen staff (made mostly of biomatons, Taryn knew), shared family-style between the students. Tonight, it was shepherd's pie, piping hot and wafting mouthwatering odors of meat and spices, along with freshly baked bread rolls and steamed vegetables. Taryn and Royal found seats at the end of a long table. Royal served up large helpings of supper for them both, shouting to be heard over the din of the other boys all chattering to one another.

"How is your clockwork project coming?"

They had to fabricate automatons for the final of their clockwork engineering class, without blueprints or instructions. Taryn had never attempted to build something on her own before, and the most complicated piece she'd ever worked on was her own arm. Taryn shook her head. "Not so well. I do much better with blueprints. How is yours coming?"

"I believe my idea is good, but I am struggling to make it work," Royal replied. "I think perhaps it is too complicated for my second year."

"Surely, you can figure it out?" Taryn questioned. As she spoke, she poured two cold, frothy glasses of apple cider for them both. "You are at the top of our class."

Royal smiled his lopsided smile. "If I do not figure it out, it will not be the end of the world. I *will* be disappointed, though."

Taryn nodded, thoughtful. She savoured the good food and sharp cider. More than that, she savoured not having to worry about where her next meal would come from. Though she'd only lived on the streets for a year, the experience had shaped her profoundly. Whether this was because it had forced her to become who she was today simply to survive, or because it was the first thing she remembered after the missing years of her life, she did not know. Perhaps that great emptiness in her mind that came before the streets made that year all the more vivid to her.

"Hello, street rat." A grinning boy with white-blonde hair sat too close on Taryn's left, so close he bumped against her clockwork arm. She quickly moved it to her lap, turning as much of her prosthetic away from him as she could so he would not accidentally discover her secret. She knew how much of a loudmouth this boy could be.

"Hello, Bennet," she muttered.

"Are you busy tomorrow night?" he questioned, pressing his leg against her skirt.

Taryn squeezed closer to Royal, feeling her face go red in frustration and embarrassment. "Yes, I am."

"What about the evening after that?" He reached over and grabbed her glass, drinking from it without asking. Taryn felt her fists clench.

"I am not going to supper with you, Bennet," she said slowly.

"Oh, come on, darling. It will be fun."

"I said no," Taryn answered. "I have told you *no* so many times now. And yet you *still* keep asking me. Why?"

He grinned, his remarkably straight teeth reminding her of a predator's snarl. "Because you are beautiful. I shall not stop asking until you say yes."

"I will not say yes," Taryn growled. "You may leave now."

He slipped an arm around her waist, tugging her toward him again. "Now, do not be so aloof. What is so wrong with me?"

Taryn shoved him away from her, so frustrated she temporarily forgot her secret. "Do not touch me!" she cried. The table fell silent, all eyes turning to watch the confrontation occur. Taryn could sense the hundreds of eyes like hot brands boring into her back. She hated the attention.

Royal leapt to her rescue. "She already said no, Bennet. Stop harassing her."

Bennet backed off, but not much. "Do you really need your benefactor's son to fight your battles for you?" he questioned, sneering at her.

Taryn glared. "What would your father think of you courting a street rat?"

Bennet smirked. "He does not need to know."

Taryn stood, head held high and eyes alight. "I am not some bawd to treat as you please," she hissed. "I will thank you not to approach me again."

Taryn turned and strode from the dining hall, amidst whoops and catcalls from the boys who'd observed the argument. Though she never would have believed it, she was very beautiful, and the boys at Grafton's were not blind to it. In a school full of boys, petticoats were bound to catch the eye— especially when worn by someone both feminine and strongly independent. But Taryn's attractiveness went beyond just her intelligence and the exotic hybrid of upper and lower class in her accent. Her eyes were a brilliant emerald green, and they sparkled brighter than the precious jewels they resembled when she laughed or got excited about a subject. Her copper hair fell nearly to her waist, and shone like fire in the sunlight. Her face was still gaunt from her years on the streets, keeping her cheekbones sharp and high. She seemed aloof and unattainable most of the time, which made her all the more desirable. She had been prepared for the attention before she came to the school, but even so, the boys' competitive advances sometimes became aggravating.

"You certainly told him!" Royal exclaimed, racing after her.

Taryn shuddered. "Bennet is a pig."

Royal nodded. "He cannot leave you alone, can he?"

She rubbed her forehead, exasperated. "That is the third proposition I have received from him this week."

"Tiger, you know you are no longer a street rat, right?" Royal said, his voice gentle and cautious.

"Of course. But that does not change what I am to them." She smiled wryly. "None of them see me as a true lady. There is not one boy here who would seriously consider courting me, let alone marriage." She scoffed. "No, to them I am merely a game, a girl to take to dinner to prove to your friends that you can."

Royal scowled. "That is not true. Not everyone thinks of you that way."

Taryn raised an eyebrow. "Show me one student who does not still see me as a vagabond, and I will believe you."

"*I* do not see you that way, Tiger."

She turned and looked at him, smiling crookedly. "You do not count. It is only because of you that I am not still living on the streets. You have never seen me as a street urchin."

Royal seemed to breathe a sigh of relief.

"But next time, if you told Bennet to bugger off a bit earlier, I would not mind." She sounded cross, but offered him a teasing smile.

"Next time," Royal answered, the slightest hint of something dark tinting his voice, "he will not even get close enough to touch you."

CHAPTER THREE

ON TUESDAY, CLASSES WERE CANCELLED FOR THE SECOND HALF of the day, as the professors were in meetings about a new grading style that had been introduced. Taryn found Royal in the library, where he was poring over a large, red leather-bound book.

"Look at this!" he hissed to her, tapping the page with a fingertip. "This is the biomechanick I met!"

Taryn leaned over the page, examining the black and white portrait of the man. He looked proud and bold, with hair that curled back over his temples and a slight smile that seemed almost arrogant, as if he held all the best cards in a high-stakes poker game. Taryn felt a rush of *déjà vu* as she examined the portrait. She shook the feeling off, telling herself it was silly. "I was going out for a walk," she said quickly. "Would you like to join me?"

Royal looked up at her. "Yes! Thank you, Tiger. I would enjoy a walk with you."

He stood, closing the book. Together, they left the library and walked across the open courtyard to one of the side doors in the wall that surrounded the campus. Taryn walked beside

Royal, breathing in the cool, damp air, the stench of the city strangely comforting to her. She could feel her clockwork churning beneath her skin, her heart throbbing beneath her breastbone. She felt alive, out here on the streets, in a way she never did when she was inside. That was the wonderful thing about Grafton's, she thought. The location was so central, and London so vast, all one needed to do was step out of the gate in order to lose herself in the labyrinthine streets.

She glanced at Royal, considering him, allowing herself to remember the first day they'd met, when he'd been no more than a boy in a preparatory school uniform, racing past the corner she'd hidden behind. Taryn had expected him to throw rocks at her, as the other boys his age did, or make crude comments, but instead, he had offered her his hand. She'd snapped at him, growling like a tiger, earning herself the nickname he was still so fond of using. But when he'd explained that he wanted to help, she'd felt inexplicably compelled to accept.

They turned a corner and entered a square, only to run into a wall of people. The crowd created a barrier of bodies and sound, beyond which Taryn could not see. A pit formed in her stomach.

"What is it? What are they doing?" Taryn questioned Royal, who stood a whole head above her and could see better over the crowd.

He hesitated a moment too long, his face going pale. "It—it is an auction, Taryn. Come, we should not be here." He took her arm, trying to pull her away.

"An auction of what?" she questioned, standing on tiptoe, trying to see. "Why are there so many people?"

"We should not be here," he repeated. "Let's go, Tiger, please."

"Why will you not tell me what is going on?"

The crowd shifted, and Taryn suddenly understood.

A makeshift platform had been set up in the middle of the square, raised above the crowd. Upon it stood four young men, as well as several larger, older men. The young men were standing near the front of the platform, their hands cuffed at the waist, chains tethering them together. They were naked from the waist up, their heads bowed, their feet unshod, but they looked clean and tidy. Each boy had a glittering prosthetic limb.

Sickness welled in Taryn's gut. She spun on her heel and ran, turning her back on the hideous sight. She did not even care if Royal followed her. She gathered her skirt up in her fists, aware that it was improper and yet no longer sane enough to care. She did not know why the sight had bothered her so—she had seen the auctions plenty of times before—but this time was different. This time she wanted to murder every person in that square in order to set those biomatons free.

"Tiger! Taryn! Slow down! Wait!" Royal exclaimed, racing after her. *"Taryn!"*

She slowed, or rather, forced herself to slow. Shaking and breathing hard, she clenched her hands into fists to hide their trembling. She stopped, her feet stumbling across the cobblestones, and stared at the ground, aware that Royal had stopped a few feet away. She could not raise her eyes.

"They were just boys," she said softly, her voice cracking. "Practically children."

"They were biomatons," Royal answered gently. "That is their lot in life."

Taryn shuddered. "But why? Why should they be forced to live like that? It is disgusting—" She broke off, covering her mouth with one hand. She knew she was becoming hysterical, but she could not help the horror that continued to flood her chest.

"That is just how it is, Taryn."

"But how can you just accept it? *Why* must we accept it?"

"Because it is the way of things," Royal replied, his voice low. "Because, if we do not accept it, we will fight in vain our entire lives. Sometimes we must accept things because that is all we can do."

Taryn did not agree with him. She believed in fighting for whatever one believed in, no matter how hopeless it seemed. But on the other hand, she knew there were already things she no longer fought, things she had not always believed in, but had been forced to accept. She'd once felt that way about her plight as a street urchin, her societal identity as a Victorian woman. But still, accepting something as appalling as the way biomatons were treated simply because she could not change it felt like giving up.

Taryn sighed, wringing her hands, fingering the chain of the pocket watch Royal had given her the year before for her birthday. "I am sorry for my reaction. I do not know why it shocked me so. I have seen the auctions before."

"I am not angry with you, Tiger. I knew it would bother you. That is why I tried to pull you away."

"If only they were not treated so poorly, perhaps it would not bother me so much," Taryn murmured, more to herself than to him. It was like telling herself a lie.

"Come on, Tiger. Let us get you walking again. Perhaps that will help you get your mind off it."

He took her by her right elbow, pulling her along down the street. She was surprised he had actually touched her, and realized he must have been truly perturbed by her outburst. Normally, she reacted so furiously if he touched her—terrified that if he did, he would discover her secret—that he very rarely reached out to her at all anymore, allowing her to initiate touch. At times she felt guilty for pushing him away like that, but she knew it was better this way. It kept her safe. It kept him safe. Gently, she pulled her arm out of his grasp, but she smiled to show him she was not upset.

They walked in silence for a time, enjoying one another's company and the city they lived in. They walked away from the auction, leaving the people and the biomatons behind. Taryn tried to drive it from her mind, but was unable to fully forget. Instead, she thought about her classes, about the essay she still had not rewritten, about going to Switzerland with Royal and his father.

Around them, the townhouses and shops grew and tilted, like giants rising from the ground, leaning against one another to ease the weight of age on their shoulders. They passed a clock-maker's shop, the ticking of hundreds of clocks loud enough to be heard on the streets, and then a soaring residential home, its high brick walls accentuated with glass and copper. London was thriving, and Taryn knew it was thanks, in part, to biomatons.

"Your collar is not straight," Taryn said after noticing as they turned a corner.

Royal grinned his lopsided grin as he reached up to fix it. "What would I do without you, Taryn?"

She smiled back at him. "You would be a slob."

He mocked hurt, as if her words had really cut him. "I would not! I would manage very well. You offend me, my dear. I can take care of myself!"

"Of course, you can," Taryn teased. "Just as soon as you learn to tie your own cravat."

He gasped, and she ran ahead, tripping off the curb into the street before turning back to face him, laughing. "You know it is true!"

Royal grinned, and then his face paled, changing to an expression of abject horror. "Taryn!"

He was not looking at her, but through her. Behind her. Taryn turned, trying to see what had frightened him so. A huge black horse was barrelling toward her, the driver of the cab harnessed behind it yelling at her to get out of the way.

Taryn froze as panic welled inside her, turning her to stone. Someone grabbed her around the waist, tugging her out of the horse's path.

Taryn raised her eyes to the stranger, panting. Adrenaline muddled her mind, making her tremble. He stood a head taller than she, gazing down at her with the most piercing ice blue eyes she had ever seen. His hair was black, not exactly curly but wavy, and fell over his forehead but not quite into those piercing eyes. He wore a dark blue coat in the naval style, though he did not strike her as a military man. His jaw was sharp, as though it had been chiseled from stone. Taryn found herself mesmerised by his gaze, unable to tear her eyes away from his. Her right hand still rested on his chest where it had fallen when he'd pulled her from the street, but it was only when she realized she could not feel his grip on her that she understood what had happened. He had grabbed her by her clockwork arm.

Taryn's eyes flicked to her left arm, to his large fingers still holding her tightly, and then back up to his ice blue eyes. Her heart was speeding, but it wasn't just because she'd nearly been trampled. Deep in his eyes there was a knowing look, and it terrified her. Hurriedly, she pulled herself from his grasp.

"You ought to be more careful, miss," he said in a surprisingly gentle voice, without an ounce of the sinister knowledge she expected to be there.

"Y-yes, sir," she stuttered. She clutched her left arm to her chest. "Thank you for pulling me out of the way."

Was the knowing look really there, or had she just imagined it? Surely, it had been obvious that her arm was not flesh and bone. Hadn't it? She had to get away from him.

"May I ask your name?" he asked.

"Taryn Roft," she answered breathlessly, glancing back to

find Royal coming toward them, his face still pale. "Thank you. I must be going. Thank you."

Hurriedly, she grabbed Royal's arm, still keeping her false limb tucked against her chest. She pulled him down the street, trying to put as much distance as she could between them and the man with the ice blue eyes. She could feel him watching her until she turned the corner. She released a breath she hadn't realized she'd been holding.

"What was that?" Royal questioned, half laughing at her. "For a moment, I thought perhaps you knew him!"

Taryn let go of his shirtsleeve. "No." She slowed down, forcing herself to breathe. "I was surprised. That is all."

"You ought to thank him," Royal said, chewing the side of his thumb. Taryn recognized the tic as a sign of stress and fear. He'd really thought she was going to be trampled. "He just saved your life."

"I thanked him," Taryn muttered. She knew Royal needed reassurance that she was all right, but she herself was still too shaken to give him much more than that.

"Well, I am glad he was there. I would have pulled you out of the way, but I was not near enough," he mumbled, almost beneath his breath. He was chewing hard on the side of his thumb.

"I am not upset you did not try to rescue me," Taryn said, almost incredulously. "Do you think I am angry with you?"

He shrugged, but said nothing. There was sadness and worry in his expressive brown eyes.

"Roy, I am not mad at you!" She tried to smile. "I am shaken. That is all."

"Still, I wish I had saved you, and not that stranger," Royal admitted.

"Shall I throw myself in front of another cab, so that you may rescue me?" Taryn questioned teasingly, though her heart was not in it.

"No!" Royal finally pulled his thumb away from his mouth, rubbing it against his pantleg. "No, I am just glad you are safe."

She smiled half-heartedly. "Thank you, Roy. I, too, am glad I am all right." *And I am glad I shall never see that man again. I am afraid he knows what I am.* "Well!" she said much too emphatically, "I believe that is enough adventure for one day. Shall we return to school and see if we can find some safe, quiet activity to occupy our time?"

"Aye," Royal answered. "That would be nice."

Together, they walked back to the school and the relative safety therein, each lost in their own thoughts, neither recognizing the turmoil the other was experiencing.

CHAPTER FOUR

TARYN COULD NOT GET THE MAN WITH THE ICE BLUE EYES OUT of her head. His spectre followed her over the next few days, and she found herself acting paranoid, jumping at shadows. He was not coming after her, Taryn told herself, but she did not really believe it. He began to invade her dreams at night.

Royal noticed how edgy she had become, how she kept her left arm hugged more tightly to her body than usual. She tugged at the glove more often, checking to make sure it was covering everything from her fingertips to her sleeve. "Are you all right, Taryn?" he asked on Friday afternoon when they had a moment between classes. "You seem preoccupied lately."

"I am fine," Taryn lied.

"Are you sure?" Royal insisted. "Your arm—"

"It is fine," she snapped. "Sometimes it hurts. That is all." She turned to go, trying to get away from his questions.

Royal grabbed her right wrist, stopping her. "Why can you not tell me the truth?" He grasped her tightly, his fingers like iron bands.

"I have!"

"What are you hiding?" he demanded.

"I have told you," she hissed. One or two students had stopped to stare at them. "I wear the glove to hide the scars from the night my parents died. Sometimes it still pains me. What is it about that explanation that upsets you?"

"I do not know." He released her wrist. His face fell. "I am worried about you, Taryn. I do not know how to help you."

Taryn hugged her left arm to her chest. "I am all right, Royal. I am just tired."

Royal nodded, meekly. "If there is anything I can do to help, please let me know."

"I shall."

He accepted her agreement, and they dispersed to their classes. Shaken by the confrontation, Taryn's attention wandered during the lecture. Her right hand rubbed over the joints of her prosthetic arm, feeling the way the wires fit together, the movement becoming almost hypnotic. Royal knew her too well. He was beginning to guess she had not told him the whole truth. He had accepted the threadbare lie this time, but she did not know if he would again. She wondered how much longer she could hide her secret. Could she have a normal life? Was she mad to even try?

But the alternative was slavery, and she didn't dare allow herself to even imagine what would happen if she turned herself in. That was not an option.

She spent the afternoon in a cloud of worry and wonder, and before long she found herself following the crowd toward the dining hall. Halfway there, she realized she had forgotten her books in the classroom. Taryn turned back, racing up the stairs to the upper right wing of the building. The hall was deserted by the time she got there, and somewhere far off, she could hear the clock at the heart of the school tolling six. The wood-panelled halls were warm and friendly when they were filled with students, but now the silence was almost sinister.

She shook off a chill, telling herself she was just being paranoid.

As she passed an office, someone stepped from the doorway, brushing against her shoulder. A low voice muttered, "I know what you are."

Taryn froze, her heart threatening to beat out of her chest. Slowly, she turned around, jaw clenched. The man who'd saved her in the street days before stood behind her, a cold smirk on his chiseled face. His ice blue eyes drilled into hers. He was standing in a relaxed, cocky position, hands by his sides and one knee slightly bent, one foot turned out. Taryn's mouth went dry. "Who—who are you? How did you find me?"

It was almost as if he did not hear her. That uncanny smile danced on his lips as he spoke in his strangely gentle voice. "Unless you want me to tell everyone here what you are, you are going to do exactly what I say."

Taryn's mind went numb. She nodded, not trusting her voice. Her fists clenched by her sides, partially to hide their trembling, and partly as a leftover fighting instinct from living on the streets. But she'd gone soft since then, she knew, and she would be no match for this man.

"Good. In a moment, you are going to turn around and walk. You will enter the third door on your left. I will follow you." He nodded. "Go now."

Taryn turned, struggling to remain calm. She counted the dark oak doors, aware of his footsteps following close behind her. Questions regarding who this man was, why he was here, and what he wanted with her spun through her head. The third door was closed, and Taryn shoved it open with a trembling hand. Inside was a small office, furnished with a desk near the far wall on her left, a few wooden chairs, and a bookshelf against the wall to her right. The wall directly in front of her had tall, narrow windows that looked out on the yard. The grey evening light filtered through the windows, waning quickly. Two gas lamps on either side of the door assisted the fading light from outside. Taryn moved into the centre of the room, afraid of allowing herself to be cornered by him. The man—he held himself like a man, though he could hardly be older than she—stepped into the room behind her and closed the door softly. Taryn stared at him, her wide green eyes betraying her fright.

"Who are you?" Taryn questioned again, trying to make her voice sound stronger than she felt.

"My name is Ace Highmore." He pulled up his sleeve, revealing a white brand in the shape of gears and crossed cutlasses on the inside of his right forearm. "I am a privateer in the Queen's navy. For now, that is all you need to know."

"What do you want from me?" Taryn's mind spun as she struggled to think of anything she might have done to draw attention to herself, any reason a privateer would be interested in her. She hadn't done anything wrong. Yet, she knew that her mere existence was wrong in most people's eyes. A painful, gaping pit opened in her stomach, threatening to swallow her whole. She almost wished it would.

He stared at her stonily. "Show me your graft."

Taryn shook her head, hugging her gloved prosthetic to her chest. She had never shown anyone her deformity voluntarily; the last time her clockwork had been exposed, she was twelve years old and assaulted by a group of school boys for her inhumanity. And even though this man—this *Ace*—already knew her secret, she could not bear to reveal it.

"*Now,*" he said, his voice losing the gentle quality and suddenly going stone cold. He swept back his dark blue frock coat, revealing the butt of a pearl-handled flintlock pistol holstered on his hip.

Taryn's head spun. He was threatening her? She did not know whether the threat was genuine or feigned, but it frightened her too much to gamble with. Barely breathing, she pulled her glove from her clockwork fingers; slowly, so slowly, she pulled back the glove, feeling as though she were peeling off her own skin. Her graft shone dully, gold and copper and silver, rust and fresh metal mixed together, clicking in tune with her heartbeat.

Ace grabbed her wrist and firmly pulled her arm closer, examining it with what seemed to be a practiced eye. Taryn kept the rest of her body as far away from him as she could. She felt naked. Violated. Exposed. She'd never felt so helpless before, not even on the streets. She clutched her glove in her right hand like a lifeline.

After what felt like forever, he released her. Taryn backed three small steps away, cradling her graft against her stomach, staring at him warily, like a cornered fawn facing down a hungry predator.

"What do you know about your creator?"

"I suspect God created me," she replied, but her voice betrayed her, cracking in the middle of her quip.

"No, your creator. The man who made you a biomaton. What do you know of *him*?" he growled. There was no hint of the earlier gentleness in his voice.

"Nothing," she answered quietly, honestly. "I cannot remember."

"Do not lie to me." His voice tightened, and it scared her more than if he'd shouted. Fire flamed inside his cold eyes.

"Truly! I do not know. I cannot remember anything about him. There are years of my memory missing, simply blank." Her eyes stung with tears, despite herself. "I am sorry, but I cannot help you. Now, if you are quite done threatening me, I am missing supper." She moved to pull her glove back on, but he caught her wrist, holding it at the level of her eyes with such force that she could not do anything but stand face to face with him, chest heaving above her corset. Her wide green eyes locked with his, filled with fire.

"You are not leaving just yet, Miss Roft," he told her, his voice husky with something she did not recognize. "You will not leave until I say you may. If you do, I will not hesitate to inform the headmaster of your *deformity*. I am sure Lord Stokker will be pleased to hear he has been sponsoring a biomaton's education."

Tears prickled the backs of her eyes again, and she fought to breathe past the lump that had formed in her throat. "Please. I do not understand what you want from me. Let me go. I am doing no harm to anyone."

"No harm?" he scoffed. "You are in violation of the law simply by being enrolled here."

"I am no different from you!" she exclaimed, her voice cracking.

His expression hardened. He released her wrist, raising his hand. She thought he was going to strike her. "Biomatons are *not* human. I could arrest you right now, if I wished."

"What is it you want from me?" she asked again. She wasn't crying, but tears hung from her lashes, blurring her vision.

"I want to know about the man who made you."

She shook her head. "I cannot remember. I am sorry."

He was silent for a long moment, his ice blue eyes examining her. "Very well. I need you to come with me."

Her mouth went dry. She stared at him in horror, unable to comprehend his words. "What?"

"You will come with me to my airship."

"I cannot leave!" she exclaimed. "I am attending classes. I have schoolwork—"

"You are leaving, biomaton. Whether that is freely with me or in chains when I reveal what you are is your choice."

Taryn wrapped her arms around her stomach, trembling. This could not be happening. Yet, it was. She had known this could not last forever. She dipped her head, voice softening. "You leave me no choice."

"We leave tonight. I will come to your window at nine o'clock. If you are not there, I *will* reveal your deformity to the headmaster."

She kept her eyes down. She pulled her glove on slowly, covering the clockwork graft that marked her as a slave. "Yes, sir," she mumbled.

He stepped aside, clearing a path for her. "You may go." Taryn slunk past him, but he caught her wrist, forcing her to turn back to him. "Not a word of this to anyone, understand?"

"Or you will tell everyone about me. Yes, I know," she answered, hiding her fear beneath bravado.

He scowled, his lips curling in disgust as he thrust her away from him. She stumbled toward the door. As quickly as she could, she hurried away from the man, away from his threats and his ice blue eyes that seemed to stare right through her. Away from the one person in the world who had figured out her secret. She ran down the stairs, out of the building, to her dorm. She slammed the door behind her and pressed herself against it as though she could keep the world out, as though she could stop time. As though if she pressed hard enough and long enough, Ace and his sinister knowledge would disappear. Her trembling knees gave out. She slumped to the floor, her head hanging. Fear and shock tumbled about inside her, so overwhelming that she could not even bring herself to cry. What would be waiting for her when she left the school? Slavery? Death? How exactly did Ace expect her to help him without her memories? And how would she even survive away from the relative safety of Grafton's, away from her best friend?

Royal. She had to at least tell him what was happening. She couldn't just disappear without telling him, without at least saying goodbye. Perhaps—perhaps he would know what to do. But no. Her mind returned to all their arguments about the biomatons, and she knew he would scorn her. Worse, he might even report her, or force her to turn herself in. No, she could not tell him. But she could at least tell him goodbye. She could at least give him that.

⚙️

"Tiger!" Royal waved to her from across the dining hall, shouting so he would be heard over the low roar of hundreds of boys chattering at once. Taryn forced a smile and moved toward him. Despite herself, she kept her left arm hugged tightly to her chest, wary of every wayward look, terrified that Ace had told someone about her secret. She reached Royal's table and stood, chewing her lip, her fingers twisted in her skirt. Royal smiled, offering her a seat. "Where have you been, Tiger? I have been waiting for you!"

"May I talk to you?" she asked, barely lifting her eyes to look at him.

"Of course." He stood, seeming to detect the nervousness of her mood, the urgency in her voice. "What is it?"

Taryn silently led him from the dining hall, barely breathing until they were out in the corridor, alone. Her own heartbeat sounded too loud in the empty stone hallway, echoing off the walls as though there was someone behind her, breathing down her neck.

"Tiger, what is going on?" Royal asked, hesitantly reaching out to touch her right shoulder.

"I—I am going away, Royal," she said quietly. His hand was warm and soft on her arm.

"What?" Horror and surprise flashed across his expressive face. "Why?" His hand tightened on her shoulder.

"I have been called away," she said carefully, concocting the lie as she spoke. "I was offered an apprenticeship repairing biomatons for a lord in Wales. I cannot turn it down."

"Really?"

Taryn nodded, surprised by the sudden joy she saw in his eyes.

"What a coincidence!" Royal exclaimed, grinning his crooked smile. "I have been offered an apprenticeship with a biomechanick! He has promised to teach me all he knows. He is very talented."

"And you have taken this apprenticeship?"

"I did not know whether to take it or not. I did not want to leave you, but if you have been offered one also…"

"You must take it, Royal," Taryn insisted. "This is a wonderful opportunity." As immense as her trepidation was, it began to fade at his news. She was really, truly excited for him. It was everything he wanted.

"I shall, on one condition. You take your holidays off and spend them with me."

"Roy—" Taryn tried to protest.

"No, Taryn, you *must* promise. I have yet to take you to Switzerland." He grinned his lopsided grin.

Taryn melted, ducking her head. "Very well. I promise." She knew she would most likely be unable to fulfill her promise—God only knew what her future held—but she made it anyway, because she knew it would satisfy him. Somehow, that was enough.

Royal hugged her tightly then, and rather than push him away, she returned the gesture. It was a rare moment, and, knowing she might not see him again, she savoured it, allowing it to touch her so frequently cold heart.

"Good luck," she said softly as she pulled away from him.

He smiled that lopsided smile she knew so well. "And good luck to you, Taryn."

"Thank you." She offered him a wry smile of her own.

"And you must write!" he exclaimed. "Promise me."

"I shall write," she answered numbly.

"Good. I shall write you every day. Every day, Taryn. Without fail."

She did not know what to say. There were tears burning at the back of her throat, but she made an effort to swallow them down. She nodded silently, unable to speak for several moments. Finally, her tongue seemed to become unstuck. "Farewell, Royal. Thank you. For everything."

"Farewell, Tiger. I will see you soon."

She turned to go and he caught her wrist, pulled her back, and kissed her forehead. Taryn flushed and hurried away, the feeling of his soft lips against her face burned there like a brand. If only he knew what she was, he would never have dared to kiss her like that. But she treasured it, knew she would keep the memory of it for the frightening unknown that lay ahead. Perhaps she would never see Royal again, but his impulsive gift to her would ensure she wouldn't forget him. She would keep it deep in her memory, the final touch of the boy who had always treated her as human, no matter what happened next.

Back in her dormitory, Taryn had one last farewell to compose before she could truly cut her ties with Grafton's School of Mechanicks. She sat at the small desk near her bed, drew a fresh sheet of paper from the drawer and lay it upon the surface, smoothing it with her clockwork hand. Almost reverently, she selected a fine silver fountain pen from the drawer of the desk. The pen had been a gift from Lord Stokker for her birthday, the year she'd graduated from finishing school. Along with the pen had been the announcement that she had been admitted to Grafton's School of

Mechanicks. Taryn could still remember the day vividly. The moment had been a joyous one, spent together with Royal and his family. Taryn supposed that was what a family was like. It was certainly the closest she was ever going to get. Her stomach flipped and she forced herself to focus only on the task at hand.

Taryn placed the tip of the pen against paper, beginning her letter with the flowing, handsome script she had learned in finishing school. She had never become as adept as some of her classmates at penmanship—her hand and eye always better at the mechanickal details than the aesthetic—but her handwriting was steady and fine, with straight, flowing lines that never wandered from the invisible boundaries she imposed upon the page. One professor had described her handwriting as being a "line of soldiers, all in a row." Taryn liked the scratch and hiss of the metal nib over the thick paper, and she liked the lines of dark ink that appeared as her hand carefully traced the letters. In all, it had been one of her better subjects at finishing school.

Dear Lord Stokker, Taryn began, then paused, lifting the nib so as not to leave a splotch of ink as she considered what to say to her benefactor. She could not leave the school without writing to him; and yet, even as she attempted to write him a letter explaining why she was leaving, her mind closed to the prospect. How could she write this without seeming ungrateful? How could she say all she wanted to in a single letter?

These past four years, I have been your ward and protégé. All I have, and all I am today I owe to you. This was not entirely true, Taryn mused, flexing her prosthetic, but it was as honest as she could be. *I write, first of all, to thank you for the hospitality your family has shown me over the years. You have never failed to make me feel like one of your own, rather than a poor orphan you found in the gutter and rescued from a life spent destitute and alone. I consider Royal my closest friend.*

But there comes a time in every girl's life when she can no longer rely on her benefactor for her every need; when she must strike out into the wide world on her own, carrying with her everything she has learned. I am afraid I am writing to tell you that time has come. I have been offered an apprenticeship—

Taryn again paused, the lie tasting as bitter on paper as it had on her tongue. Still, it was this or the truth. She knew the truth would devastate Lord Stokker, at the very least. At worst, he would punish Royal for not realizing her secret, or something else just as mad. No. She would keep the lie to protect her last friends in the world.

I have been offered an apprenticeship with a lord in Wales. He has asked me to live at his manor home. I shall repair his biomatons and any other mechanickal devices he has about. It is not a glamourous positon—it pays only a little besides room and board—but if I am careful, I shall be able to save up, and with experience, I may get a better job somewhere nearer to home in the future.

This last was utter fantasy. Who was she kidding? She might be dead in a week, or enslaved somewhere, or worse. How could she invent such fantastic circumstances on paper? But she did it for the sake of those who had been so kind to her. They would want to know she was safe somewhere, content.

I have promised Royal I shall write, and I shall not forget to keep you in correspondence as well. I once again thank you for all you have done for me. I shall never forget your kindnesses, and I only hope I may one day repay you. I do hope I have been worth all your generosity.

Thank you for all I am today.

Sincerely,

Taryn Roft

She signed her name with a flourish and pulled her hand away, feeling tears press at the backs of her eyes as she watched the ink dry. It felt final now. It *was* final now. Even if she returned to the school in three days with her secret intact, there would be no more scholarships, no more money from Lord Stokker. She had cut her ties with him, at least as his ward. She sighed. It was better this way. It was better to never come back. She had stayed far too long already.

As soon as she was certain the ink was dry, Taryn painstakingly folded the paper as she'd been taught, closing the thick page around its precious contents. She rose and lit a stick of red sealing wax with the gas lamp upon the wall. She let the wick burn until she had a small puddle of wax upon the page where it folded against itself, then blew out the flame and pressed a seal into the centre of the puddle. It cooled quickly, and it was only moments before it had dried upon the page, leaving the shape of the seal permanently impressed on it. The seal was an old one Royal had given her, with a calligraphic letter *R* and little excess decoration, but Taryn had used it since she started finishing school at the age of fourteen. She knew this was the last time she would use it.

Taryn finished addressing the back of the paper, then set it outside her door where she knew it would be picked up in the morning along with all the other outgoing letters. Then, she locked the door. Without really knowing why, she returned to her desk.

Taryn lay her head upon her arms and wept.

CHAPTER FIVE

The fog rolled in thick that night, so thick that by the time Ace tapped on Taryn's window, she felt she could have sliced through it with a knife. She lifted the sash, allowing both the stranger and the chill to enter her room. The fog pooled around Ace's feet as he pulled himself through the window, as if he were a creature of darkness himself.

He spoke softly, barely above a whisper. "It is time."

Icy fingers closed around Taryn's heart. Quickly, she snatched up the birthday pocket watch from Royal. She looked around at the small bedroom the headmaster had given her at the empty end of the boys' dormitory. She had lived here for the past two years. Her school books were scattered across her desk, her mechanick's tools piled on the floor. The wardrobe hung open, revealing a row of dark blue uniforms. This was her home, as much as any place in the world could be. She could hardly bear to think she might be leaving it for good.

"Let's go," Ace muttered, his low voice bearing just a hint of impatience.

Taryn shut her eyes for one last moment, holding the

pocket watch tightly in her palm. The casing was cold and solid, grounding her. She silently promised Royal that she would return. She would see him again. Then, she turned and slipped through the window behind Ace.

He caught her about the waist as she dropped to the ground. His ice blue eyes caught hers and held them until she shoved his hands away, scowling. Ace placed a finger to his lips. She understood, even without the gesture. *Not a word.* He gestured for her to follow him as he rounded the corner of the building. Taryn hurried to catch up, lifting fistfuls of her heavy woolen skirt. He led her across the yard, toward a side gate not frequently used by students, but also very rarely locked or patrolled. Taryn briefly wondered just how long he'd been watching her. He practically knew the campus better than she did.

The gate was mostly unused for one reason: it led to a filthy back alley well away from any of the main streets. It had a reputation for being rather seedy, and even the most thrill-seeking students avoided that kind of adventure. As they crept through the gate, Taryn was startled to see a human figure sitting in the shadows just outside. She shied away when it stirred, struggling to its feet.

"Taryn Roft?" the figure asked in a slurred, but familiar voice. "Ish that you, my pretty?"

Taryn winced. "Hello, Bennet. Have you been drinking?"

"A little," he said, swaying toward her. Taryn backed away. She bumped into Ace, who stood directly behind her. "What're you doing out sho late?" Bennet seemed to finally notice Ace, his bleary eyes watering. "Who'sh this? You did not tell me you were courting anyone."

"He is not a suitor." Taryn ground the words out between clenched teeth.

Bennet's face twisted. "Not your shuitor? Then where are you going? It'sh late and you should not be out…"

Taryn heard a click behind her. Ace stepped forward, his silver flintlock pistol held casually at his waist. "You had best be moving along, Bennet. I do not want things to get messy."

In his drunken stupor, Bennet glanced from the pistol, to Ace, to Taryn dumbly. "Ish thish man bothering you, sweetheart?" he slurred.

"No, Bennet. It is quite all right. I think you ought to do what he says."

Bennet looked at her for a long moment. His eyes went again to Ace and the pistol. He lunged forward suddenly, reaching for the pistol in a gesture Taryn could only interpret as muddled chivalry. Ace moved faster than her eyes could track. One moment, Bennet was upright, and the next, he was on the ground, blood rapidly pooling from a wound on his temple. Taryn slapped a hand over her mouth in horror.

Ace grabbed her arm, tugging her away. Taryn fought him. "What did you do to him?"

"He will be fine. In a few hours, he will wake, having slept off most of the alcohol. I do not envy the headache he shall have, though."

Taryn shuddered. "You did not have to knock him out. He is mostly harmless."

"If I had not, he would have drawn attention to us," Ace answered matter-of-factly. "And we do not want that, do we, biomaton?"

Taryn could feel the knot of disgust in her chest quickly hardening into hatred. She wrested her arm from his grip, following him through the streets of her own volition. He kept out of the glow of the street lamps, moving from shadow to shadow like a true creature of the night. He barely cast a glance back to her to ensure she was following a few steps behind him, but Taryn had the feeling that if she tried to run, he would know immediately. They passed from the fine, wealthy part of London into a dingy, industrial district. Here, the fog mixed with smoke and steam from the smokestacks, at times reducing visibility to only a few feet ahead of them so that Taryn had to stick close to Ace in order not to lose him in the fog. They passed dirty factory workers stumbling home after long shifts. Once, a man tried to grab her skirt. Ace sent him skittering away with a flash of his pistol, tugging her over the cobblestones until she recovered herself. She hadn't the faintest idea where they were headed. She began to shiver, her frock soaked with the damp of the fog.

Finally, they came into the airshipyard near the Thames, where dozens of airships hung over London, moored to heavy iron rings cemented to the cobbles. Airships of all sizes hung in the air above their heads, from small yachts to the huge naval warships that belonged to Her Majesty's Navy, their immense hydrogen balloons tugging them upward in opposition of gravity. At the centre of the yard, a tall metal tower rose like a beacon, with smaller airships tethered around it. The docking tower was one of three metal structures rising into the air above London, even taller than Big Ben, with airships constantly buzzing around them like bees. Taryn had been here before, during the day, but the airshipyard never ceased to amaze her. Ace did not even stop, leading her straight through the yard between the thick, taut mooring ropes. Taryn paused, staring up at the hulking ships above her head, astonished once again that they could hang there, practically weightless. The ropes mooring the balloons to the hulls of the ships snapped as they drifted in the breeze.

"Biomaton!"

Taryn dragged her gaze away from the airships, back to Ace, who was standing a few feet away, looking impatient. "Please, announce what I am to the whole world," she hissed furiously.

Ace strode back over to her, grabbing her wrist, pulling her along. "We haven't time for gawking."

"I was not bloody gawking!" she exclaimed, stumbling along behind him. It wasn't as though he gave her any choice.

He led her to a ship moored near the bank of the Thames. It was a large ship, though not as massive as some of the naval warships Taryn could see in the distance at the other end of the shipyard. The wood of the hull was scratched and chipped, signs that she'd seen battle, perhaps many times. The balloon above her was made of dark blue canvas, patched in places where the cloth had been torn. The canvas was sealed on the inside with rubber, Taryn knew, to keep the hydrogen from escaping. The figurehead on the prow was a carved centaur, weather-worn and grey with age, its equine forelegs rearing away from the ship. On the side of the ship, in faded gold letters, were the words *H.M.A. Dauntless*.

Ace put his fingers to his lips and whistled. A rope ladder tumbled over the side of the ship. He grabbed it and held it steady for her. "Welcome to the *Dauntless*, Miss Roft."

Carefully, Taryn climbed the rope ladder, her stomach lurching at the way it swayed, untethered in the wind. As Ace began climbing behind her, Taryn picked up her pace, painfully aware that from his vantage point he could easily look up her skirt.

When she reached the top, a young man took her hand and helped her onto the deck of the ship. "Welcome to the *Dauntless, mademoiselle*," he said, his voice coloured with a lilting foreign accent. He was short and wiry, with ash blond hair and sharp features, but it was his eyes that were the most striking, large and grey as a stormy sky and unlike any Taryn had ever seen. He was still holding her hand, and lifted it to his mouth, kissing her knuckles with soft lips. Taryn jerked away.

"Leave her alone, Emmett," Ace growled as he pulled himself onto the deck of the ship.

"You did not tell me she was so beautiful!" the young man

exclaimed. His eyes glowed with a mischievous, teasing light. Taryn noted his clothes with a cursory glance: a striped, red vest over a loose cream blouse, brown breeches and black boots, with a scarlet cravat about his neck. The odd combination made her smile inwardly. This young man was everything she had imagined an air pirate to be.

Ace frowned. "She is a biomaton. Do not forget that." He began to stride across the deck of the ship. "Come with me, Miss Roft."

With a final glance at the young man who'd called her beautiful, even if only in jest, Taryn hurried after Ace. It was her first time aboard an airship of this size, and she quickly discovered the deck moved about beneath her feet in a manner not unlike a sailing ship. She found it difficult to maintain her balance, but Ace walked smoothly, his hips rolling with the movement of the deck. Avoiding the heavy lines that moored the hydrogen balloon above them to the deck below their feet, Taryn stumbled across the deck, barely keeping pace.

"Slow down!"

They had boarded near the bow of the ship, and he led her toward the stern, where an open door revealed a rickety set of stairs leading into the labyrinthine underbelly of the *Dauntless*. Ace navigated the steps easily, but Taryn had to keep one hand on the wall to steady herself.

Belowdecks was a maze of halls; the walls, ceiling, and floor made of wide-grained, well-worn wood. Copper pipes with pressure gauges and cut-off valves lined the ceiling, occasionally dripping condensation. The space smelled of old wood, metal, and leather. Though Taryn could not hear it, she could feel the thrum of the massive steam-powered engine below their feet. She wanted to stop and examine the complicated mechanickal workings that made up the ship, but Ace rushed her through the halls. They stopped at a pair of wide double doors. Ace shoved them open. Taryn's jaw dropped.

They entered a massive control room at the bow of the ship. The curving far wall was, in reality, a colossal window, looking out into the night. In front of the window was a series of wooden panels, curving with the contours of the front of the ship, covered in gauges, levers, and all sorts of buttons. Men bustled around the space, preparing the ship for flight. In the centre of the room stood the one thing Taryn had missed above deck—a gargantuan ship's wheel. Standing in front of the wheel with her back to them, a woman commanded the room.

"Captain Storm!" Ace shouted over the din of the sailors. "I have brought the biomaton."

A flash of anger flooded Taryn's chest, hotter than the dull smoulder of hatred in her stomach, just as the woman at the wheel turned, and Taryn got a good look at her for the first time. She wore *trousers.* It was the very first thing Taryn noticed. The woman wore brown leather breeches, with a corset and a white blouse, and a long navy coat similar in style to the one Ace wore. Her high-heeled boots laced all the way up to her thighs, the leather scuffed and worn. She had long, dark brown hair cascading over her shoulders in wild curls. Taryn could see she had bits of ribbon, bone, feathers, and coins tied into her hair. She had a thin white scar on the right side of her jaw, and the same ice blue eyes as Ace. On her left hand, she wore a vicious metal gauntlet.

"Captain?" Taryn questioned, trying to hide her fear and hatred beneath a layer of false bravado. "Surely, you are jesting."

The woman clenched her fist with a *clank* of metal, her other hand going to the sword at her hip. "Welcome aboard the *Dauntless,* Taryn Roft," she said coldly, then turned back to the men who stood about the room, awaiting orders. "Haul anchor! We are leaving!"

"Wait!" Taryn leapt forward, confused. Ace had said nothing about leaving. "I cannot leave! I am attending school—"

Storm turned her gaze back to Taryn, a sneer on her face. "Did I say you could speak, biomaton?"

Taryn winced. Despite herself, the accusatory tone hurt. "I cannot leave London. I am attending classes. I have friends—"

Storm interrupted her with a scoffing laugh. "Friends? Do any of them know what you are? Do they know you are not even human?"

Taryn swallowed hard, dropping her gaze to the floor. "I *am* human," she muttered, so quietly no one heard her.

"That is what I thought," Storm growled. "Ace, please show the biomaton to her quarters."

Taryn clenched her fists, but said nothing. She could not change what Storm thought about her; it was what everyone thought. Ace grabbed her arm—though not as roughly as he had before—and led her from the room. Storm had already dismissed them, ordering her crew to prepare the *Dauntless* for launch. Taryn felt the engines change pitch and strength below her feet as they were stoked. She was leaving London, and there was nothing she could do about it. As Ace led her through the dim underbelly of the ship, Taryn couldn't help but think that perhaps she was leaving London for good.

CHAPTER SIX

ACE LED HER DEEP INTO THE BOWELS OF THE SHIP, DOWN WHERE the very atmosphere thrummed with energy from the engines, and heat and steam leaked up through the floor. Taryn could taste the ozone scent of hot metal. It coated the back of her throat, suffocatingly strong. Ace led her to a small door, opening it with a flick of his wrist. Nothing was visible in the murky darkness beyond.

"Please explain to me what is going on," Taryn pleaded. That dark maw hung open ahead of her, gaping, ready to swallow her whole.

"You shall find out soon enough," he answered coldly.

"Please." Fear crept into her voice, her green eyes full of desperation.

Ace sighed, perhaps surprised by how much humanity those eyes could portray. "Your creator is a man named Anthony Erikkson. He is an incredibly skilled mechanick. But he is also suspected of treason."

The name rang a bell in the back of her head, but she couldn't place *why*. "What does that have to do with me? I don't even remember him."

"He created you. We are taking you to a man who can tell whether you have been built illegally or not."

Taryn's stomach tied itself into knots. A slow, mind-numbing dread crept across her body like frost. "I am never going to be allowed to return to school, am I?"

"You should never have been attending classes at that school at all," he said in a voice that cut her like a knife, but his eyes had softened, melted into twin blue pools.

"Because I am nothing but a slave, right?" Taryn growled, struggling to swallow back the tears that pricked the backs of her eyes.

"That is what you were built for," Ace answered, sounding like he was speaking more to himself than to her.

Taryn bit her lip. She didn't trust herself to say anything else. She shoved past him, stepping into the dark room he'd deemed hers so that he wouldn't see her fighting back the tears. Ace closed the door behind her.

Blind in the darkness, Taryn stood stock-still, tears slipping down her cheeks. She couldn't stop them. Her whole world had just been pulled out from under her, and she had discovered herself to be utterly helpless. As her eyes began to adjust to the darkness, she struggled with the way she'd been treated, with the way Ace and Storm had spoken to her. Taryn had never felt any different from the people around her who were "whole." Yes, her arm was clockwork, but did that mean anything else about her was different? Was she really fit only to be a slave?

There came a strange ticking, rustling sound to her left. Taryn froze, eyes straining in the darkness. "Hello?"

There was another rustle and the distinctive *click* of clock-work. A small yellow sun burst into flame. Taryn was momentarily blinded by the brilliant flame. The light moved through the air to ignite a gas lamp, then drew away. Taryn blinked, waiting for her eyes to adjust to the sudden glow illuminating the room. A dark-skinned man who looked to be in his mid-twenties sat upon a wooden crate, staring at her. He had dark, wavy hair that hung down over his shoulders, and wore a black leather greatcoat over a navy blue shirt. Most striking were his eyes: almond-shaped with brilliant green irises, though the left one looked cloudy, duller than the right eye.

"Who are you?" Taryn questioned nervously, wiping the tears from her cheeks.

"Did I frighten you? I apologise," he said, his voice a gentle rumble.

"Who are you?" she asked again, too stunned to think of any other question.

"My name is Seraphim." He offered her a shy smile, which revealed a flash of silver. The smile was too quick for Taryn to see where the silver had come from. "I am like you."

"Like me?"

He nodded, and again she heard the click of clockwork as he stood. Unfurling behind him were two enormous mechanickal wings. Taryn's eyes widened, stunned by the intricacy of the machinery. They were exquisite, made all of bronze, right down to the tips of the feathers. His wingspan filled most of the tiny cabin.

"Gor," she whispered, impressed. "May—may I?"

Seraphim nodded and turned, allowing Taryn to examine his wings. They were hinged at the base and at approximately the one- and two-thirds marks, allowing him to fold them exactly as a bird would. Taryn had heard of angels before, and had seen paintings, but this was something altogether new. This was, perhaps, the closest she would ever get to an angel. Hesitantly, Taryn reached out and brushed the metal feathers with her fingertips. The edges were sharp, and Taryn pulled her hand away in surprise. Every feather doubled as a blade.

"You are a weapon," she whispered.

Seraphim turned back to her, folding his wings once more. "That I am. But it is, perhaps, better than being a mindless slave."

"Who did this to you?"

"Lord Erikkson," he replied. His deep voice was slightly accented.

The back of Taryn's mind tingled, like a nearly forgotten memory was struggling to emerge. But nothing came. No memory lifted itself from the darkness of her mind. Taryn tried to push the feeling away. "At least you remember your creator," she said sulkily.

"It is not all good," he answered gently. "May I see your graft?"

She nodded, slowly removing the black glove she wore to cover her graft, revealing the small, rusted, delicate prosthetic. Seraphim took hold of it with large, gentle hands, examining it carefully. He ran his dark hand over the clockwork. Strangely, Taryn felt no fear or shame in showing *him* her prosthetic. Perhaps it was because he was a biomaton as well. There was a feeling of familiarity that danced in the back of her mind when she looked at him, though she knew she would have remembered someone so unique.

"You were very young when you received this?" he asked.

She ducked her head in assent. "Aye."

"But someone has worked on it."

"I have." She tried to smile. "I was learning to be a mechanick."

"A mechanick?"

"Aye. But that was before—" Her voice cracked.

"Before what?"

"Before bloody Ace found me and brought me here."

"Ah. I see." Seraphim shifted, releasing her wrist. Taryn pulled her glove back over her clockwork fingers. "Why did he bring you here, miss?"

"Taryn."

"What?"

"My name. Taryn."

"Miss Taryn. Why did Ace bring you here?"

"I do not quite understand. He said that I may have been… illegally built. I do not know. Apparently, they are attempting to entrap the man who built me."

Seraphim nodded. "I see."

"How can they even tell if I was—" she winced at the words, "*built illegally?* I understand the law requires biomatons to be built with dampers in their brains, but how can they tell?"

"On the back of your head, there is a metal plate a little larger than a playing card, is there not?" Seraphim asked.

There was. Until now, Taryn had believed it was nothing, a metal plate required by her injuries, perhaps. She had never imagined that her brain had been fundamentally altered.

"Then I do not think anyone will be convicted because of your grafts," Seraphim concluded, reading the answer in her face.

Taryn sat heavily on the wooden barrel near the wall. A headache was blossoming between her eyes as she struggled to recall something, *anything* about her life as a biomaton. She couldn't remember. She could *never* remember. "Why do they treat us this way?" she moaned.

"Because we are different."

"We are not so different! Are we?" She lifted her eyes to him.

In response, he lifted his lips, displaying his teeth. In place of his canines were two sharp silver fangs. "You tell me," Seraphim replied, hiding his fangs once more.

Taryn shook her head, horrified. "I do not belong here. I should not be here."

"Your life is no longer your own, Miss Taryn. It would be best if you accepted it."

Anger filled her, flooding her chest with a fight or flight instinct so powerful she could barely contain herself. Her heart sped up, pumping red-hot blood through her body. She clenched her fists, her fingers warming with the beat of her heart. "We are *just* as human as they are!" She knew her outburst was stupid, but she was tired and angry and no longer thinking logically.

"Take your argument to Ace or Storm," Seraphim muttered, his voice edged with bitter sarcasm. "I do not disagree with you."

"Very well. I shall." She stood, headed for the door.

He caught her wrist, stopping her, holding her firmly but gently. "Miss Taryn, they will not listen to you. Do not risk yourself like this. They hate us, and nothing you say can change that."

Taryn frowned, knowing he was right, hating the knowledge.

"Do not do this," Seraphim begged again.

Taryn yanked her wrist out of his grasp. "I—I need some air."

She hurried from the claustrophobic room, afraid of what she might do, afraid she might confront these people if she did not control herself. Whatever happened next, she knew she would regret it. She rushed through the halls of the *Dauntless*, praying she would find the door and get herself above deck before she came across any of the people who had forced her to come here.

CHAPTER SEVEN

Before she knew what she was doing, Taryn found herself marching across the deck of the ship, the cold wind whipping her hair across her face and tangling her skirt around her legs. They were moving quickly now, the airship skimming over London like a silent angel in the night as the people below slept soundly, unaware of the activity above their heads. The airship soared just above the fog bank, and the air was clear and cold. All across the deck, crew members worked, calling to one another and scaling the balloon nimbly to fix the ropes stretched across its taut surface. Storm stood in the middle of it all, calling out orders and watching the crew, her shoulders thrown back and her hands on her hips. She appeared utterly at home on this ship of the sky.

"Captain Storm," Taryn called over the noise of the wind.

Storm's lip curled when she saw Taryn approaching. "Did I not order Ace to take you to your quarters?"

"He did not tell me I was meant to share them," Taryn yelled.

"Oh, the biomaton has sensibilities?" Storm sneered. "If

you do not like your accommodations, I can always clear a cell for you in the cargo hold."

Ire rose in Taryn's gut, hot and fierce and ugly. She shoved her hair back from her face, but it did little good with the ferocity of the wind. "You have no right to kidnap me like this. Put the ship down."

"I beg your pardon?"

"Put the ship down!"

Storm scoffed. "And what exactly do you expect to happen if we return you to London?"

"I shall return to school." Taryn bit down hard on the inside of her lip, the pain dispelling the fear but fueling her anger. "I was not harming anyone."

Storm took a threatening step nearer, her face masked by the shadows of the night. "No harm?" she hissed. "It is not about *harm*. It is about humanity. Did you believe that with enough smarts you could make yourself human? That with a fancy enough education you could fool everyone into believing you were human?"

"I *am* human!" Taryn screamed.

Storm's hand flashed across Taryn's face, striking her cheek hard. Taryn stumbled backward, her hand to her face. It had been years since someone had dared to slap her, and more than anything, her pride stung.

A crowd was gathering, the crew abandoning their duties to watch the confrontation. Everyone wanted to see what this biomaton would do and how the captain would punish her. Storm turned to the accumulated crew, throwing an accusatory finger at Taryn. "*This* is what happens when we allow biomatons to live unfettered! They forget their place and try to pass themselves off as human. Human? Hah!" She turned and spat at Taryn. "Show us your graft, biomaton."

Taryn shook her head, pulling her clockwork arm to her chest.

"Now," Storm ordered. Her hand rested on the hilt of the sword that hung at her hip.

Hesitantly, Taryn took off her glove, revealing the prosthetic for the third time that day. There wasn't any point in hiding it; they all knew what she was. Still, she felt naked with all their eyes on her deformity. She could see no friendly face in the gathered crowd as her clockwork glittered in the dim light.

"Now we see what you really are," Storm muttered, moving toward Taryn. "You can *never* be human." Taryn backed away a step, aware that somewhere close behind her the cargo hatch lay open, as the sailors were loading new supplies through it up until the very moment they had taken off. She didn't dare look away from Storm to find it, though, or let down her guard for a second. Storm was more vicious than Taryn had ever expected.

The captain snatched the glove from Taryn's fingers, raising it aloft. Taryn leapt forward, trying in vain to grab the item from the taller woman. "Hey!"

Storm shoved Taryn backward, her metal gauntlet leaving bloody scratches across Taryn's neck and chest. "Biomatons should not masquerade as human." Storm seized the glove with her sharp armoured fingers, rending it into shreds.

Taryn shrieked in anguish before she could throw a hand over her mouth to stop herself. She watched in horror as Storm dropped the one thing that had allowed her to live a semi-normal life, torn beyond repair. "Why are you doing this?" Taryn's voice took on a pleading quality she could not hide.

"You really do not know?" Storm sneered. A ripple of murmurs ran across the deck. "Biomatons are built with physiological changes to their brains. The man who built you changed your emotion centre. You are built to feel the way he programmed you to feel. Your humanity has been removed.

You cannot *ever* be truly human. It was stripped from you at your creation."

Taryn's knees went weak. She'd known about some of that already, but she'd never had it all spelled out for her so explicitly. "But—"

Storm placed a hand on her sword. "I am getting tired of your insubordination, biomaton."

Taryn took another step backward, and her heel slipped on the edge of the open cargo hatch. She tried to correct herself, but found the tip of Storm's sword at her throat. Taryn froze, heart galloping. The crew fell utterly silent, every sailor waiting to see what would happen.

"Now, what have we learned?"

Taryn swallowed hard but remained silent, refusing to give Storm the satisfaction of seeing her crumble. She did not dare move, with the abyss behind her and the sword's point straight ahead.

"Come now, we haven't all night, *slave.*" Storm spoke the word cruelly, her voice dripping with contempt.

Taryn winced and lowered her eyes to the rough wooden deck of the ship. "I am not human," she said, barely audibly.

"Louder."

"I am not human." Taryn's throat was so tight it hurt to speak.

"Do not forget it," Storm sneered. "Consider this a warning. Next time, I shall throw you overboard." She struck Taryn so hard across the chest with the flat of her blade that her foot slipped. The momentum carried her backward, and she wheeled her arms in a desperate attempt to regain her balance until someone caught her left wrist. Taryn looked up to see Ace hanging on to her as she dangled over the cargo hatch.

"Let her go, Ace. It may teach the freak a lesson," Storm said carelessly.

Ace's blue eyes flickered for a moment. Taryn started to choke out a plea for help—

And then she was falling, tumbling into darkness, her breathing too loud in her ears. The world slowed as though she was only watching herself fall, yet she could feel her body turning, her heavy prosthetic oriented beneath her. She only fell twelve feet down, and it lasted mere seconds, but they might as well have been an eternity. She felt her brittle prosthetic hit the floor first, felt it crumple beneath her weight, and then pain slammed through her body. A blinding light burst across her vision.

The world went dark.

CHAPTER EIGHT

A CE THREW OPEN THE GILDED DOUBLE DOORS TO THE CAPTAIN'S quarters, surprised by the anger that coursed through him. "You cannot do things like that, Storm."

She sat in a wingback chair by the portcullis window, her feet thrown over one arm as she polished her gauntlet with a grey rag. She had a reputation for being cruel and relentless, a reputation Ace was all too familiar with, but this was somehow different. "What do you care? She is just a biomaton."

What *did* he care? All he knew was that he did. "You could have killed her!"

"I was not the one who dropped her," Storm answered nonchalantly, returning her attention to her gauntlet. "Perhaps you ought to be down in the cargo hold, making sure she is all right, rather than here telling me what I can and cannot do."

"I have been down there already. She is unconscious but seems otherwise uninjured," he paused. "Her prosthetic has been crushed."

"Is that a tinge of sympathy I hear?" she questioned tauntingly. "Do not tell me you have gone soft over a biomaton. What, did those big green eyes capture you?"

Ace's jaw clenched, his pulse throbbing in one temple. His eyes stared right through her, to the wood paneling behind her and the rounded edge of the brass portcullis when he snapped, "She is of no use to us broken."

She sighed and stood. "Oh, brother dear, I hate it when you are logical." Storm set the gauntlet down on the desk beside her armchair, letting it lie across crumpled maps and assorted papers. Ace had never known a time when she'd voluntarily cleaned her own space, preferring instead to let things accumulate until she had to dig through piles of clutter in order to find whatever she was looking for. He did his best to tidy up for her, but he'd been on assignment these last few weeks, and it was clearly taking its toll. Near the top of the piles, he noticed one opened letter with an unfamiliar seal: a gear overlaid with a calligraphic letter *E*. He made a mental note to ask her about it later.

"What is it you wish me to do, Ace?" Storm questioned, staring out of the portcullis into the night. "I shan't apologize to a biomaton."

"You nearly killed her!"

"Have you forgotten what the biomatons did to us?" She spun around, her eyes—which matched his so closely—alight and her mouth twisted into a snarl.

"*One* biomaton," Ace answered, his voice dangerously soft. "Not *all* biomatons."

"So you are willing to apologize for this girl?"

He was quiet for a long moment, his face unreadable while he held an internal debate. He knew she would not like it, and despite everything, he still sought Storm's approval. She had a kind of power over him, and it was not just because she was the captain of the ship. It was because he wanted his big sister to be proud of him. "I do not think she intended any disrespect. She genuinely believes she is no different from anyone else. She does not remember her time as a slave."

"Then I would say I have done her a kindness, by reminding her of her place. If we continue to allow her to think she is human, imagine what they will do to her at the Black Castle."

Ace's stomach leapt into his throat. He sat heavily in the armchair Storm had abandoned, trying to breathe through the waves of nausea that had come out of nowhere. "You plan to leave her there."

"Why not? It is where she belongs."

Ace shook his head, wringing his hands together. "They will destroy her."

"Why do you *care* so much?" Storm sounded disgusted as she leaned on the arm of the chair, then hissed in his ear, "Harden your heart. If you cannot, I shall harden it for you."

Ace rose, anger colouring his words. "You were not always so cruel, sister. What has changed?"

He made to leave the cluttered room; he would be better spending his time elsewhere than there arguing with her. Before he slammed the door, she called after him.

"You grew soft!"

"Hush, my child. Lie still. Everything is going to be all right."

Taryn awoke to a pounding headache and pain that radiated through her whole body from her scalp down to her toes. She moaned, blinking her eyes open as she adjusted to the dim light. It took her a moment to understand where she was; silvery moonlight painted a square on the wooden slats upon which she lay. Then she remembered: she was in the cargo hold aboard the *Dauntless*. She had fallen through the cargo hatch. Slowly, she sat up and realized her left arm would not move at all. Her breath caught in her throat as she lifted her right hand to examine her prosthetic.

It was crushed. The prosthetic was bent and twisted, the delicate clockwork within mangled and bent beyond repair. Even the familiar ticking had ceased, leaving a silent void in its place. Numbness flooded her as she ran her hand over the cold, broken piece of machinery. What would happen to her now? Not only was she a biomaton, but now she was broken. What would she do without her left arm? It would have to be removed, of course. And then she could not even pretend she was human.

Taryn rubbed her temple with two fingers. They came away sticky with blood. She was bleeding, but the cut was small. Her whole body ached.

She thought about what Storm had said about biomaton's brains being fundamentally different. *Was* she different? She still did not know. And, if she was honest with herself, she did not really want to know. She closed her eyes again.

A cautious voice came from behind her. "*Mademoiselle* Taryn?" She turned to see the young Frenchman she'd met earlier that evening standing in the doorway, holding a shuttered lantern. "Are you all right?"

She nodded, turning her left shoulder further away from him so he would not see how her arm had been crushed. "Yes. I am all right." She nearly choked on the final word, and forced herself to stop and breathe.

"Are you certain?" he asked, taking a few steps into the room. He lifted the shutters from his lantern, allowing it to illuminate the space and reveal the barrels and boxes around them.

She nodded, the light warm on her face. She didn't trust herself to speak.

"*Chérie,* you are bleeding," he said. He set the lantern atop a nearby barrel and knelt beside her to brush her hair back from her temple. Taryn shoved him away, both surprised and offended by his boldness.

"It is nothing," she snapped.

"It is not *nothing,*" he insisted. "Let me help you."

She shook her head and watched him warily, once again struck by his stormy eyes, but all too aware that her crushed prosthetic was completely visible to him. "Why are you trying to help me?" she asked, unable to keep the bitterness out of her voice.

"Because you are hurt," he answered gently.

"I am not *hurt,*" Taryn exclaimed, her right hand going to the immobile prosthetic. "I am *broken.*"

He frowned. "You mean your arm is broken."

"Which in everyone else's eyes means *I* am broken."

His scowl deepened. "Who told you that?"

She cast her gaze down. "Captain Storm."

"Do not listen to her, *Mademoiselle* Taryn," he said as a gentle, friendly smile touched his lips. "She has been hurt by a biomaton before, and thus treats them all poorly."

"She was hurt by a biomaton?" Taryn asked.

"*Oui.* A clockwork assassin called Petrichor killed her parents. Now Ace is all the family she has left."

"Ace is her brother?" It made sense; they had the same eyes.

"*Oui.*"

Taryn's expression twisted into one of disgust. "Of course those two vipers are related. I should have known."

"Do not hate Ace."

"He dropped me!"

"He is not a bad man. He is pressured by Storm to stay tough and cruel."

"I do not think he needs much encouragement," Taryn

snarled. She forced herself to her feet, her entire body screaming at her, her prosthetic dangling uselessly by her side. She turned to leave and froze, scowling. Ace stood in the doorway, staring at her.

"Are you all right?" he asked.

"Aye, no thanks to you," Taryn snapped, clutching her broken prosthetic.

"You are bleeding," he said, his ice blue eyes examining her temple.

"I wonder *why*," Taryn said with a sneer. "Are you going to keep standing there, or may I return to my quarters?"

"Let me help you," Ace offered, stepping toward her.

"Why?" She felt wild, like an animal who knows it is cornered. "So that you can finish what you started and kill me?"

"Taryn, I am sorry I dropped you."

"No," she snapped, her throat tight. "You do not get to use my name. You have not earned the *right* to use my name. Call me 'biomaton' like your sister does. That is all I am to you anyway."

Ace's face twisted into a scowl, but there was something almost like hurt in his eyes. "Sit down, biomaton," he commanded.

Taryn bit down hard on the inside of her lip. She sat on a barrel, glaring at Ace. "What is it you want from me?"

"Right now, I want you to shut your mouth and do as I tell you," Ace growled. His hand rested on the butt of the pistol at his hip as he walked toward her, closing the space between them. His boots were too loud on the rough-hewn wood of the deck. "Are you ready to listen to me?"

Taryn's jaw clenched so hard she feared she would bite right through her lower lip. She nodded.

"Good. Can you move your arm at all?"

Taryn shook her head.

"I thought not." Ace glanced at the Frenchman, who had silently watched the exchange up to this point. "Bring the lamp over here, Emmett."

"What are you doing?" Taryn cried, jerking away as Ace touched her shoulder.

"Our ship's mechanick can attempt to fix your prosthetic, but I need to remove it. It is useless to you like this, anyhow."

Taryn wanted to say no, wanted to deny him the right to even touch her, but she knew it would make no difference. She teeth gritted tightly. "Do what you need to do."

She turned her face away from them as Emmett brought the lamp over so that Ace could see the twisted, broken prosthetic. Taryn's sleeves buttoned over the shoulders, and Ace unbuttoned her left sleeve hesitantly, pushing the fabric away, baring her skin. Beneath the leather pad between her shoulder and the prosthetic, her skin was livid, the tissue puckered and discoloured where the clockwork joined her body. Emmett leaned over Ace's shoulder to watch while Ace's fingers fluttered over her shoulder, examining the places where the clockwork met her skin.

"This is well-made," Ace said, pulling a number of tools from the pocket of his great coat. "Tell me if you experience any pain; I do not want to hurt you."

"There is no need to lie," Taryn hissed. "I know what I am to you."

Ace sighed, but did not say anything else as he began to work in earnest on the prosthetic. Taryn sat quietly, her right hand twisted in the folds of her skirt. *It used to be so elegant, and now it is broken.* She appreciated the offer to have the ship's mechanick try and fix the prosthetic, but she doubted it could be repaired. Her fingers moved to the chain of the pocket watch from Royal. The watch was still intact, and she thanked God that the one thing she had left of her previous life had not been destroyed. At least she could hang on to that, even if she was being forced into slavery.

"How did you lose your arm, *chérie?*" Emmett asked, his French lilt pulling her from her dark thoughts.

"There was a fire," Taryn replied quietly, utterly emotionless as the images from her nightmares flashed behind her eyes. "My father came home very late and very drunk. My mother was furious. She said if he was going to come home like that, he ought not to come home at all. I was only six. I do not quite remember what happened, but the oil lamp fell. My parents died in the blaze. I should have died, too, but someone pulled me out. Apparently he thought I would make a good slave."

"This man—he was kind to you, *non?*" Emmett asked.

"I do not remember," Taryn answered flatly. "I haven't any memories of my time with him."

"You remember nothing?" Ace asked, looking up from his work on her arm.

She shook her head. "Nothing before I lived on the streets five years ago, save the fire and a few foggy memories of my parents."

Emmett appeared saddened by her words. "I am sorry, *chérie.*"

"Your creator was Lord Anthony Erikkson," Ace said.

"You said that once before. That means nothing to me," Taryn said, but something deep, deep in her mind was stirring. Images flashed behind her eyes too quickly to read or even really remember, making her feel claustrophobic in her own head. Ace's fingers fluttered across her skin, and at the same moment a memory struck her. As clearly as if she'd been physically transported there, she saw herself in a room with golden light streaming through a window draped with gauzy curtains. She was sitting on a large four-poster bed. She was distinctly aware of someone sitting on her left side, but when she turned to look, the vision faded. She found herself staring at Ace as he worked with painstaking patience to remove her crushed prosthetic.

And then he looked at her, too. "This is more difficult than I expected."

Taryn looked away, something catching in her throat. She felt like a broken toy under his hands, like a marionette, limp and empty. She was broken and small and *nothing*, and here was Ace, his careful fingers dancing on her shoulder, as though she was simply a machine. A wave of loneliness washed over her. Not for the first time, she missed Royal immensely.

"Ah, finally. I think I have got it," Ace said. His fingers slipped between her shoulder and the leather pad that protected it, gently pulling it off with the prosthetic. Taryn looked down at the small pieces of clockwork protruding from the stump of her shoulder. Those small gears and metal pins were all that made her arm operate, connecting to the muscles and tendons inside her shoulder. She ran her fingers over the pieces, mourning the loss of her limb. Quietly, she pulled her sleeve back down and buttoned it, hiding the damage in an empty sheath.

Ace set her clockwork arm aside, where it looked dull and dead, twisted and deformed. "Well, let us hope you do not have another encounter with Storm like this one. I would avoid her from now on, if I were you."

Taryn frowned at him. "*You* are the one who dropped me."

"Just stay away from Storm," Ace snapped. "I shall take your arm to our mechanick and see what she can do."

Taryn did not thank him. She stood, her head held high. "I am returning to my quarters."

"*Bonne nuit, chérie,*" Emmett called as she left the room. Taryn did not even turn.

Ace watched the biomaton go, limping from the cargo hold, and struggled with the feelings within his chest, feelings he could neither explain nor understand. She was a *biomaton*. She wasn't human; she had not been human since she'd nearly died all those years ago. Someone had chosen to pull her from the edge of oblivion and turn her into a slave, and when he'd finished with her, he'd wiped her mind and dumped her on the streets. It was *sick*, but it wasn't illegal. Ace couldn't do anything about the cruelty Taryn had experienced, especially if she could not even remember what had happened. Besides, who knew? Perhaps her creator hadn't abandoned her at all. Perhaps she had run away all on her own.

But what Ace could not ignore was the sheer *humanity* he had seen in those emerald eyes. This was a frightened young woman they had taken from everything she knew and dropped into a world of fear and hatred. She had no one here, no friendly face to look to for help—and that was Storm's intention, he supposed. Isolate her. Make her understand her place. But something inside him rebelled against the very thought of Taryn ending up like the other biomatons he had known. It would be wrong, so wrong, for her to lose all that fire and become the hollowed shell she was meant to be. It would somehow mean the death of a beautiful creature, and everything within Ace hated that. He recalled Storm's words. *Harden your heart.* They were the same words he'd been telling himself for years, the same words he told himself even now, as he stared at the girl's broken prosthetic. His compassion would not save her from the fate dictated by law. And he couldn't afford to be in any more trouble with Storm than he already was.

"I want you to keep an eye on her," Ace said quietly to

Emmett. "Make sure she is safe. She is very important to our mission."

"*Oui, Capitaine,*" Emmett said, grinning. "I will ensure she is safe."

Ace could tell he was smitten as well.

CHAPTER NINE

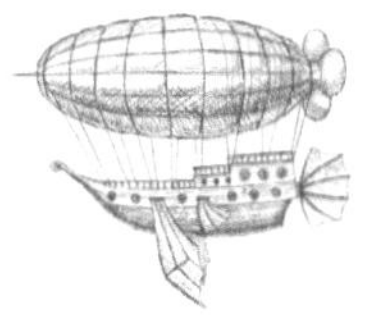

Taryn did not sleep. They had provided her with a hammock in the small cabin she shared with Seraphim, but between her aching body and the troublesome thoughts swirling in her mind, she spent the hours tossing and turning. She gave up just before daybreak, and rose to head above deck. It was chilly in the predawn air, and a stiff breeze swept her skirt about her legs. The sky was still a deep indigo blue, but as she gazed out over the rail, she could see the horizon was just beginning to lighten, turning pale blue and yellow with the rising of the sun. The air was crisp and fresh, and Taryn allowed it to wash her lungs clean of the night's worries and fears.

The light rose quickly, bathing the world in salmon pink and revealing the *Dauntless'* position above the clouds. Below them, a blanket of white cotton hid the ground from view. In places, she could see a hillock or craggy ridge peeking through, but for the most part, the fluffy clouds hid any clue as to their location. Taryn sighed, watching the sky turn orange as the sun prepared to breach the horizon.

She heard voices behind her and turned to see three men clamber onto the deck, chattering amongst themselves. She was disappointed the silence had been broken, but there was nothing she could do about it. Taryn returned her gaze to the horizon. It had been a very long time since she'd seen a sunrise, and she had never before experienced one from this height.

"Well, look here!" one of the men cried. "It is the firecracker biomaton what believes she is human. What happened, Firecracker? You are missing an arm!"

Taryn turned slowly, keeping herself calm and steady as she regarded the men. The one in the centre, a huge blond who had to be more than six and a half feet tall, was grinning. The other two chuckled, so Taryn was certain the big man had spoken. She considered replying—but no, she would not give him the satisfaction. She started to return to her quarters instead.

The other two airshipmen laughed. "She is having none of that, Terrence!" The corner of Taryn's mouth twitched ever so slightly at the man's humiliation while his friends laughed loudly at his expense.

The big man—Terrence—stepped in front of Taryn, blocking her path. "I asked you a question, biomaton."

"Please step aside," Taryn said calmly, trying to keep herself from being afraid.

"You think you are better than us, don't you?" he hissed.

Taryn shook her head, her heart pounding. "No, sir." She choked the words out, hating herself for even saying such subservient things. She tried to duck past him, but a meaty hand closed around her wrist, yanking her back around to face him. Terrence was huge, so close, and his livid face towered above her.

"Did I say you could go?" he hissed.

"Let go of me," Taryn said, her voice tight. She tried to pull away, only for his grip tighten until he was squeezing her wrist so hard that Taryn yelped in pain.

"Perhaps we ought to teach you another lesson."

In desperation, Taryn cried out. "Leave me alone!" She tried to push him away with her left hand—only to remember she had no left hand. She tried to back away, only to discover the other two airshipmen had surrounded her. Her fingers were going numb.

"Release her." Taryn recognized Emmett's voice immediately. No one else on board that she'd met so far had a French lilt like that.

Terrence's eyes had moved to somewhere over Taryn's shoulder. "We were just about to teach the biomaton lesson. Do not get in our way."

Emmett stepped between Taryn and Terrence, forcing him to let go of her wrist. Taryn stumbled backwards, her eyes locked on the confrontation between the small, wiry Frenchman and the massive airshipman. Emmett's body was tensed, a bundle of sheer muscle ready to fight, ready to leap into action. To Taryn's surprise, Terrence backed down.

"If you so much as come near her again, I shall kill you. *D'accord?*" Emmett hissed.

The sailors scowled, but nodded, saying nothing.

"*Bien.* Return to your duties." Emmett turned to Taryn as the sailors moved off, and all of the fight drained out of him even as she watched, his grey eyes softening until he was the lean Frenchman again, kind and friendly. "Did they hurt you, *chérie?*"

Taryn released a breath she hadn't realized she'd been holding. She shook her head meekly. She was just beginning to regain feeling in her hand, like someone was pricking the tips of her fingers with a needle.

"I am glad. You should not allow them to push you about. It gives them too much power."

Taryn frowned. After what Storm and the others had done to her, the last thing she wanted was confrontation. Let them do what they liked, let them walk all over her, just so long as they stopped hurting her. This was far worse than any bullying she had experienced at Grafton's. This was pure hatred.

"I tell you the truth, *chérie.* Do not allow them to rule you."

Taryn merely shrugged, looking away to where the sun had already risen fully above the horizon. She had missed the sunrise after all. "Thank you for stopping them," she muttered quietly, turning to return belowdecks and take her place in her quarters until they arrived wherever they were headed. It seemed the only place she was at all safe.

"*Mademoiselle,* wait," Emmett called after her.

Taryn stopped, chewing her lip. "What?"

"We ought to tell Ace what happened. He can do more to prevent it than I."

Taryn shook her head. "No. We do not have to bother him. I am all right."

"*Mademoiselle* Taryn, I must insist. He can protect you."

"I do not need protecting!" Taryn exclaimed. Her exhaustion was kicking in, making her irritable. "I need to get off this bloody ship!" She bit hard on her lip, refusing to break down in front of him.

"*S'il vous plaît.* Let us at least inform him of what happened. *D'accord?*" He offered her his hand.

Taryn did not take it, but she followed him below decks, to a first class cabin that contained two bunks against one wall, neatly made and tucked in with military precision. Ace was there, preparing for the day. He was not yet wearing his navy coat; it lay neatly on the lower bunk, ready for him. His nimble fingers were buttoning his waistcoat. Taryn felt strange seeing him in his shirtsleeves, as if she were intruding.

"Taryn was attacked by three of the crew this morning." Emmett got right to the point. "Their intentions were not honourable."

Ace raised an eyebrow, his face otherwise stony and still as a statue. "And you swept in on your white horse to rescue her? Perhaps you should have allowed them to have their way with her. She is only a slave, after all, and should understand her place."

Taryn's irritation boiled into full-blown anger. "I did not ask to be this way!"

"Shut up!" Ace cried, his face turned red with anger for the first time in her presence. Taryn shut her mouth, almost frightened by his outburst. "You are not in your safe little school any longer. No one is fooled by your human act, and no one cares that you feel attacked. No one may *ever* care how you feel again. The sooner you learn to swallow your feelings and remain silent, the better your chances of survival. Do you understand? Your life no longer belongs to you. And though it may not seem like it, I am actually trying to help you."

Taryn fell silent, too stunned to bring herself to argue with him. Ace stood just inches from her, his eyes locked with hers, blue ice melting slowly. His face suddenly held some sort of pain she did not understand, and he turned away, overcome.

"I do not want to see them tear you apart," he muttered beneath his breath, so quietly she almost did not hear. Louder, he said, "Have I made myself clear?"

"Yes, sir," Taryn muttered, dropping her eyes. She did not know what else to say. She shuffled her feet on the wooden floor.

Ace looked at Emmett. "If you are worried about the crew being hostile to her, then remain with her. She is important to our mission. If you want to be her protector, please, do so." Ace worded it in such a way that made it sound like Emmett had a choice, but his tone suggested it was a command, not a suggestion.

Emmett nodded. *"Oui, Capitaine."* He took Taryn's hand. "Come, *chérie.* Ace has things to do."

He had to pull Taryn from the cabin. She was still too stunned to speak or move on her own.

✾

Emmett pulled her through the halls to the lower deck, into a converted cargo hold. Inside was a steam-powered bread oven and a black iron potbellied stove filled with hot coals. Barrels of salted pork, pickled herring, and fresh fruits and vegetables stood all around the room. Onions, chains of garlic, dried herbs, and pots and pans hung from the ceiling. Beside the stove swayed a man Taryn could only describe as *large.* If Terrence had been big, this man was nearly twice his size. He had dark skin, and hair cut so close to his scalp as to appear nonexistent. He wore an apron that might once have been white, but was now grey.

"Cook!" Emmett called with a grin. "I expect you can make us a fitting *petit déjeuner?"*

The man turned to see them come in. He had the warmest, most welcoming smile. "Emmett! Come in, my friend! I think I can cook something up." His deep baritone voice was tinged with a lovely, unfamiliar accent Taryn could only guess was from some part of Africa.

There was a makeshift bench made up of a large plank of wood perched atop two barrels, and the cook pulled down a frying pan from where it hung, setting it atop the bench. "Introduce me to your lady friend, Emmett, please," he said as he retrieved an onion and a slab of cured bacon and began chopping them.

"This is Taryn," Emmett said, tugging her over to two barrels that sat in lieu of chairs. "Ace brought her aboard."

"Pardon my saying so, Miss Taryn," the big man intoned, meeting her eyes, "but you do not seem like Master Ace's type."

Taryn scoffed. "I am *not* Ace's type. I am only here for his mission."

"Ah, another mission," he grinned, shaking his head. "We are always going somewhere to do something. I do not bother myself with it any longer. Just so long as I have my supplies to cook for the crew."

"What may I call you?" Taryn asked, watching his large hands work deftly to chop the vegetables and meat. He did not even need to keep his eyes on his task.

"Cook. Just Cook." He nodded his head toward her left side. "May I ask what happened to your arm?"

Taryn shuddered, her fingers going to her empty sleeve. "I had a run-in with Storm," she answered flatly.

"Taryn is a biomaton," Emmett explained.

"I thought so," Cook replied. He cracked eggs into a skillet, using only his right hand. "Watch out for the captain, Miss Taryn. She is rather hostile toward your kind."

"I have discovered that," she muttered.

The sizzle of cooking food filled the air as Cook placed the skillet on the stovetop. Succulent smells began to fill the hold, making Taryn's stomach rumble. She hadn't realized just how hungry she was. The last meal she ate was breakfast the morning before.

"I like her," Cook said after a moment. "Be watchful, Emmett. Do not let Ace steal this beauty from you."

Taryn's cheeks grew hot in embarrassment, and she lowered her eyes, allowing her red hair to fall over her face.

Emmett laughed. "You have made her blush!"

"I apologize, miss," Cook said gently. "I did not mean to be forward."

Taryn shook her head, but did not look up, her cheeks still burning. She chewed her lip, wondering how Cook could even say she was beautiful when she felt so broken. She was missing her left arm. She was so very clearly not whole. She did not feel beautiful in the least.

"Here, eat," Cook said, passing them two plates filled with fluffy yellow omelettes. "It will help you feel better."

Taryn carefully balanced the plate on her lap, forcing herself to take small, ladylike bites even though she wanted to scarf down the delicious omelette.

"*Merci,* Cook! *Ç'est trés bien,*" Emmett exclaimed, his mouth full. "*Délicieux!*"

Cook smiled, the corners of his eyes crinkling. He wiped his hands on his apron and started chopping veggies for a stew. "Thank you, Emmett. Miss Taryn, if you ever get hungry, come down to see me. I shall fix you up in no time."

Taryn nodded and smiled, enjoying the kindness of these strangers and the good food. "Thank you, Cook." She finished the omelette off and sighed, satisfied. It was nice to feel accepted, to feel like they were not judging her for what she was. She could almost pretend she was normal, save for the strange phantom sensation of her missing arm's fingertips prickling.

"Miss Taryn," a deep, silky voice intoned from behind them. Taryn turned to see her roommate, his long black hair tied away from his face.

"Yes?"

"May I speak with you?"

Taryn nodded, waiting, but Seraphim hovered in the doorway, wings fluttering nervously. Only then did Taryn realize he meant speak *alone,* and stood to follow him. Seraphim was odd, yes, but she sensed no danger from him. "I shall return in a moment," she told Emmett before leaving the room with Seraphim.

He led her a little way down the hall and then stopped, glancing about as though he were afraid of someone eavesdropping. "You must get off this ship, Miss Taryn."

"What?"

"Quickly." He glanced over his shoulder again, and his voice grew urgent as his hands twisted into knotted fists at his waist. "I did not recognize you last night, but now I do. If you do not leave, a great many biomatons will suffer."

Taryn did not understand. "I would like nothing more than to leave this ship and return to my life, but look at me!" She gestured to her empty sleeve. "I would be in chains as soon as my feet touched the ground. I can no longer pretend I am whole or human."

Seraphim's eyes flashed. "You shall be enslaved as soon as we reach our destination, and many other biomatons will die!"

Taryn shook her head, shrinking away from him. All this talk of suffering terrified her. "No. No, I am not important. I am no one. The world will not change simply because I have been put in my 'place.'"

"You do not know how important you are." Seraphim's voice dropped to a whisper. "Remember: Sedition."

Taryn jerked as though she'd been slapped. The word sent an image hurtling through her mind the image of a man's face, auburn hair, urging her on. But the image was so fleeting she hardly saw it at all, just *felt* it before it vanished. Still, she *knew* it was a memory. It was the same man she sometimes saw in her dreams. "What did you say?"

Seraphim just shook his head. "I did not say anything."

Taryn struggled to recall what she'd seen, desperate to regain anything, any *scrap* of memory that might rise to the surface. "You said you know who I am now. What did you mean?"

Seraphim shook his head again. "It is not yet time. When you are ready, it will become clear." He began to walk away, his wings shut tightly and no longer fluttering.

"Time for what?" Taryn questioned, racing after him. "Seraphim, what do you know about my past?"

"Get off this ship, Miss Taryn. It is not safe for you here."

"What do you *mean?*" she demanded.

But he would not answer her. Taryn gave up as Seraphim disappeared into the maze of corridors. As she turned to retrace her steps, she realized she was lost. *Very* lost. She kicked her heel across the wood floor, feeling sick and alone. Perhaps it was because of her isolation there in the labyrinthine belly of the ship, but how painfully alone she was hit her like a brick wall, and all at once she could barely breathe. She swore, cursing the day Ace had discovered her secret.

"Those are rather harsh words, biomaton."

Taryn spun on her heel, surprised to discover Ace standing behind her, half a grin on his face. Taryn slapped her hand over her mouth, her face flushing with embarrassment yet again. "I—I was not aware you were there."

"So you felt your verbal abuse was appropriate because I was not here?"

Taryn watched him warily. He did not seem angry, but he was volatile. What if he hurt her for her thoughtless words? "I am sorry," she said, but it was more out of fear than remorse.

Ace watched her for a moment, his face betraying nothing. "What are you doing down here besides using language fit for a sailor?"

"I got lost," she admitted. "I was trying to find my way out."

"Above deck?"

She nodded, still afraid of somehow angering him.

"You are not far. Follow me."

Ace led her around a corner and down a hall to a flight of stairs. Taryn stopped halfway up to examine a dial on the wall, its needle trembling slightly as it moved with the steam pressure created by the engine thrumming beneath their feet. She ran her fingers over the dial, an ache blooming in her chest. She'd had a dream, once, of being an airship mechanick, but that dream died when she'd discovered girls weren't allowed on the naval ships. And yet, here she was, aboard an airship that flew for the Queen. It wasn't at all like she had imagined.

"Biomaton?" Ace questioned, looking back at her with a puzzled expression on his face.

Taryn jerked her hand away from the dial. "I—I used to dream… I am sorry."

"Come with me," Ace said, as if he hadn't heard her. She followed him up the stairs, onto the upper deck of the ship. The day was clear and cold, and Taryn realized this was her first time above deck in true daylight. The balloon above their heads was taut and bulging, the lines that kept it tethered thicker than her arm. The wood of the deck was even more weathered than she'd thought, grey with age and wear. Where the tether lines met the deck, the wood was worn smooth from the tread of sailor's feet. The crew scuttled about the deck, performing their various duties. Taryn and Ace had emerged on the quarter deck, and she gazed over the ship, feeling something like awe that she was actually here. *Royal will never believe this,* she thought before a pang of sadness washed over her again. She might not ever see Royal again.

"Seraphim said you intend to make me a slave," Taryn said quietly, almost surprised she had said anything.

Ace's expression hardened. He was silent, looking away from her while his jaw worked.

"You were never not a slave," a sharp voice interrupted. Taryn flinched upon recognizing Storm's voice. She turned warily, watching as Storm's eyes lit on Taryn's empty sleeve, then traveled back up to her face. She clicked her tongue. "You are barely even a biomaton any longer. It is unfortunate they changed your brain too much for you to be considered human."

Taryn's fist clenched tightly as anger climbed up her throat. She wanted to retort, but thought better of it when she remembered what happened the night before. "What do you want?" she asked, her voice dripping with venom.

Storm smirked, but it failed to reach her ice-cold eyes. "I only wanted to make sure our little biomaton was still fit for her mission. I would hate to find out that my brother had killed her."

"You would not care if I died in that fall. We both know that," Taryn growled.

Storm's eyes narrowed. "Actually, you are wrong yet again, biomaton. You are *very* important to this mission. So I need you alive for a while yet." Her sneer became menacing. "Still, it does not seem you learned your lesson, freak. Shall I teach it to you again?" Storm's gauntlet closed with a clank.

"Let her alone, Storm," Ace interjected, though he sounded detached, disinterested. "We shall reach the Black Castle by tomorrow morning, and then you may gloat as much as you like."

Storm's lip curled in revulsion. "Still protecting her?"

Still? Taryn looked from the captain to her first mate, wondering at the implications of that single word. What had Ace said or done on her behalf to make Storm so angry?

"You may call it what you like." Ace's tone was icy. "I am not going to argue with you."

Storm snorted. "I thought you told the Frenchman to look after her."

"I did. She was lost. I was just taking her back to him when you interrupted."

Storm narrowed her eyes. "Take her to him, then meet me in my cabin. I need to speak with you. Alone."

Ace nodded. "Yes, Captain." Taryn could hear the contempt in his voice; it practically dripped off his tongue. But beneath it, there was something else, something familiar in the tilt of his head and the slope of his shoulders: submission. "Come, biomaton. We shall find Emmett."

Taryn followed Ace back belowdecks, turning the confrontation over and over in her mind. She marveled that Ace had apparently stood up for her. She was beginning to see two sides of him. There was the fierce, cold privateer who cared for no one and nothing and did his captain's bidding without question, who was as bad as his psychopath sister. The second was different, hidden—only apparent when Storm was not around— and not exactly kind, but near it. If only she could keep him away from Storm, perhaps she could get to know the second, almost decent man she thought he could be.

"You protected me," she said softly after a moment.

He glanced at her. "You have enough ahead of you without her abuse. She treats you cruelly because she enjoys it. I am tired of watching."

Taryn observed him quietly, unsure of what to do with this side of him. Finally, she said, "You never answered my question. Are you going to sell me into slavery?"

Ace did not look at her, but his jaw tightened. "I do not know what will happen. I do not like the thought of leaving you there. That place is cruel, *evil* without measure. They are not the kind of people anyone should be subject to, regardless of their humanity or lack thereof."

Taryn's throat constricted and she rubbed at her shoulder, feeling the metal protruding from her skin: the spot where she was more machine than human. Once again, she thought of Royal. How different her life could have been, if only she were whole. Royal cared about her. They could have been happy. Not married—no, she had never dreamt of marriage, even in her wildest daydreams. He was an aristocrat, after all. He stood to inherit his father's title. And she was nothing, even without the clockwork that branded her a slave. Besides, she did not love him, and perhaps *could* not—she no longer knew. But they could have been friends. She could have been the mechanick for his biomatons, and they could have been happy. There was no hope of that left. The last few years had been a lie. A dream. It could never last, and she'd known that. But now it was all over, and the harsh reality of the world they lived in had come crashing down around her. It had only been a matter of time.

"You know," Ace offered, waking Taryn from her thoughts. "I lost my parents when I was young, too."

Taryn stopped in her tracks, stunned to hear him admit something about himself. "You did?"

He nodded. "I was twelve. Storm was sixteen. We inherited the *Dauntless* from them." He avoided her eye. "They were killed by a biomaton assassin called Petrichor."

There were no words that seemed appropriate. Taryn looked at this man, this man who had seemed so hard and cruel when she met him, yet now seemed so thoughtful and filled with sorrow. A biomaton assassin? She had not known such a creature existed. And why would Ace entrust her with this information? "I—I am sorry," she said feebly, knowing it wasn't enough.

"We believe Petrichor was built by Lord Erikkson," Ace continued. "You are our only link to him. Please, help us bring him to justice so he cannot hurt anyone else."

Taryn's stomach flipped and bile crept up her throat. Ace's sob story was yet another manipulation tactic. He did not care about her; he cared about what she could do for him. She shoved past him, struggling to hide her fury. She should not have been so stupid as to think she could actually see a friend in him. She should have learned her lesson when he dropped her. He was a pirate, after all. Only a fool trusted a pirate. And she was learning just how great a fool she could be.

Ace caught her wrist. "Taryn—that did not come out as I meant it to. I only meant that he hurt you, too. And all the other children he turned into biomatons. I thought you, of all people, would want to stop him."

Taryn hated herself for wanting to say *yes,* for wanting to exact revenge on the man who had saved her life only to turn her into a machine. She hated the fact that she wanted the same thing her captors wanted.

"What does it matter what I want?" she spat at him. "You will get what you want in the end, and all because you are human and I am not. I hope one day you are forced to stand in my shoes. I hope *you* are turned into a bleeding biomaton!"

She wrenched her wrist from his grasp and stormed off. Ace called her name, but she refused to stop. If he cared whether or not she found her way back to Emmett, he would follow her.

"Taryn, I am sorry. I deserved that. Honestly, I shall do everything in my power to protect you," he claimed as he chased her. "But ultimately, it is not up to me. Storm is in charge. Even I fear her. She may be my sister, but she would not hesitate to keelhaul me if she thought it would send a message."

Taryn pretended she could not hear him. He was trying to manipulate her; she understood that now. It was all a game to him. Get her to trust him, even *like* him, just to say he could: just to have a laugh with the crew about how utterly naive the biomaton was. He would brag to Storm about this interaction later and they would laugh at the poor, helpless biomaton. Well, she would not give him the satisfaction.

"Taryn!" Emmett came running up the corridor, a look of relief creasing his brow. "You disappeared! I was afraid—" His grey eyes flickered over Ace. "What happened?"

"I got lost," Taryn answered flatly. "Ace *helped* me get back." Her intonation made it very clear she certainly did not believe he had helped her.

"*Merci, mon ami,*" Emmett said, giving Ace a nod. "*Merci* for bringing her back to me."

Ace inclined his head. "*De rien,* Emmett." He turned back to Taryn. She thought she read hurt there, just beneath the layer of ice, but she quickly told herself she was seeing things. "Do try to stay with Emmett, biomaton. He will protect you."

He turned to go, his face sliding back to the inscrutable neutral expression it normally held. He'd reconstructed the walls just as quickly as he had taken them down to let her in. Of course he did not care to make up for what he'd done, she told herself. He was as cold and cruel as his sister.

"*Chérie,* what happened between you and Ace?" Emmett questioned, touching her shoulder tenderly. Taryn glanced at him, and at such close quarters she could see the individual freckles scattered across his cheekbones.

"Nothing."

"*Vraiment?*"

"*Oui,*" she nodded.

His stormy eyes lit up, his entire face glowing with excitement. "*Tu parles français?*"

"*Un peut,*" Taryn admitted. "I learned in finishing school, before I attended Grafton's. I am afraid I am not very good at it."

"Ah, I do not care if you are any good!" Emmett exclaimed. "*Ç'est merveilleux* to hear it from another tongue!"

"Does no one else on this ship speak French?"

"Only Ace, and his French is just passable," Emmett replied, his features drooping. "How I miss being amongst my own people."

"*Je suis désolé,*" she whispered.

He shrugged and smiled at her. "What would you like to do, *chérie?*"

Taryn paused, considering. "May I see the engine?" She had been curious about the engine since she'd boarded the *Dauntless.* Since before that, if she was honest. She wanted to see the powerful engines that thrummed in the depths of the ship like a heartbeat.

Emmett nodded, but Taryn noted that he'd lost some of his colour. "*Oui.* Follow me, *mademoiselle.*"

He led her through the corridors of the ship, down several flights of stairs to where the very atmosphere thrummed and Taryn could feel the power of the engines vibrating in her chest. The air was thick and humid from the excess heat given off by the massive engines. Finally, Emmett led her through a door and out onto a metal mesh catwalk. Below their feet lay the giant engines, singing joyfully like a living thing.

Taryn stared at the engines, in awe of their size, how complicated they were. The huge furnace providing steam and power to the engine filled the room with red-orange light. It was brighter closer to the engines, but up on the catwalk, the reddish glow provided little illumination. Heat and steam hung thickly in the air. Taryn marveled at the immensity of the engine, the *sheer power* of it. It had been one thing to read about them in textbooks, but it was another thing entirely to stand just above an engine of such grand scale and power. She looked at Emmett excitedly, so eager to share her awe with him she did not notice how pale he had become, how still he stood upon the catwalk.

"This is incredible!" she cried.

"I am glad you find it interesting," Emmett answered, his voice shaking.

"Are you all right?" she asked. He did not sound like himself.

"I do not like this room. I am afraid the floor will fall."

Taryn smiled, his fear both surprising and somehow endearing. She would not have guessed he was afraid of anything.

"Emmett! What're you doin' 'ere?" A new voice came from the shadows at the far end of the room. A figure appeared, walking with a slight swagger: evidence of one who spent more time strolling with the sway of an airship than on solid ground. The girl wore a heavy leather apron over her dress, whose hem had been trimmed to end halfway up her calves. She had dark skin, and dark, wiry hair held back from her face by a pair of welding goggles. Around her waist was a belt that held the tools of a mechanick, large enough to suit the huge gears of the engine below them. Her hands were coated with grease and grime.

"*Allo*, Bolts," Emmett said, trying to sound chipper, but Taryn could see how petrified he still was. "I brought our new mechanick to see the engine."

Bolts' dark eyes moved to Taryn, a crease between her eyebrows. "Mechanick?"

Taryn shook her head. "Try biomaton."

Bolts seemed to relax. "Of course! You're th' one I'm fixin' th' arm for! Pleasure to meet ya." She held out a hand, giving Taryn a firm, warm handshake. "That bit o' mechanicks 's more intricate than any I've seen." Her voice was heavily accented with the familiar, warm tones of a cockney street urchin, an accent Taryn herself had fought so hard to lose. "But I'm makin' progress."

"May I see it?" Taryn asked, eager to be in the presence of another mechanick.

Bolts nodded, stepping into the shadows once more. Taryn followed her, with Emmett tagging close behind as he walked gingerly across the catwalk, as though it could cave at any moment beneath his weight.

Bolts led them out of the engine room and into a small cabin beyond that had been converted into a workshop. Several lamps burned, casting warm yellow light on the bare wooden walls. The engine noise was muffled slightly here, but Taryn could still feel its power vibrating the floor beneath her feet. On a workbench against the wall to their left lay Taryn's broken prosthetic. It had been pulled apart, broken and bent cogs scattered across the workbench, organized roughly according to their place in the original design. Taryn's throat closed unexpectedly. She ran her fingers over the prosthetic's pieces, wondering at how it could look so small and lifeless there on the table. She barely believed it was the same arm she had worn for most of her life.

"I do not 'ave enough parts ta fix it prop'rly," Bolts admitted, moving a few of the cogs about with her fingers. Taryn noticed her fingernails were short and ragged, perhaps chewed.

"Are you sure?" Taryn asked. She wanted—no, *needed*—to fix her arm. She needed it back, if only to stop feeling so alien in her own skin. If only to stop everyone from staring when she walked past.

"Aye. We 'ave large parts for repairin' th' engine, but not small parts like this."

Taryn fingered the chain on her birthday pocket watch, wondering if the parts inside its golden case would fit her prosthetic. It wouldn't be the first time she'd swiped parts from a clock to fix it. But no, there were not enough gears there, and she did not want to lose her one connection to Royal. "Well, I suppose I cannot ask you to do any more than your best. I appreciate you trying, anyhow." She sighed. "Thank you for showing me the engine room."

"You are welcome down to visit anytime," Bolts smiled. Her teeth were a brilliant white, and perfectly straight behind her full, rosy lips. "It can get lonely down 'ere wit' th' engines."

"Thank you." Taryn smiled, but the expression did not reach her eyes. She did not understand the knot of mournfulness that bloomed in her chest the longer she stared at her broken arm. "I am sure they will take my arm off your hands soon. I do not think I shall be aboard the *Dauntless* much longer."

"What?" Emmett questioned, his voice sharp at the edges. Taryn had nearly forgotten he was standing behind her.

"Do not act surprised, Emmett," Taryn said dryly. "Wherever we are going, Storm is planning to leave me there."

"*Non!*" Emmett cried. "They cannot leave you there!"

"They have made it clear that is what they are planning," Taryn replied bitterly. "Besides—" She gestured to where her crushed, dead arm lay, her lip curling in disgust.

"They cannot intend that! *Sûrement!*"

"Where else am I to go?" Taryn asked. "As soon as I touch ground I shall be arrested and enslaved." Her voice fell, until she was speaking more to herself than to Emmett. "And then Royal shall know my deceit and hate me, and I cannot bear that."

"You may remain on *la belle Dauntless.*"

"And endure Storm's torment?" Taryn asked, horror creeping into her voice. She raked her hand through her copper hair. "There is no safe path for me. Pray you do not ever become a biomaton," she said firmly to them both. "It is a living hell."

Emmett's expressive grey eyes spoke volumes of pain and sympathy. He offered her his hand, and though hesitant,

Taryn took it. He pressed her hand between both of his. "*Chérie,* I will do all I can to change the mind of *mon capitaine.*"

Taryn searched his eyes. "Why are you so kind to me?"

"No one deserves to be alone," he said gently, smiling a little at her. "I will be gone a few minutes. Is that all right?"

"She can stay 'ere with me," Bolts offered. "I'll show you the engine up close."

"*Bien.* I will return, *ma belle*. Do not be afraid."

And then he was gone, and Taryn followed Bolts down to see the powerful engine, her heart in her throat.

<h1 style="text-align:center">CHAPTER TEN</h1>

"Are you *attempting* to undermine me?"

Ace did not flinch at Storm's scream, so used to her fury by now that it no longer ruffled his feathers. They were alone again in her cabin, her favourite place to berate him—besides in front of the entire crew. His hand went to the pistol at his hip, taking comfort in the way it fit in the palm of his hand.

"Or are you simply so *stupid* you do not care you are being insubordinate?"

"Once, we made decisions together," he said quietly, his expression calm, almost glassy.

"We did. Do you remember why I quit taking recommendations from you, brother dear?" Storm asked, rancor dripping from her tongue.

Ace searched for anywhere to look but at her, his roving eyes betraying his guilt.

"Well?" she spat.

"We changed," he muttered.

"No, *you* grew sloppy!" she screamed. "How many airships did we lose that day?"

Ace swallowed hard but remained silent although pain

flickered behind his eyes. His fingers tightened on the butt of his pistol, knuckles going white and bloodless. He remembered that day all too well. They had lost three airships to his stupid miscalculation. Three airships, and three crews of good British privateers, including Storm's best friend: the captain of the *HMA Fidelis*. Storm held it over his head like a death sentence, kept it as leverage for any flaw in his perfect privateer's programming.

"You used to be the *best*, Ace," she hissed, slamming her metal gauntlet down on the desk among the maps. If possible, her cabin was even more cluttered than it had been when he'd last been there. "Now you cannot even handle a mission as simple as gathering incriminating evidence on Erikkson! Rather than working *for* us, you are protecting a biomaton! A *machine!*"

Ace lifted his eyes for the first time since she'd begun yelling at him. The icy blue irises mirrored the ones staring back at him, except that one pair was utterly calm, and the other was filled with mad fire. "Even she does not deserve the way you treat her."

He felt the words leave his lips and immediately wished he could take them back. His sister would gut him like a fish sooner than tolerate insubordination, even from her own flesh and blood.

Storm's face became a mask of darkness, one he could no longer read. "I ought to leave you in that place with her, since you care so much about her," she hissed.

Anger began to boil just beneath Ace's skin, but he kept it caged, like a wild animal locked inside his ribcage. "But you will not."

Her lips curled into a sneer. "And how can you be so confident?"

"Because, though you hate to admit it, you still need me."

"Then prove to me there is value in keeping you around!"

she screamed at him, face red, the muscles in her neck so taut they stood out beneath her skin like cords.

Ace's skin crawled with the tension in the room, but he was the perfect calm to her hurricane of fury. He raised his pistol, his focus narrowing to a single pinpoint as the entire world around it faded into a kaleidoscope of meaningless colour. He drew a single breath, the sound too loud in his ears, and counted the individual heartbeats pulsing in his fingertips. *One, two, three...* Aware only of his target and the gun, cold and solid in his hands, he fired, the bullet spinning out of the pearl-handled flintlock pistol faster than the eye could see. It drilled through an Oriental coin tied in Storm's hair, but did no harm to Storm herself; it didn't even so much as split a single hair before it embedded itself in the wall behind her. Ace lowered the pistol, releasing the breath he'd been holding. The barrel was warm, the scent of gunpowder familiar and comforting.

"You. Still. Need me."

She fingered the coin thoughtfully, her short, dirty fingernails rubbing the still warm metal. A slight smirk crossed her face. "You have proven your point. I am listening."

"Allow me to handle the biomaton until we reach the Black Castle. I will ensure she does not cross your path, nor will she bother you. You do not even need to know she is on this ship at all."

The corners of Storm's mouth creased in another scowl. "So that you may pamper her? She needs to learn her place. If that means I must punish her, so be it."

"You are not doing this for her sake!" Ace raised his voice for the first time. "You are doing this because cruelty gives you *pleasure.*" He spat the word at her, as though the taste of it was bitter in his mouth. He'd crossed so far beyond the familiar line that he no longer knew what would or would not anger her; all he knew was he was tired of constantly feeling guilty. He was tired of turning his conscience off for her.

She looked ready to spit fire at him again, but before she could start, the door banged open.

Emmett stood in the doorway, his face contorted in an expression of fury and his eyes brimming with compassionate tears. "You cannot be planning to leave her there, *Capitaine!*"

"And what if I am?" Storm sneered, her body language shifting from a fighting stance to one of cool, collected power. Ace noted the change, storing the information away for another time. She felt threatened by him, despite everything. Perhaps that was why she had demoted him.

"They will kill her!"

"No, they will *break* her and put her back where she belongs." Her lip curled haughtily. "I would not expect you to understand, Frenchman, since you are not even advanced enough to *have* biomatons in France."

"Capitaine, s'il vous plaît—"

Storm slapped him. Emmett's hand went up to his reddening cheek in surprise. Ace clenched his fists to stop himself from jumping in.

"I *told* you to stop speaking in French, *frog.*"

Ace winced at the racial slur. He read the hurt and anger in Emmett's eyes, in the clench of his fists, and in the tense stance he'd taken, his body a coil of potential deadly force.

"It is not my fault I am aboard this ship," Emmett replied huskily. His left hand pressed over his hip, at the exact place Ace knew he still bore a scar from the old wound, inflicted with the express purpose of coercing him to join them so long ago.

"No? Well, perhaps I shall sell you to the Black Castle and rid us of your foreign filth."

Ace could not endure it any longer. He stepped between them, holding out his hands in a gesture of peace as well as to restrain them both. "Storm, do not act so hastily. Emmett has not been around many biomatons. She has clearly charmed him, that is all." *She's charmed us all,* he mused, but did not dare speak the words aloud. "Remember, we shall need Emmett's abilities as much as mine."

"Then both of you should get over your squeamishness," Storm growled. "I do not suffer insubordination on my ship."

Ace nodded, intent on defusing the situation. "Yes, Captain."

"Get out of my sight."

They left the cabin together, both watching the other's shoulders relax visibly as Storm's aura of fury dissipated. Emmett stopped Ace in the hall outside the control room, grabbing his arm. "You are protecting her?"

Ace nodded, blue eyes difficult to read, focused on something far away, or perhaps deep within himself. "Someone has to," he replied, his voice low. But it was more than that, he knew. Deep within him, a thirst for redemption was welling up, as though someone had finally budged the stone that had blocked the wellspring of his spirit, if only a little. He did not know if it was born of Storm's reminder of his mistakes, or if it was something that had begun before, when he first saw Taryn's big emerald eyes. All he knew was that Taryn had everything to do with him wanting—perhaps for the first time in his life—to be better.

"Do not let Storm leave her there, *mon ami*," Emmett murmured.

Ace glanced at the young Frenchman who'd quickly become his best friend since he joined the crew three years before. "I do not know how much influence I have over her right now, Emmett. She still has not forgiven me for the incident with the pirates last year."

Emmett frowned. "She is still angry about that?"

"Aye, and rightly so. A lot of soldiers died that day," Ace

replied bitterly. "She demoted me then and she has not given me any power since. She no longer trusts me, or my advice."

Emmett's face fell. "Please try. You must. They shall destroy her there."

Ace nodded. "I will try. But I can make no promises." *And you know I am a coward when it comes to defying Storm,* he thought, but could not find the courage to say. He realized suddenly that he had left Emmett to watch over Taryn, but the biomaton was nowhere to be seen. "Where did you leave her?"

"Do not fear," Emmett said, smiling. "She is in the engine room with Bolts."

"The engine room?"

"*Oui,*" Emmett replied. "Would you like to see her?"

Ace bit the inside of his cheek. He *did* want to see her, but the memory of her words the last time they spoke gave him pause. She had been furious with him. "No, that is all right. Take care of her, Emmett. Whether or not I am able to convince Storm not to leave her, she has a difficult journey ahead of her."

⚙️

Evening fell over the *Dauntless,* and lanterns coated the ship both above and below deck in warm golden light. Emmett and Taryn stood above deck and watched the clouds streak with orange, red and pink; the sunset was as beautiful as any Taryn had ever seen. The colours seemed more vibrant here above the clouds, with the endless sky enveloping them. Cook and a few other crew members were preparing to serve dinner across the deck, a huge batch of stew they had lugged up from below in a large iron pot. Taryn felt almost happy here, though she kept a wary eye out for both Ace and Storm. She knew they could appear at any moment and ruin her brief respite.

"Are you hungry, *chérie?*" Emmett asked, touching her shoulder gently.

Taryn nodded, looking at this Frenchman who was so quickly becoming her friend. His face was cast in sharp lines by the twilight and the lanterns as he grinned at her.

"*Bien.* I shall fetch us both something to eat."

Taryn watched him hurry across to where the crew were already queuing up to receive their meals. She looked back out over the rail at the landscape below them, rubbing her fingers over the wood, worn smooth from so many hands doing the same thing she was.

"Did you enjoy seeing the engines?" a voice asked behind her.

Startled, Taryn spun around to find Ace standing a few feet away, his expression unreadable. She turned away from him, refusing to answer. Her copper hair whipped into her face, and she shoved it away, huffing a little.

He came and stood beside her. "Look, Taryn—"

"I told you to call me biomaton," she snapped.

"I need you to listen to me," he answered quietly, almost begging her to hear him out.

"So you can berate me again? So you can continue to dehumanize me? You have won, Ace. You have what you want. I have been humiliated. I am here. We are headed to whatever cruel place you will take me." Desperation came into her voice. "Please, just give me this last evening as a human being. Please let me be for one more night."

He sighed and nodded. "As you wish."

Taryn listened to his footsteps on the wooden planks fade away and found herself shaking with emotion. She hugged herself with her one good arm, shivering. He had respected her request. He had left her alone. But she was so scared of where they were going, she had nonetheless lost all her contentedness with the evening.

"Was that Ace?" Emmett asked, returning with two steaming bowls of hearty stew topped with thick slices of brown bread.

Taryn nodded, still trembling. She took the bowl of stew from him and sat on the deck, her back to the rails as she balanced the bowl in her lap.

"Is everything all right?" Emmett asked, sitting cross-legged beside her. He cradled the bowl of stew in one hand against the swaying of the airship.

She nodded, trying to eat and get her mind off her terror. The stew was delicious, rich and hearty, packed with chunks of vegetables and morsels of tender meat, but she barely tasted it. After just a few bites, she set her spoon in her bowl. "I am frightened, Emmett."

"*Pourquoi?*" he asked, looking at her with compassionate eyes.

"I am afraid of what is going to happen to me."

"Do not fear, *belle* Taryn," he said gently. "Ace has said he will do all he can to keep you safe. You are not alone."

"Ace does not care about me," she said quietly. "He only cares what I may do for him. I am only a tool to him." Her voice had grown husky and bitter.

"*Ce n'est pas vrai,*" Emmett replied, touching her shoulder tenderly. "Ace is fighting for you."

Taryn shook her head. She could not believe it. She couldn't. Exhaustion hit her hard, the sleepless night before making her drowsy, uncomfortable, irritable. A headache throbbed in her forehead and her eyelids weighed ten times more than normal. "I do not think so."

Emmett was silent for so long Taryn almost thought he had given up trying to argue with her. Then, when she'd nearly finished her slice of hearty bread, Emmett pointed across the deck to where Ace and Storm seemed to be engaged in a confrontation. Ace's usually stoic face was folded into a frown, and Storm's position was defensive, her gauntlet raised, her weight balanced low in her hips. "Look, *chérie*. He is fighting for you."

She watched them argue for a moment, contemplating. She couldn't hear what they were saying, but she could hardly believe they would get into such a heated argument over her. It could not be. Neither of them cared enough about her for that. She finished her final bite of stew, then set the bowl beside Emmett before carefully rising. She took a deep breath. "I am going to my cabin, Emmett. I shall see you tomorrow."

"Very well," he replied. "*Bonne nuit, chérie.*"

She offered him a wan half-smile, then moved across the deck, feeling dead on her feet. When she finally reached her cabin, she fell into her hammock with a sigh. She was asleep just moments later.

°⚙°⚙°○°○°

Ace watched Taryn cross to the door and disappear belowdecks. Her gait was still a little wobbly, as if she could not read the sway of the ship. It was not a gift everyone possessed. He scanned the deck for Storm, raking a hand through his thick black hair. She was nowhere to be seen. He breathed a little sigh of relief. She'd chewed him out in no uncertain terms more than once this evening, and he wasn't eager for another lashing. If the *Dauntless* had a mast, he'd probably be tied to it for his cheek. As it was, she'd made it abundantly clear that if he so much as made one wrong step in the morning, she would demote him so far down the chain of command he'd be swabbing decks with the cabin boy. It wasn't an appealing prospect.

Ace crossed the deck to where Emmett was sitting, bowl cradled in one hand and his legs slid between the wooden spindles of the rail, dangling over the clouds. "May I join you?"

"*Oui, mon ami*," Emmett answered, smiling. "Please, sit down."

Ace sat, dangling his own legs between the spindles of the rail and watching the world drift by far below. It always looked fake, no matter how many times he gazed down at the English countryside on a golden evening like this. The land became a storybook, open and inviting. From this high off the ground, anything seemed possible. That hillock could be a sleeping dragon. That ruined castle, a vampire's lair. They were stupid, fanciful thoughts, but Ace allowed himself to think them, if only to escape the reality of his own cowardice for a brief moment.

"You are not going to stop them when they come for her, are you?" Emmett asked after several minutes of silence.

Ace started, surprised by Emmett's words. His fists clenched around the spindles until his knuckles were white and his stomach lurched. For an instant he thought he was falling, but it was only the *Dauntless* hitting a pocket of turbulence. He forced himself to take a deep breath. "I have tried every means I can think of to convince Storm, but she will not listen. Besides mutiny, I can think of no other way to protect the biomaton from what is to come."

"Then perhaps that is what we should try," Emmett muttered.

"What?"

"Perhaps you should lead a mutiny. I know there are many on this ship who would gladly follow you."

"Emmett, I am not mutinying over a single biomaton girl! She is not worth it, no matter what my conscience may say."

"Ah, so you *do* still have a conscience," Emmett replied, looking at him with knowing grey eyes. The Frenchman shifted, wincing a little as he adjusted his position on the deck of the ship. "I was afraid you might have cauterized it, *mon ami.*"

"If Storm had her way, I would," Ace muttered. "And perhaps that would be easier."

"Do not let Storm forget that we are not pirates. We are representatives of the Crown. She must not lose sight of that."

Ace shook his head. "Ever the idealist, Emmett."

"Non, *mon ami*, I just refuse to give up hope."

Ace got up then, the weight in his chest becoming almost too much to bear. "I have done all I can for the biomaton, Emmett, and it was not enough. I am sorry. But I did warn you when I brought her aboard. Her fate has always been slavery. It was not I who determined that."

"Someday you will not be able to blame your failings on the choices of others," Emmett retorted. The words were like a blow to Ace's ribs. He swallowed hard and turned away.

"I am not proud of this, Emmett. But I'm afraid I don't have the power to stop it."

He turned away, hurrying belowdecks before Emmett could catch up with him. He headed for Storm's cabin, his feet carrying him there even though his mind was otherwise occupied. He had the niggling feeling he should be doing more for the biomaton, but it wasn't strong enough to drive him to action. He was a coward, and he knew it. But maybe it was worth something to admit it?

Ace entered the cabin, wrinkling his nose at the piles of dirty clothes, papers, unwashed dishes, and general clutter that littered the captain's space. Her bed was unmade, the blankets arranged in a sort of nest, but he didn't dare touch that. The last time he made her bed, she'd yelled at him. Apparently, she preferred her blankets in disarray.

Still, he could tidy up some of the other clutter, starting with the desk, which was stacked high with haphazard piles of papers, maps and notes. He began to sort them, making neat stacks, and came across the letter he'd glimpsed the other day, printed on fine, thick cream-coloured paper and sealed with red wax. It was so fine he'd thought at first it might be from the Queen herself, but as he peeled it open, he realized he'd been wrong. It was an anonymous note in a fine, spidery hand.

Dear Captain,

It has come to my attention that you are seeking a biomaton built by Lord Erikkson. One is closer than you may think. A girl, seventeen years old and redheaded, has been attending Grafton's School of Mechanicks in London. She is in her first year there. She is masquerading as human, but this is not the case. Her left arm is made of clockwork. She was built by Lord Erikkson.

The letter was unsigned. Ace read it once and then again, his mind racing. His heart began to pound, and his palms were sweaty. What kind of a person reported a girl like Taryn to someone like Storm? He'd known Storm had found out about Taryn somehow, but this anonymous letter felt like a betrayal to him, like a personal attack against Taryn. Besides, she'd claimed to have fooled everyone in that school. Who could have known about her, let alone that she was built by Erikkson?

"What are you doing?"

Ace had been too engrossed in the letter to notice Storm enter the room. He jerked his head up and the paper fell from his shaking hand. "I—I thought I would tidy up a bit in here."

"Are you reading my correspondence?" she asked without preamble. She set her hands on her hips, revealing her flintlock pistol in its holster. She was blocking the door, the one escape route from the cabin. Ace couldn't breathe.

He stooped to pick up the letter, setting it atop the nearest stack of papers. His hands were trembling. "No, I—" He sighed. Better to tell the truth and accept the consequences than try to lie. "When did you receive this letter, Storm?"

"It was delivered to me when we were in Paris several weeks ago. Why?"

"Did you not think it strange? An anonymous letter revealing the one undiscovered Erikkson creation, a girl who had hidden herself so well even her benefactor did not know what she was?"

Storm shrugged. "So there was someone out there who knew what she was. Is it so surprising?"

Ace shook his head. "The whole thing stinks of a plot. You should have shown this to me."

"A plot?" she scoffed. "If this is another of your tricks to fool me into having compassion on her, brother dear, save your breath. What plot could there possibly be against that waif?"

He shook his head. "I do not know, but this does not feel right to me."

She crossed the room, her gauntlet sliding shut with an audible *clink*. "She is going to the Black Castle tomorrow, and that is final. If you disobey me, I will keelhaul you in front of the crew. And if you survive that, I will make sure you never get an assignment again. Do you understand me?"

Ace nodded, his throat dry. "You made yourself clear."

"Good. Run along." She waved her hand, dismissing him. Ace swallowed hard and headed for the door of the cabin. That was it, then. He'd done all he could. And it hadn't been enough.

CHAPTER ELEVEN

"*Mademoiselle* Taryn!" Someone shook her shoulder. "*Levez-vous!*"

She blinked her eyes open, sleep clouding her mind. Emmett leaned over her, shaking her shoulder. Fear and urgency were written across his brow.

"What? What is going on?" she groaned, pressing her hand over her face.

"We are nearing the Black Castle," Emmett answered. "Ace and Bolts are coming to reattach your arm."

Taryn sat up, rubbing her eyes and shoving her copper hair away from her face as her fear reappeared. She sensed her life falling to pieces around her, and she stood helpless in the centre of it all, unable to stop it. The momentum the ship had carried for the past two days was slowing, the constant sounds of the engine changing, fading. "I am afraid, Emmett."

"Do not be." He sat beside her and took her hand in his, squeezing it tenderly. "I will make sure you are safe."

She tried to smile at him, but she knew the expression came out pained and forced. Fear conquered everything; not the heart-pounding, breath-stealing kind of fear, but the kind that worked its way into the mind and nested there like a virus, spinning a web of lies about itself. She squeezed Emmett's hand in return.

Ace entered the room, carrying Taryn's crumpled clockwork arm, with Bolts following close behind him. Taryn allowed her expression to display all of her loathing for both Ace and the broken prosthetic he carried. Ace's ice blue eyes were hard and cold, meeting hers without a hint of him backing down. Even Bolts looked somber, her big brown eyes unable to meet Taryn's and her lips pressed into a tight line.

Ace stopped right in front of Taryn, his face a sheet of stone. "Bare your shoulder."

Taryn glared daggers at him, but complied and slipped the sleeve off her left shoulder, once again baring the scarred, puckered stub: all that was left of her left arm. She turned her face away as Ace and Bolts began to reattach the broken pieces, rebuilt by Bolts but clearly damaged far beyond repair. Taryn sat rigidly, her right hand clenched around Emmett's so tightly her fingers began to go numb. Each time Ace's fingers brushed across her skin, Taryn jerked involuntarily and hated herself for it. Chewing the inside of her lip, she prayed Ace and Bolts finished soon; she no longer even derived comfort from Emmett's hand in hers.

She flinched again, and Ace took his hands away. "Are we hurting you?" he asked.

Taryn shook her head.

"You are flinching, Taryn."

To her surprise, she read genuine concern on his face. But it wasn't enough to keep her from snapping,

"Just finish with my bloody prosthetic and stop pretending to care."

"Taryn," Emmett chided quietly, cupping her hand in both of his.

Ace stared silently at her, his blue eyes watery as they

drilled into her, as though he could stare right into her soul. Bolts waited quietly, watching. Taryn looked away first, chewing the rough place on her lip where she could already taste blood welling, and Ace sighed as he began to work on her arm again. Holding perfectly still, Taryn focused all her energy on not moving at all when he touched her. The coppery saltiness of blood coated her tongue.

Finally, Ace and Bolts finished attaching the useless prosthetic to Taryn's shoulder. It hung at her side like a dead thing tethered to her. Ace rose from his crouch, handing his tools back to Bolts. She placed them in her belt.

"Follow me," Ace commanded.

Taryn pulled her sleeve over the broken clockwork arm. It did nothing to hide her deformity—she did not think anything would hide the disfigured prosthetic any longer—but the garment made her feel slightly less vulnerable. She stood, holding her head high and promising herself that she would not reveal how afraid she was, no matter what happened. Ace led her out of the tiny cabin, his hands set in loose fists by his sides and his jaw set. As Taryn stepped past Bolts to follow, the girl muttered "I'm sorry," under her breath. Emmett followed them all, his grey eyes watchful.

Storm was waiting for them on the quarterdeck. The rising sun lit her hair with a halo of fire and she wore a triumphant smile across her angular face. Three men Taryn did not recognize stood with her, their attention trained on the approaching group. One of them sneered.

"That's it? She doesn't look like much." He had a low, gruff voice. From where she stood, Taryn saw that there was dirt under his nails, and his hair was shorn close to his scalp. His clothes were expensive, but they were tattered and filthy, as though he had fallen from a position of wealth, or had perhaps stolen them from someone who was.

"Looks can be deceiving, Mr. Sloane." Storm's voice was oilier than ever. "Cuff her."

The two men who had not yet spoken grabbed Taryn, forcing her arms behind her back and shackling her wrists together. Her prosthetic twisted at an odd angle because of the way it had been smashed, and it felt as though the clockwork inside her shoulder wanted to tear away from her flesh. Taryn gritted her teeth as indignancy boiled inside her.

"*Capitaine*," Emmett interrupted. "Are the restraints really necessary? She cannot even use her left arm."

"They are a requirement of Lord Bellham," Storm retorted with a hard look. "Move, biomaton."

Terror and fury flooded Taryn all at once. The men pulled her forward, but Taryn held her head high, ignoring their hands, and led herself down the stairs with as much pride and grace as she could muster. She would not allow them to steal her dignity as well.

"I am coming with you," Emmett told Storm.

"Very well. But you may wish you hadn't, Frenchman."

Emmett shook his head. "I am coming." He ran down the steps to stand beside Taryn, brushing the hair from her face. "It is going to be all right, *chérie*."

But Taryn couldn't look at him. She'd suddenly grown aware of the entire crew of the *Dauntless,* standing around them in a large half-circle: spectators to her downfall. She noticed Terrence and his friends sneering at her on the right. Cook was there on her left, towering over everyone else with sadness in his eyes. Seraphim stood by the rails, his face a mask.

And then she saw it. They were hovering by the battlements of a castle built of black stone—*the* Black Castle. Mooring lines kept the *Dauntless* close, and a wooden plank bridged the gap between the ship and the imposing structure.

"Biomaton, I asked you a question." Someone struck her

on the side of the head, not hard, but hard enough to snap her from her thoughts. "Who is this?"

Taryn glared from her captors to Emmett, who looked angry.

"Do not touch her!" he exclaimed.

The men laughed. "A foreigner? What, you could not seduce a sensible Englishman?"

Taryn didn't answer, though she bit down on the inside of her lip so hard she drew blood again. One of the men shoved her. Without her arms to balance herself out, Taryn could barely remain upright. She stumbled forward, reeling, until Emmett caught her. This seemed to be somehow immensely funny to the men, and snickers rippled through the onlooking crew. Cruel laughter rent the air like knives thrown.

"Enough," Ace commanded.

Taryn turned to watch him and Storm descend the steps. Storm was gloating, authoritative, with a smirk on her lips. Ace looked more serious; his face was a mask, but his eyes still held that watery, pained expression from before.

Storm pointed Taryn toward the plank between the ship and the castle. "On your way, biomaton. Ace, go with her."

"No."

The deck fell so silent that Taryn could hear Emmett's breathing beside her. Everyone waited, holding their breath, to see what Storm would do about Ace's refusal.

"What?" she snapped.

"No. I do not need to see this. I do not *want* to see this. Surely, the four of you can control one biomaton with a broken arm."

"Ace—" Storm said warningly.

"No. I wash my hands of this."

All of the anger bubbling inside Taryn boiled over, and she lunged at Ace. "Coward!" she screamed, spittle flying from her lips. Sloane caught her by her shoulders, his strong hands holding her back. Taryn struggled against him, kicking her feet, shaking her shoulders. "You coward! You bring me here and cannot even face the consequences of your actions? You are a bloody coward!"

Ace looked at her stoically. "We all have our roles to play, biomaton. Mine is finished."

Sloane laughed, his face too close to Taryn's ear and his fetid breath hot on her cheek. She forced herself to stop struggling.

"I hate you," she growled as her entire body shook. Whether with anger or fear, she did not know. "I *hate* you."

Sloane shoved her toward the rails, toward that plank and the Black Castle. Hesitantly, Taryn moved toward it; all other choices had been stripped away from her. She could not breathe, as though Ace had physically struck her as well. She saw him turn and walk away, leaving the deck even as she was forced to walk across the plank. Ace's cowardice resonated with her own as she stepped down onto the battlements, her last friend in the world by her side and her last vestiges of freedom falling away.

CHAPTER TWELVE

They brought Taryn into a study with the remains of a fire crackling in the hearth. Tall cherry bookshelves lined the walls. A plush Persian rug lay across the stone floor. There were leather chairs near the fireplace, and a desk by the far wall that was stained a deep, almost blood red color. The study smelled of wood fire, old books, and tobacco smoke.

The room seemed almost normal, save for the chains that hung from the walls near the centre of the room. They shoved Taryn into the middle of the room like she was an offering to the man who sat behind the desk.

He stood, watching her with pale, sunken eyes. His face reminded her of a bird of prey, with a sharp, hooked nose, thin lips, and a receding hairline. What hair remained upon his head was dark and peppered with silver. His clothes were handsome and expensive, rich, and made from silk in all sorts of vibrant colours.

"What have you brought me, Captain Highmore?" His voice was low, coloured with the slightest twinge of a Welsh accent. Taryn wondered how far north they had traveled.

"She is an Erikkson, Lord Bellham," Storm replied, resting her gauntlet on Taryn's shoulder.

"An Erikkson? This tiny slip of a thing?" He moved from behind the desk, his intense, colourless eyes drilling straight through her skull. Taryn stared back, trying not to betray how afraid she really was. "She is rather damaged. What happened?" Bellham's sharp features twisted into an ugly smile. "Did you drop her?"

"*Précisément,*" Emmett muttered.

Bellham chuckled, a sound that contained no joy nor mirth. He slipped long, gnarled fingers beneath Taryn's chin, forcing her to look at him. "What happened, girl? Did you disobey your captain?"

Defiance rose from somewhere deep within Taryn and she shook her head, forcing him to release her. "She is not my captain," she growled.

He looked at her for a few silent moments, examining her as a tiger examines its prey. "I assume you have a reason for bringing her to me?"

"We are trying to take down Erikkson. We believe she was not built with the proper dampers, but we need a biomechanick to confirm." Storm lowered her voice. "She believes she is human."

Again, the three men snickered and jeered at Taryn. She heard Emmett swear in French, defending her honour. Bellham shot the men a furious glare. "Well, Mr. Sloane, if you please."

One man grabbed Taryn's shoulders, keeping her still. The other two moved to the chains, lifting them and walking toward her. Taryn struggled, shouting wordlessly, refusing to let them chain her up without a fight. Her struggles did little, as she was no match for three strong men. They released her wrists from the cuffs one at a time, dragging her arms out and clamping the chains around them. Her left shoulder ached with all the ways her clockwork had been abused beneath her skin, and it was difficult to breathe with her arms spread like that. Her chest heaved above her corset. She closed her eyes, trying to keep calm in spite of the pain.

"Now, let us see what Erikkson did to you, girl," Lord Bellham intoned, moving around behind her. She nearly panicked as he left her line of vision, but forced herself to stay still. Taryn's blood ran cold as Bellham's fingers pulled her hair up, away from the plate on the back of her head. His strong hands forced her head down, and Taryn heard the click of something metal; he had opened the plate on the back of her head. Taryn's terror mounted inside her when she could no longer feel both of his hands on the back of her skull, just the one keeping her hair up and her head down.

"This all seems to be in order, Captain," Bellham said after a moment.

"What?" Storm sounded furious. She moved, and Taryn sensed her behind her. Storm's gauntlet clamped around the back of Taryn's neck, so cold it stung. "That is impossible."

"All is in order. Her dampers are all properly in place. The settings are here."

Storm's gauntlet tightened, the sharp tips of her fingers digging into Taryn's throat until she yelped involuntarily. "Are you certain?" Storm questioned, as if she did not even notice Taryn's discomfort. "Could the control panel be a facade?"

"We can test it," Bellham replied.

There was a click from the back of her head, then blinding white pain flooded Taryn's mind. She couldn't see. Everything hurt. She screamed, fighting the chains in an animalistic attempt to get away from the pain.

"*Arrêtez!* Stop! You are hurting her!" Emmett cried, but his voice sounded far away.

The pain stopped as quickly as it had come. Taryn sagged, panting. The chains around her wrists jangled, and it felt as though a dense fog was draining from her mind, taking her strength with it. She could barely catch her breath.

"Clearly, it is not a facade," Bellham breathed, his voice betraying his fascination.

Storm scoffed, but finally released Taryn. "Very well. We shall find another Erikkson."

"And this one?" Bellham was unable to hide his eagerness. "If she is of no use to you, I shall buy her from you."

Sick terror flooded Taryn at the prospect of being sold off to a man who could inflict that much pain without a second thought. How *had* he inflicted that much pain? What other horrors lay behind that small metal plate, no bigger than a playing card, on the back of her skull?

"How much are you willing to pay?" Storm asked smugly.

"*Non!*" Emmett cried. There was desperation in his words. "You cannot leave her here!"

"I shall do what I like, Frenchman, and if you get in my way I shall not hesitate to sell you as well."

"No!" Taryn finally found her voice.

"Shut up, biomaton," Storm growled. Taryn gritted her teeth, still struggling to breathe. Her whole body stiffened as her blood turning to ice in her veins.

"I am staying with Taryn," Emmett insisted.

"Very well." Storm grinned. "How much?"

Bellham walked around Taryn once more, examining her hungrily. His pale eyes rested for a moment on her broken prosthetic. "One hundred pounds."

"I beg your pardon?"

"She is broken and defiant. She will require repairs and reprogramming."

Taryn glared furiously at Bellham. She already hated him. She could hardly believe she was being forced to suffer the indignity of listening to them haggle over her life.

"Two hundred pounds," Storm said flatly.

"If you include the boy," Bellham returned coldly. Taryn twisted, her chains clanking, trying to see Emmett. She could hear a struggle, and caught a glimpse of the man called Sloane forcing Emmett's arms behind his back.

"The boy is easily worth two hundred on his own." Storm betrayed no qualms about selling Emmett as well. Taryn's head spun. Try as she might, she could see no way out of this.

"He is not yet changed. That will take time," Bellham retorted. He seemed to consider. "I will give you two hundred and fifty pounds for them both," he paused and smiled unpleasantly, "but only because the Erikkson is so rare."

"Done." Storm shook hands with Bellham, her gloating sneer turning Taryn's stomach.

"It is always a pleasure to do business with you," Bellham told Storm. "See Mr. Trade on the way out, and he shall get you what you are due."

Storm nodded and gave Taryn one last sinister, patronizing smile before turning to leave.

"Wait!" Taryn cried, yanking feebly against her restraints, though she knew it was futile. "Please. Do not leave him."

Storm looked back and laughed, a high, mirthless cackle that made Taryn's blood run cold. "You can no longer pretend you are human, biomaton. No one shall believe it here."

"Ace will not allow this!" Emmett cried angrily.

"Ace is not the captain," Storm retorted. "Ace has no authority." Her ice blue eyes, so like Ace's, flickered over them both. "Good riddance to bad rubbish."

And then she was gone, as suddenly as Ace had slipped into Taryn's life just a few days ago. A few days? It felt like years. Taryn felt herself becoming fully aware of their situation; they had truly been abandoned to these people, people who did not believe they were human, and never would. They were trapped, at the mercy of strangers who had already demonstrated they had none.

"Mr. Sloane, take them away. Do not let the Erikkson out of your sight. She could be dangerous. I shall be along in a few hours to begin her processing, but I have a few things to take care of first." Bellham returned himself to the chair behind the red desk, his intense, colourless eyes still watching Taryn hungrily.

Sloane and another man unchained Taryn, only to cuff her wrists behind her back again. She huffed under her breath at the sheer idea of being dangerous. She was a schoolgirl! A mechanick! She was not dangerous. But the men's hands were coarse and cruel, and she knew there would be no sympathy for her here.

Sloane shoved her shoulder toward the door to exit the study. "Move, girl."

Taryn complied, hating herself for her obedience all the while.

❖❖❖

The men led Taryn and Emmett through the castle, down long, dark flights of spiral stairs lit by torches, into the deepest depths of the massive medieval structure. Down in the dungeon, torches sputtered, giving off feeble light and throwing twitching, garish shadows. It smelled musty and damp, like rotting stone and unwashed bodies, and beneath all that, the sharp scent of blood. The cells were little more than cages built against the rough-hewn stone walls, with solid iron bars embedded in the walls, ceiling and floor. Water dripped somewhere, echoing in the cavernous space. These dungeons were built to house hundreds, if not thousands, of people.

They were shoved toward one of the cells nearest the stairs, and one man swung the barred door open with the creak of rusty hinges. Sloane kept a grimy hand on Taryn's shoulder as the other two removed Emmett's handcuffs. The shackles fell away, and instantly they were lost in a flurry of motion. Emmett lashed out, easily catching the men off guard and even knocking one to the floor. Hope fluttered in Taryn's chest. Emmett could fight their way out of here—

Her heart sank as Sloane wrapped an arm around her neck, and she felt the cold point of a knife beneath her jaw.

"Enough," Sloane snarled. Emmett froze when he caught sight of the blade. "Get in the cell, boy, or I will use this knife."

"You will not kill her," Emmett said huskily, panting. "Not after your master paid so much for her."

"I do not need to kill her," Sloane hissed. He twisted the knife so its point pressed where Taryn's shoulder met her torso. The sharp tip of the blade cut through her dress like butter and she winced. "Now, boy, get in the cell."

Emmett hesitated, staring at Taryn for a moment too long. Sloane applied more pressure to the knife. Taryn yelped, and Emmett's face went red as he slunk into the cell. The man he had knocked down rose—a bruise was already blossoming above his eye—and spat at Emmett. "Serves you right, Frenchman."

Only when Emmett had his back to the stone wall in the back of the cell did Sloane sheathe his knife and uncuff Taryn. He grabbed the back of her frock and dragged her to the cell, shoving her inside. The door clanged shut behind her.

"Lord Bellham will be back for you in a few hours, girl. Until then, I urge you to consider how you would like your stay with us to be. You can either make this very easy or very difficult." He smiled unpleasantly. "It makes no difference to us."

The other two chuckled, and then they walked away, leaving Taryn and Emmett alone in the cell. Somewhere far off, someone screamed. The sound echoed in the huge space and Taryn shuddered. She pressed her palm to the small wound in her shoulder, trembling as she closed her eyes. For the first time since they left Grafton's, she began to cry.

"*Chérie,* you are bleeding." She heard Emmett's voice close by, felt his tender touch at her elbow. She did not open her eyes and her throat was so tight she could not speak, so she nodded feebly.

"Let me help you." Emmett lifted her hand from her shoulder so his gentle fingers could pull her sleeve away, and Taryn winced as it scraped over the wound. Emmett was quiet for a few moments, examining the place where Sloane had stabbed her. "It is not deep. *Et voilá.* You see? It has nearly stopped bleeding. You will be all right."

Taryn nodded, silent, pulling the collar of her dress back over her shoulder. She sank to the floor, and her left arm hung limp and dead by her side. It scraped across the stones when she moved. A low moan rose in her throat, and she could not keep it from escaping her lips.

"*Chérie, s'il vous plaît,* it is going to be all right," Emmett whispered, kneeling beside her, his fingers brushing her copper hair back from her face.

Taryn lifted her puffy, swollen eyes. "How can you say that? We are trapped here. We are slaves now, Emmett. How can you even say things shall be all right?"

"Because this is not how it ends. *Ceci n'est pas finis.*"

"Yes! This *is* how it ends! We shall die here, or worse—" She choked on a sob and stopped, pressing her hand over her mouth. It smelled of blood. Taryn's stomach roiled.

"Hush, *belle,* calm down," Emmett whispered. He pulled her into his arms, tucking her head to his chest and rubbing her shoulder tenderly. "We will be all right. I am here."

Tears fell from her eyes once more. "I am sorry I brought you into this, Emmett."

"I do not regret my decision," Emmett said, stroking her hair. "Do not blame yourself."

Taryn's shoulders shook with a barely suppressed sob. Embarrassed by her tears and by his kindness, she pushed him away. It was improper to allow him to hold her like this—improper for her to cry like this, too. She barely knew this man! She stood, wiping her eyes with the back of her hand. She strode over to the bars, resting her forehead against the cold metal and gripping the bar so tightly that the sharp, pockmarked iron cut into her palm.

"How did you do that?" she asked quietly, thinking again about how Emmett had fought their captors.

"*Quoi?*"

"How did you learn to fight so well?"

"That is my power, my *skill*," Emmett said, and Taryn could hear the smile in his voice. "I can see my foes' actions before they perform them, as clearly as if they were telling me aloud." He paused. "I have studied since I was very young."

Taryn rubbed the sore spot on her shoulder. "If he had not grabbed me, could you have gotten us out?"

"*Peut-être*," Emmett replied. "*Mais... Je ne sais pas.* I would have had to fight far more than those three men. There are many cruel people in this place, *chérie*. I do not think I could defeat them all." He came and stood beside her, gazing out at the gloom. She turned and studied him for a moment: the neat, long lines of his face, his wiry frame offset by the flickering torchlight. His tousled ash blonde hair hung over his brow, hiding the bruise over his eye. She wished she knew him better.

"What is this place, Emmett?" Taryn asked. The question hung in the air between them, like a sinister spectre keeping watch over them both.

"*Le Château Noir*—the Black Castle it is called—has been the most lucrative dealer of biomatons since the law allowing their sale passed. Lord Bellham is the patron of this," he swore darkly in French, "this *place*. They sell more biomatons than anyone else in England." Emmett glanced at her, his grey eyes flashing in the torchlight. "It is likely you were here before, *chérie,* when you were a—" He paused awkwardly. "When you were young."

Taryn shook her head. "I would remember this place." She felt tears threatening to fall again and pressed a hand over her mouth, realization hitting her like a fist to her stomach. She hadn't cried over her memories in years—there wasn't any point in it—but now she could barely hold it back. It had suddenly become painfully clear that she had no idea what had been done to her. She had probably been in this cruel place before and could not remember one second of it. It did not matter what they did to her here; if they wanted to, they could wipe her mind and start over. Her throat ached with the knowledge. She sank to her knees, eyes wide and staring, her fingers desperately gripping the chain of her pocket watch.

"Taryn?" Emmett sounded concerned.

Taryn shuddered as if icy fingers were running down her back, raising gooseflesh on her single real arm. "I do not remember, Emmett," she whispered, voice dry and crackling. "Nothing. I haven't any idea what happened to me, here or anywhere else. Perhaps—" She fell silent, staring straight ahead. No more tears would come. She had spent them all, and now found the part of herself inclined to weeping emptied of all emotion. "Perhaps at the end of this they shall wipe my mind again and I shall forget all this, too. Forget the school and the airship, forget Storm's cruelty and Ace's cowardice—forget Royal…"

"Do not talk like that, *chérie,*" Emmett murmured.

A strange, wry smile twisted her lips. How ironic, that even the torture they put her through could be wiped from her mind in an instant. That was the point, she supposed. The perfect slave was one whose mind could be manipulated at will. But it was discordant, also, that the very methods of control they used could be wiped from her mind in order to manipulate her. Perhaps it was better that way. She had seen the biomatons in the rich homes of Royal and his friends. Perhaps they remembered nothing but being a slave, and that was easier. But then she thought of Royal again, and of what it had been like to have a real friend, and she knew she did not want to lose that, no matter how painful it was. No, she could not imagine what she would be without Royal. She did not want to. Her throat ached as she thought of the kindness he had invariably shown her. She shifted, sinking to the floor and pulling her knees to her chest. Her broken prosthetic dragged across the stone floor as she moved, the grating sound setting Taryn's teeth on edge. She shuddered.

Emmett sighed and moved to the back of the cell, setting his back against the wall as he settled to the floor. "I will try to find us a way out of here, *chérie*. This is not the end. *Je promets.*"

Taryn did not respond. She did not know what to say. She could not find it in herself to trust his optimism. Somehow, this felt like the end of everything, like the end of Taryn. Someone new was waiting to take her place, but she had not yet revealed herself. Taryn wondered who this new person was, hatching inside her. Would she be like the other biomatons, subservient and hollow-eyed? Time would tell, she supposed. She slumped against the bars, feeling she had already endured a lifetime of fear, loathing, and mistreatment, and yet her troubles had only just begun.

CHAPTER THIRTEEN

"You *what?*" Ace screamed. This time, Storm had gone too far. He knew she would be furious with him for confronting her in front of the crew, but he was too livid to care.

"Leave us," Storm commanded the crew gathered on the bridge. They all shot nervous glances at Ace as they left, and he read both curiosity and trepidation on their faces. Storm waited until they had all gone, and then, without even deigning to look him in the eye, she spoke. "What does it matter?"

"What does it matter?" Ace repeated indignantly. "This is not a biomaton you have sold into slavery. This is Emmett! A whole, *human* being! This is not only illegal, it is immoral!"

She looked at him, icy calm—too calm for any sane person who had just condemned another to slavery. "And who is going to convict me, Ace? You? You cannot prove I sold him. You were not there. And the court does not accept the testimony of biomatons."

"It does not weigh upon your conscience at all?" Ace questioned, his voice saturated with horror as he realized what kind of monster his sister was. "Perhaps it is *you* who is the biomaton."

Her eyes filled with anger, her face going red. "Do not *ever* say that about me again."

Ace threw his arms wide, exasperated, and began to pace the floor of the control room, if only to expend some of the furious energy locked within him. He caught a glimpse of his own reflection in the glass of one of the control panels and turned away, ashamed of the wild look in his eyes, the colour in his cheeks. "You just sent my friend, my *only* friend, to his death! Can you see nothing wrong with that?"

"He will not die there."

"It shall be as if he did! The Black Castle is a fate worse than death, a living hell that even the worst criminals do not deserve to endure. You cannot just sell people off because you are irritated with them!" He was not only angry, he was frightened for his friend—and for Taryn, Ace realized with a start. Though he would not have guessed it, he feared almost as much for the biomaton as he did for Emmett.

"Well, perhaps things would have turned out differently if you had come along. You have always been better at diplomacy than I—"

"No!" Ace interrupted. "Do not blame this on me! None of this is my fault. It is *you,* your doing! Their blood is on your hands." His face twisted in disgust. "I hope you are happy."

She tugged a bag of coins from the inside pocket of her coat, dropping it onto the control panel with an audible *clank.* "Two hundred and fifty pounds has satisfied my conscience considerably," Storm answered with an ugly smirk.

"What conscience?" Ace growled, then turned and stormed from the room, slamming the doors open, unable to bear being in the same room with her any longer. He needed to breathe, needed to think.

He found himself above decks before he fully knew where

he was going, but chose to scale the balloon. Swinging himself up one of the thick mooring lines with all the agility of a spider monkey, he soon reached the top and settled himself on the swaying canvas. It gave a little beneath his weight, but he was familiar enough with the large hydrogen balloon to know which parts were safe to rest upon and which could give way. The wind blew across his face, drawing tears to his eyes and blood into his cheeks, crisp and cold and fresh. He sat there, watching the Black Castle fade into the horizon, growing smaller by the moment. Though he knew it was impossible, Ace imagined he heard a shriek echo across the air, the sound of a life abandoned. A hideous image flashed behind his eyes, of Taryn screaming, tied down to an operating table, her red hair like a pool of blood behind her head. Ace shook the image away, only for it to be replaced by the same vision, but this time, it was Emmett tied down and screaming.

Ace's hands clenched on his knees in white-knuckled fists. He yelled into the sky, the sound tearing from his chest like a living thing. He was, perhaps for the first time in his life, completely helpless. There was nothing he could do for his friend, or for the girl he'd led to the slaughterhouse, knowing precisely what was in store for her. If only he'd been there, if only he'd fought… But no. He would not allow himself to do exactly what Storm wanted: to blame himself for this, to bear her guilt as he had so many times before.

If you cannot harden your heart, I shall harden it for you. Storm's voice echoed through his head. Ace grimaced, chewing the inside of his cheek. She *had* warned him. He should have done something. He should have known. But it was too late.

Or was it? He could not stop them changing Emmett, but perhaps he could go in and get Taryn and Emmett out. The least he could do was try.

And if you fail?

Ace shoved the thought away. He would not allow himself to think that way. He would have to wait until they arrived back in London, but then he would take a small yacht, and he would return to the Black Castle for his friend. And Taryn? He'd return for Taryn, too, if for no other reason than that she made him feel something he'd no longer believed he could, something he no longer thought he deserved. This would be the redemption he had been searching for.

Clang!

Taryn jerked awake at the crash of metal against metal. She sat up, scrambling backwards almost before her eyes were even open, and blinked blearily in the dim torchlight. She had no idea what time it was, as the light had not changed. It could have been the middle of the night for all she knew. She reached for her birthday pocket watch, only to be shocked into motionlessness by another loud *clang*. She lifted her eyes to the door of the cell, and instantly the horror of the situation flooded back to her.

Outside stood Bellham and Sloane, along with two other men she did not recognize. Sloane was holding a pair of manacles in one hand, his fist wrapped around the chain so that the cuffs dangled on either side, yawning open. The sight disturbed Taryn more than she could have expressed.

Smirking wolfishly, Bellham beckoned her with a skeletal finger. Taryn rose, petrified; she could see no other option but to cooperate. If she did not obey them, they would force her to. Behind her, Emmett had also risen, his small, wiry frame a knot of fighting strength ready to pounce.

"Let her out," Bellham ordered as Taryn reached the door of their cell. One of the guards—a man with greasy hair and a mermaid tattoo on one thick forearm—withdrew a key and unlocked the door. Taryn stepped out of the cell, digging her nails into her palm to steel herself. Before Emmett could follow her, the man slammed the cell door in his face.

"Taryn!" Emmett cried. She turned to look at him, and the other unfamiliar man grabbed her arms, restraining her.

"Do not worry," Sloane hissed, his voice slimy with contempt. "Your turn shall come soon enough, boy."

"Leave him alone." Taryn intended the words to be strong and commanding, but they came out strained and scared.

"What did you say?" Sloane turned his attention away from Emmett, leering at Taryn.

"Leave him alone." Her throat had constricted so tightly she could barely speak.

"You think you can give me orders, freak?" Sloane questioned. He raised a hand to strike her, but Bellham caught his wrist.

"Enough, Sloane. There shall be time enough to break her insolence. Cuff her. Dr. Harper is waiting for us."

Taryn locked eyes with Emmett as her hands—one real, one false and broken—were manacled behind her back. She read concern and fear in his stormy gaze.

Lord Bellham grabbed Taryn's right arm and pulled her away. She had to hurry to keep up with his long stride as he led her up from the dungeon. The three men followed behind; even if she *had* been a fighter, there was no hope of escape.

They led Taryn into a part of the castle she had not yet seen, away from the lavish richness of the study and the other occupied parts of the building. This new section was spartan, with bare stone walls and floor; what few windows Taryn saw were small open slits, though the fresh air they let in could not entirely hide the coppery smell of mechanicks. Oil lamps hanging at regular intervals on the walls provided enough light to navigate passages that did not have the luxury of windows. There were people here, far more people than Taryn had expected to see in this place. She passed young gentlemen and ladies dressed richly, dripping with silk, jewels, and expensive Parisian fashions, all there to get their biomatons repaired or to inspect the new merchandise. There were doctors clad in white coats and dirty mechanicks, their hair held back from their faces by welding goggles and their hands coated with oil and grime. And everywhere there were more doe-eyed biomatons, their heads bowed as they followed after their human masters submissively. Her stomach rolled each time she caught sight of glittering clockwork. Then and there, Taryn swore she would never become the docile slave she was intended to be. She would rather die.

After walking what seemed like miles of this, Bellham steered her into a room that reminded her of an operating theatre. Expensive arc lamps placed across the ceiling lit the room as brightly as the sun, and there were no windows in this room. The heavy wooden door closed behind them with a *thump.* Along the walls were shelves covered with arcane objects, tools for both clockwork and medicine. Diagrams of the human anatomy hung tacked to the walls. On one shelf, rows of bottles stood: some labeled, others blank. Taryn recognized chloroform and ether, but the unnamed milky white substance was a mystery to her.

Despite all the strange tools, Taryn found her attention inexplicably drawn to the metal slab in the centre of the room like a table, with leather straps trailing from it like spilt entrails. The metal was stained in places with something dark and rusty brown, despite the obvious attempts to polish it away. Taryn's stomach twisted once more, adding to the pressure at the base of her throat.

A woman wearing a white lab coat over her dress came over, her dark eyes alight with interest behind her spectacles. "Is this the Erikkson?"

Bellham nodded. "Yes."

Somehow, Taryn had missed four other people standing in the room. Two were clearly mechanicks, and the other two wore white coats similar to the first woman's.

She walked around Taryn, her calculating gaze skimming her body as though she was a book. "What is this?" The woman ran her fingers over Taryn's twisted prosthetic, looking disgusted.

"Captain Highmore dropped her."

"It is not just the damage. Uncuff her," the woman commanded. Almost at once, Taryn's handcuffs fell away. The woman lifted Taryn's wrist, turning it to display the way the differing metals caught the light. "Someone has attempted to rebuild her, perhaps several times."

Bellham grabbed Taryn's chin, forcing her to meet his colourless eyes. "Who did this?" he hissed. "Who knew about you?"

"I did," she answered, meeting his gaze with what she hoped came off as bravery. "No one else knew."

He slapped her hard enough to leave her cheek stinging. "Tell me the truth!"

"That *is* the truth! I did it! I was going to school to become a mechanick!"

Bellham's eyes hardened and Taryn waited, expecting him to strike her again. And then the woman in the white lab coat began to laugh. "She is an Erikkson, all right. I recognize that fire."

Bellham was still staring at Taryn, anger burning in his eyes as his mouth turned down in an ugly frown. "Rebuild her arm and prepare her for training, Dr. Harper. She shall be broken of this rebellious streak, whatever it takes."

"Yes, sir," the woman replied. She took Taryn by the arm, leading her to the metal slab in the centre of the room. Taryn balked, her heart beating wildly in her chest. "On the table, girl."

As Taryn lifted herself onto the metal slab, a thought occurred to her. Dr. Harper seemed to be in charge, which was entirely anomalous with Taryn's understanding of the way the world worked. She had never known a woman could become a doctor, let alone a biomechanick—but all other thoughts fled as hands grabbed her shoulders and forced her to lie back. Taryn struggled against the hands pressing her down, and Harper tightened leather straps around Taryn's ankles, wrist, stomach and throat. Panic suddenly seized her and she screamed, struggling against her bonds.

"Be quiet!" A strong hand clamped over Taryn's mouth and she choked, heaving for breath. Dr. Harper leered over her. "Or I shall give you something to scream about, biomaton."

The doctor released her and Taryn forced herself to relax, breathing raggedly. The cold of the metal seeped through her frock, raising gooseflesh down her spine and across her arm. Overhead, the arc lamps beat down upon her, their white light too bright. And yet, the stone ceiling remained in shadow. The two men Taryn had guessed were mechanicks had already begun to dismantle her prosthetic, starting at her fingers and working their way up, dropping the broken pieces in a bag to be melted down or reused. Taryn squeezed her eyes shut; though she knew it was impossible, she could have sworn her fingers prickled with feeling, and that the mechanicks' work on her arm *hurt*.

Heavy hands grabbed Taryn's face and forced her head far to the right, so her cheek was pressed against the metal table. Her hair was shoved aside, and Taryn heard the *click* of the little metal plate in her skull being opened. She tensed, squeezing her eyes shut all the more tightly as she anticipated the great blinding pain she had felt before.

It never came. After a few long minutes, her head was

released and she opened her eyes to observe Harper cutting off her left sleeve. The biomechanicks were nearly finished with her arm and now worked like carpenter ants to dismantle the few remaining bits and pieces. Taryn tore her eyes away, shivering upon the cold metal table. She now knew what the beetle in a schoolboy's collection felt like, pinned to a cork board for inspection.

"Interesting..." Harper muttered. Her fingers traced the puckered scar on Taryn's shoulder. "He built you well, girl. Why did he allow you to escape?"

Taryn swallowed hard. "I do not remember," she replied hoarsely.

"Oh? Perhaps we can do something about that."

Taryn panicked again when she felt someone lift her skirt, and bucked against the straps holding her down. The same large hands that had held her down before now pinned her shoulders to the table. Taryn clamped her teeth down around her tongue, and her muscles stood out taut beneath her skin like twine as she flinched every time fingers brushed her skin. Her skirt was pushed up a little past her knees, and deft fingers ran down the inside of her knee.

"Dr. Harper, look at this."

The woman moved from Taryn's shoulder down to her legs, her dark, predatory eyes scanning Taryn's anatomy as though she were a Renaissance anatomist and Taryn a fresh cadaver, ripe for dissection. "An incision has been made here."

An incision? Taryn's mind spun. Why would there be any clockwork in her legs? It didn't make any sense. Harper *had* to be mistaken. "No," Taryn choked the words out. "I was caught in a fire. That must be a scar."

"Did I say you could speak, biomaton?" Harper snapped. "This is much too precise to be a burn. No. Your master has altered more of you than you thought." She finished examining Taryn's legs and covered them with her skirt. Her eyes traveled up Taryn's body and she paused, her brows knit. She grabbed the gold chain that hung from one of the buttons on Taryn's bodice, tugging it out of her pocket. The fine pocket watch dangled from the end of the chain, glinting in the lamplight. "What is this?"

Taryn fought against the leather bonds in vain, trying to snatch the pocket watch back. "That is mine!"

Harper swung the watch into her palm, her dark eyes glinting with malice. "Yours? Nothing in this world is yours."

"Please. Give it back," Taryn begged unabashedly. That pocket watch was all she had in the world, all she had left of Royal. She couldn't bear to lose it.

"I think not." Harper smirked, seeming to consider for a moment, then handed the little fob watch to one of the biomechanicks. "Perhaps we shall use it to rebuild your arm."

That was the last straw for Taryn. She struggled again, screaming in wordless fury, unleashing all the fear and pain and anger that had been building up within her. Her back arched, her wrist strained to escape, her legs thrashed.

"Hold her!"

Hands pinned Taryn on all sides, legs, arm, waist, shoulders. Even her head was once again pressed to the table, leaving her completely immobile. She gave in, lying still and frozen, panting as tears welled in her eyes.

Icy fingers brushed her hair away from her ear, and Harper whispered darkly. "Now listen, girl. You can make this easy for yourself or you can make this very, very difficult. I am going to allow you to decide." She paused, and Taryn held still, breathing heavily as her body begged for more oxygen. "Perhaps you do not understand me," Haper hissed. "If you are obedient, we will not punish you. If you continue with this insolent behaviour, you will suffer. We have many ways of making biomatons obedient. Do you understand?"

A tear slipped from the end of Taryn's nose. "Yes," she said hollowly.

"Yes what?"

"Yes, miss." She could barely bring herself to say the words. Shame washed over her in waves, chilling her to the bone. A voice echoed in her head, but it was not her own.

You serve no one.

She rebuked the words, shoving the thought away. *I do now.*

"Good," Harper said. "Now, let us see about that missing memory."

CHAPTER FOURTEEN

AT FIRST, SHE WAS AWARE ONLY OF THE HEAT: PLEASANT, wonderfully warm, like being cradled in the arms of her mother. But then it grew hotter, blistering her skin, searing into the backs of her legs, her neck. She shrieked, but the sound was smothered by the smoke, choked by the absence of oxygen in the air. She arched her back, trying to get away from the heat. Something pressed upon her chest, keeping her tiny, heaving body pinned.

Images returned to her, flashes of memory, ugly glimpses of the events that had led up to this moment. Mother and Father screaming at one another. The oil lamp getting knocked to the floor. Fire, bright orange, crackling, devouring everything in sight. Shrieks. Screams. Darkness. And now, this. This searing pain, the pressure on her chest, the smoke filling her eyes and lungs and throat. She lifted her head enough to glimpse the charred beam that lay across her chest, weighing her down. She moved her hands, trying to make it budge, only to realize her left hand did not move at all. She could not even feel her fingers.

She glanced to her left and froze, staring. Her stomach

lurched into her throat. Where her left arm should have been, there was just a bloody stump. She couldn't remember losing the limb, couldn't feel any pain, but her stomach roiled at the sight of the blood. The little girl turned her head away from the horrible sight and wretched.

A whimper rose in her throat, despite the sting of the smoke. Where were Mother and Father? Why didn't they come for her?

She understood a moment later, the knowledge like a heavy weight on her heart just as the beam was heavy on her chest. Mother and Father had died in the blaze. They were not coming. She was trapped. Alone. And *no one* would ever come for her.

The little girl coughed weakly, her tiny body expending what little energy it had left to expel the smoke from her lungs. The air was so dense with soot that her next breath was just as noxious as the last.

"Hello?" A voice broke through the sounds of crumbling wood and crackling flames: low, unfamiliar and wary.

Her eyes widened. There was someone out there! *Mother? Father?* No, the voice was more sophisticated than any she knew. She opened her mouth to cry out, to exclaim, "Yes! I am here! Help me!" But only a weak croak emerged from a throat too parched with smoke to call for help. She was beginning to see black spots dancing at the edges of her vision, their darting movements distracting her from the urgency of answering whomever had called out.

Her eyes had nearly drifted shut when the man appeared, kneeling beside her. He had auburn, curly hair and copper stubble across his chin. His kind, forest green eyes crinkled at the corners. "Hello, little one," he said gently. Strong hands lifted the charred beam from where it lay across her chest, relieving the pressure. A rush of air surged from her lips, emerging as a half-cry, half-sob.

"Shh," he soothed her, placing one gentle hand against her forehead. "Hush, my child. Lie still. Everything shall be all right."

She stared at him, small eyes wide and wondering as he gently lifted her into his arms, pausing whenever she whimpered to make sure he was not hurting her. Finally, he rose, cradling the tiny, damaged girl in his arms like a baby, and carried her from the burned wreckage of her home.

He came to a waiting carriage and set her inside, yelling at the driver to hurry as he pulled himself in after her. As soon as the carriage was moving, he tore off his ascot and used it as a temporary bandage. In moments, the cloth was soaked with blood. The girl moaned and opened her eyes, looking up at him again as she coughed feebly.

"Mother?" She seemed to see him at last, and fear flooded her. "Where is Mother?"

"Hush," the man said, stroking her forehead with a cool palm. "What is your name, little one?"

"Taryn," she answered warily.

"What a pretty name," he smiled kindly, the corners of his eyes crinkling.

"Where are Mother and Father?" the tiny girl demanded.

His expression fell. "Taryn, I need you to be a big girl for me. Can you do that?"

She frowned. "They are dead, aren't they?"

The man nodded, taking her little hand. She began to cry, feeling the tears tracing clean tracks down her soot-covered cheeks. "Shh, little one," he whispered, crouching down on the swaying floor of the cab to look her in the eye. He cradled her petite fingers in both of his massive palms. "Taryn, would you like to come live with me? I have a big house in the country. There are other children there for you to make friends with. And I shall take care of you."

Her eyes were drifting, and she had stopped crying. She

was losing too much blood, he knew, but he kept calm, waiting for her answer.

She nodded, sucking on her cracked lower lip. He waited for her to respond verbally, but her eyes finally fluttered shut, and her breathing rasped in the back of her throat.

"Do not worry, little one," he murmured. "You are safe with me."

Taryn woke with a start, her heart threatening to beat out of her chest. After a moment of struggling to get up, she remembered where she was and gave in to the restraints. Taryn forced herself to breathe calmly, staring up at the bright arc lamps overhead and focusing until her heart stopped beating too fast.

She considered what she had seen in the—vision? Memory? What was it? Had she really remembered, or had it only been a dream? But it *had felt* real, the fire and the smoke and the pain, and that man—

Taryn swallowed as his face filled her mind, his kind voice coming back to her over the great distant emptiness of her mind. His was the face she had so often seen, half-remembered, in her dreams. His was the voice that echoed in her head, sometimes more real even than her own. Lord Anthony Erikkson. Her creator. The man who had turned her into a biomaton. She had spent so many years hating him, and yet... And yet, now that she remembered him, even in just that one instance, she couldn't hate him. She couldn't. He had done it to save her. But had he known it would make her life so difficult?

"Ah, so you have rejoined us at last," a silky, feminine voice muttered. Taryn turned her head to the right to find Dr.

Harper grinning at her. "Tell me, girl, what did you find out about your master? Why did he create you?"

Taryn hesitated, knowing the answer wasn't what Dr. Harper wanted to hear. "He saved me," she said hoarsely. She looked up at the stone ceiling, picturing his face again. "He did it out of kindness, I think."

Dr. Harper actually laughed, a high-pitched cackle that was both terrifying and mirthless. "Your master is not kind, girl. However deceived you are, you cannot truly believe that."

But Taryn didn't know what she believed any longer. All she knew was that what she had seen was true. "No. I would have died without him. He rescued me."

Dr. Harper frowned at Taryn, her spectacles flashing with reflected light that obscured her eyes. "Let me tell you something about your master. Lord Anthony Erikkson does not build biomatons out of the kindness of his heart. He builds weapons. I know you met Seraphim aboard the *Dauntless*. He is an excellent example of Erikkson's work. And his great masterpiece, Petrichor, has used her enhancements to become an assassin. Do you really believe he built you to be *kind*?"

Taryn hesitated, imagining the terrifying grafts Seraphim possessed. And Petrichor—there was that name again—killed Ace's parents. But Taryn wasn't a weapon. She was a child when she was changed. Surely, she was not like the others? She wished she could remember more.

Dr. Harper released the leather straps that kept Taryn pinned to the table, one by one. "You seem intelligent, girl. I want to show you something."

Taryn sat up slowly, wary of this woman who one moment spoke to her like a human being, and the next treated her like an animal. She knew from her experience on the streets that this was the most dangerous kind of person. As she stepped down to the stone floor of the lab, Taryn tensed with the chill. The lab assistants had taken her shoes at some point.

Dr. Harper eyed her thoughtfully. "Do I need to restrain you, or are you smart enough not to run?"

Taryn stared incredulously back at Dr. Harper. "Where would I go?"

Harper grinned. "Good girl." Without waiting to make sure that Taryn was following, she led her out of the lab and back into the busy corridors of the castle. Harper walked quickly, her heels clicking against the floor, and the white coat she wore over her dress billowed behind her. People got out of the way when they saw Harper weaving her way with purpose, and Taryn felt eyes following them as they moved through the halls.

She must be important. She wondered what a woman had to do to gain such respect, but quickly realized the answer for herself. Harper was ruthless. She would just as soon vivisect a specimen as prepare it for sale, and Taryn had no doubt that countless children had lost their humanity under her knife. Such a person commanded power here, where status was determined as much by skill as it was by wealth. *And above all, one must never show they care about the lives being destroyed here.* That was how Harper earned these people's respect.

Biomatons in chains sent Taryn venomous glances as she passed. It took her a moment to realize these were not the docile, doe-eyed slaves she had seen elsewhere. These were mean, bitter biomatons straining against their chains, as tumultuous and unpredictable as she felt inside. They were muscular and scarred, and a few bore more recent injuries that were still swollen and red. And when she met their gazes, they snarled wordlessly, like animals.

Someone grabbed her frock from behind and threw her against the wall so hard her vision went momentarily black. Taryn blinked as adrenaline shot through her in a way she'd never experienced before. It was as if the blow had jogged some long-forgotten memory. Everything took on a crystalline sheen, more clear and real than it had ever been before. A hulking biomaton stood over her, his eyes alight with bloodlust. Without thinking, Taryn threw the palm of her right hand up, aiming to break his nose.

But the biomaton saw the blow coming and deflected it with an upraised forearm before catching her by the hair. Every fighting instinct fled from Taryn's body and she shrieked. This was not how she wanted to die, torn apart by some animalistic biomaton. His metal fist caught her in the gut. The blow was softened by her corset, but only slightly.

"*Dostatochno*," a voice commanded. Taryn guessed the guttural word was Russian, though she couldn't be certain. Either way, the biomaton released her and Taryn sagged against the cold stone wall, panting. Another man took the biomaton by the wrist, leading him away.

"Very interesting," Harper sounded impressed, excited. "You have the correct impulses, but something is overriding them. Perhaps you think yourself too much a lady to fight?"

Taryn could barely breathe, but she managed to choke out a question. "What is this?"

"This," Harper chuckled, though her voice sounded bitter, "is where we would put you if you were not so rare and appealing. Lord Bellham believes he can make a fortune just by selling you to a collector who likes pretty things." Harper touched Taryn's chin with a hand, turning her face to catch the light before Taryn shook the woman off.

"I am not a *thing*."

"Now, biomaton." Harper's voice was calm, cold, and chillingly sweet. "Let me make something very clear to you; no one is fooled by your act here. It may have gotten you places in the past, but you cannot pretend to be human any longer. Things are so much easier for biomatons who accept their place in the world. You do not have to sleep in that dungeon, you know." Harper smiled: a cold, cruel smile that reminded

Taryn of a wolf cornering its prey. "You are a clever girl. I am sure you will make the right choice."

Taryn did not answer, just glowered at the woman with all the venom and hatred she could muster. The trouble was, she could see the sense in obedience. She could see why it would be easier to allow herself to be ordered about by these people. But every fibre of her being rebelled against her caving into Harper's demands. Everything she was screamed that she was equal, that she did not deserve to be treated this way. Every part of Taryn—and every part of the new person waking up within her—commanded her to rebel. And yet, all survival instincts told her this was a surefire way to get killed. Her mind spun until she felt dizzy with all of the questions she still could not answer.

"Come. We must still take your measurements and get you out of that school uniform before you may return to your cell."

Harper turned on her heel and began walking back the way they came. Taryn followed reluctantly, trying her best to absorb every detail of the castle. In the unlikely event that an opportunity arose, she wanted to be ready to escape.

CHAPTER FIFTEEN

Taryn was almost thankful when she was returned to the musty dungeon hours later, having been measured and examined and touched too much for her liking. Emmett reached for her as she walked through the door, murmuring something in French, but she shoved him away with her real hand; she didn't want to be touched any more. Taryn slumped to the floor, utterly exhausted. The damp stone was rough beneath her bare feet. Harper had forced her to change out of her school uniform and gave her a thin cotton shift to wear instead. The dress was dingy brown, and so thin it barely kept out the chill. She rubbed her left side, feeling the absence of her clockwork arm all the more immensely for the cold.

"*Ça va?*" Emmett questioned, moving to sit in front of her.

Taryn just nodded, her mind too full for speech. Her fingers moved absentmindedly to the place where she always kept her pocket watch, but there was no pocket, and no watch, either. Tears that she had kept dammed behind mental walls spilled over her cheeks, as unstoppable as a flood. She pressed her hand over her face, trying in vain to hide the sobs racking her shoulders.

"*Belle?*" Emmett's voice was full of empathy and concern. He took her into his arms, tucked her head to his chest, and rocked her as a mother rocks a newborn. "What did they do to you?"

She kept her face buried in his collarbone, barely trusting herself to speak. Her hand gripped a fistful of the fabric of his shirt, dirty from the damp and grime of the dungeon. "Why?" she sobbed.

"*Quoi?*"

"Why did he drag me back from the edge of death? Why would anyone enslave another person?" Her knuckles were stark white against his shirt. "I should have died."

Emmett cradled her wordlessly, allowing her to cry into his shoulder without attempting to explain away her feelings. Taryn cried until all her sadness and fear and anger were spent, trembling in his embrace like a child. She cried until she was emptied, and yet somehow, she felt full. She was thankful for his silence. She drew away from Emmett at last, embarrassed, and scrubbed her face with her fist.

"Do you wish to talk about it?" Emmett asked gently.

Taryn looked at him and shoved her long, copper hair out of her face. It was tangled, the normally straight locks a web of knots. She gave him a crooked, pained smile. "I am frightened, Emmett. I am more frightened than I have ever been." Her fist tightened in her hair until pain prickled across her scalp, sharpening her senses. Instantly, she became hyper-aware of her surroundings, right down to the thin, acrid scent of smoke from the torches mounted outside the cell. It was strange, the sharp gleam everything had taken on, as if she was only now seeing everything for the first time. The attack from that biomaton had woken something up inside her, given her new eyes. "I have always hated being given orders. This—this place is the worst I could possibly be in."

"Can you not just—" he hesitated.

"Obey?" A dry, pained laugh crackled in her throat, heavy with irony. "It is as if everything I am refuses to obey. I do not know if I could obey even if my life depended on it. And it does." She pressed her hand to her forehead, the weight of the words hitting her. Yes, her life depended upon this one thing: obedience. What good did it do her to rebel? *And yet...*

Emmett's brow furrowed. He tried to take her hand, but she pulled away and stood instead. She tried to offer him a smile, but this time she could not even force her face to form the expression. "There is something else happening here. Besides the biomaton creation and the sales." She frowned. "They took me to a part of the castle filled with biomatons that seemed almost inhuman." Taryn paused, realizing what she had just said. She shook herself. "One attacked me. If they had not stopped him, I believe he would have killed me."

Emmett did not answer right away, as if he expected her to say more. He toyed with the collar of his shirt, fiddling with a loose button. Finally, he spoke. "The biomaton fighting ring. I have heard about it. There were crew members of the *Dauntless* who liked to spend their time at the fights. People place bets on their favourites." Emmett shook his head. "It is not legal, but I would guess the Black Castle makes just as much on the fights as they do on selling biomatons."

Taryn shuddered. This was not something she'd ever imagined, even in her wildest nightmares. They pitted one biomaton against another for entertainment and money. Would humanity's cruelty never end? "Do they fight to the death?" she found herself asking nervously.

"*Je ne sais pas*," Emmett replied. "Seraphim spent some time as a fighter *exotique*, but he would not talk about it." He touched her elbow. "Surely, they do not intend to put you in the ring?"

Taryn shook her head. "No. It was just a threat, I think." But she thought about what they'd told her, about the other biomatons created by Erikkson. Seraphim. And the mysterious Petrichor, the biomaton who somehow had enough autonomy to become an assassin. Why would anyone build dangerous biomatons? What point was there in that? She couldn't be like them. Could she? Even Lord Bellham had confirmed the dampers in her brain were all in place as they were supposed to be. *Whatever that means.*

"Emmett, let me try to get you released," she said impulsively, a feeble hope filling her with light.

"*Non,* I do not think you can." Emmett offered her a wan smile.

"Let me try! You must let me try. It is all I can do." And it was true. If she held any bargaining chips at all, they were only for his freedom. Her own was beyond anyone's scope.

He ducked his head. "*D'accord.* You may try, *belle* Taryn."

Taryn took his hand and pressed it to her forehead, unable to verbally express her gratitude. He had granted her one final shred of authority, of power. Of humanity, she realized with a painful twist of her gut. He was giving her one last chance to do something human.

CHAPTER SIXTEEN

Taryn woke to find Emmett curled close beside her on the stone floor, his hand twined around hers. His eyes were closed tightly, but in his sleep, his lips were parted, and he seemed almost peaceful. Carefully, she extricated herself from his grasp, doing her best not to wake him. She wondered at his kindness, his nearness, his touch, and how he cared for her.

With a jolt, she realized he must love her. Why else would he sacrifice his freedom for her? The mere thought of it made her feel sick to her stomach. Here she was, altered beyond a doubt, missing some, if not all, of what made her human. She couldn't return whatever affections he had for her; not only because she was a biomaton, and inevitably subject to the whims of her masters, but because she was saddled with the knowledge that her mind had been forever altered. No matter how human she felt, Taryn could not help but suspect she had not been so for a very long time.

She moved to the door of the cell, her eyes adjusting to the flickering orange torchlight. Her body ached, but she welcomed the pain, allowing it to wake up that new, hypervigilant part of her mind. It was as though she could feel each individual grain of the damp stone beneath her bare feet.

"Is there something the matter, *chérie*?" Emmett's voice interrupted her reverie.

Taryn turned to look at him. "Why do you care about me so?"

"*Tu es ma amie*," he answered as he stretched, rolling his neck and shoulders.

"You only met me a few days ago!"

"No one should be alone." Emmett stood and came closer, taking her hand. His hair stood up at strange angles, and the bruise over his eye had turned yellow as it began to heal. He didn't say anything else, just gazed at her with those stormy grey eyes.

Taryn's cheeks grew hot and she could not meet his stare. "Emmett, I am not human. You know that. I cannot return any affection you feel for me." She choked the words out in a half-hearted attempt to stave off any feelings he might have for her, though a part of her knew it was far too late for that.

"You *are* human, *belle*. I know you are."

Taryn shut her eyes, trying to find a way to convince him of what she already knew, what she did not want to admit even to herself. She felt guilty that the one reason Emmett was there at all was false hope, a false appearance she wore in order to protect her secret from the world.

"*Je suis lá*, Taryn," Emmett said, squeezing her hand. "I would not be here if I did not believe you were human. *Tu es ma amie, et je t'aime.*"

Footsteps approached from outside. Taryn tried to pull her hand away from Emmett, but he only clutched it tighter as her body went rigid on instinct.

"What is this?" Bellham demanded. Taryn turned slowly, her mouth dry. There were more men outside her cell along with Sloane and Lord Bellham, new faces looking at them with curious eyes. These were not Sloane's mercenary lackeys that she had seen before, but gentlemen: one young, the other older. They both wore fine clothes, the kind she recognized from upper class parties. The older man had a handkerchief pressed over his nose and mouth. Otherwise, they didn't seem bothered by the foul conditions in which the biomatons were being kept.

"Please, boy, repeat what you just said for our guests."

Emmett glared at Bellham as Taryn shook her head, her eyes begging him not to repeat his words even as they spilled out. She felt the mockery coming before it began. "I said 'I love you.' And I do. I love her."

"You love her?" Bellham scoffed. "You love a *machine*, boy. You love a slave. When she was built, her ability to love was removed. It is a part of the dampers required by law. She cannot ever return your affections. You are wasting your time."

"I do not believe you," Emmett replied defiantly.

"And have you asked the biomaton how she feels?" Bellham asked, turning his hawk-like gaze on Taryn.

Swallowing her terror, Taryn forced herself to return his glare. "I am no different from any of you."

She could practically hear the shock resonating in the four men. Sloane was already unlocking the cell door, and Taryn backed away, pulling Emmett with her, aware that they would have no tolerance for her saying something so defiant. She didn't know why she had said it. Hadn't she just told Emmett she wasn't human, wasn't capable of reciprocating his feelings? All she knew was that as soon as these slavers began mocking them, it ignited a rebellious fire she could not quell.

"Come out, girl," Bellham commanded sharply.

Taryn gritted her teeth. "You do not own me."

Emmett clutched her hand tightly. "*Chérie...*" he whispered, a hint of warning in his voice.

Bellham's expression hardened with fury. "What is it you believe you can accomplish?"

"Release my friend. If you let him go free, I will obey you."

Bellham sneered. "You have no bargaining power here. If you do not obey, I shall see you broken. I can make you do anything I like. So, either you come along now, or your life becomes very difficult indeed."

"Do as he says," Emmett murmured. "I shall be all right."

Every fibre of her being begged her to fight, to continue with the standoff until she won or they forced her to give in, but Taryn had to ignore her own feelings for Emmett's sake. Jaw set, head held high, she stepped out of the cell.

Once she cleared the threshold, Sloane slapped her hard enough to knock her to the ground. The physical abuse only made Taryn angrier. She tried to rise, her red hair cascading over her eyes, but Sloane grabbed her right arm and twisted it behind her back until it hurt too much to resist. Bellham grabbed her chin, forcing her to look up at him. "Do I have your attention?"

Taryn did not answer, seething with anger and terror she feared would spill out as soon as she opened her mouth.

"Good." Bellham's mouth twitched with a smile, but his eyes remained hard as stone. "If you *ever* attempt to defy me again, you shall receive thirty lashes for your impudence. The *only* thing that stays me from pronouncing this sentence on you now is the presence of these two gentlemen, who have come to inspect you for purchase and do not need to witness a bloody spectacle." He let go of her, his expression filled with hate. "As for your lover, I have paid good money for him, and I intend to make my investment worthwhile. His operation is already scheduled."

Taryn hung her head, her own self-loathing growing with the knowledge that she had led Emmett into this. She could not speak. Her shoulder ached with the severity of the angle at which Sloane held her arm. She hated that Emmett was going to be hurt because of her. Taryn shut her eyes, grimacing against the pain.

"Have I made myself sufficiently clear?"

Taryn tasted something bitter at the back of her throat. "Yes, sir."

"Good. Get her up," Bellham commanded.

Sloane hauled Taryn roughly to her feet. She made eye contact with Emmett, who stood at the bars of their cell with nothing but concern for her in his stormy grey eyes. Taryn offered him a half-hearted smile. Before she could speak, Sloane dragged her away after Bellham. She had to hurry to keep up with him, stubbing her bare toes on the uneven stone floor. The other men followed along behind. Taryn knew they were observing her, evaluating her. She hoped her rebellious outburst would keep them from trying to purchase her. As awful as it was here under Bellham's thumb, Taryn had no doubt it would be worse at the hands of a master who did not have the added concern of damaging his merchandise.

They dragged her through the castle along the path she recalled from the day before, passing dozens of curious eyes. Dread bubbled up in Taryn's gut as she realized they were taking her back to Dr. Harper's lab, where the doctor herself was waiting.

Lord Bellham shoved Taryn in front of the woman, who was wearing a smock stained with blood in addition to her white coat this time. "Attach her new arm and tag her. I want her prepped for training."

"Yes, sir." Harper pushed Taryn to the centre of the room, beneath the brightest of the arc lamps, and signaled to her assistants. Taryn feared she would be forced to climb back onto the dreaded metal table, but Harper positioned her in the middle of the room and told her not to move.

"Oh, and Dr. Harper?" Bellham said, giving Taryn a look that sent shivers down her spine.

"Yes, sir?"

"Prepare for the boy's operation. I want it done tomorrow."

"But—"

"Tomorrow," Bellham snapped.

"Yes, sir," Harper agreed.

Taryn did not know if it was the idea of Emmett being torn apart, or the combined smells of formaldehyde, blood and oil in the room, but waves of nausea washed over her.

"Please, do not do this to him!"

"Have you not learned your lesson?" Sloane growled, coming toward Taryn with his fists clenched. Harper stepped between them.

"Now, Mr. Sloane, while she is in my lab she is mine to control. I do not need you muddling things up for me. Besides," Harper turned back to Taryn, turning her chin with strong fingers, "unless I am mistaken, you have struck her already today."

"She needs a firm hand," Sloane growled.

Harper cocked her head, still examining Taryn's cheek and not even deigning to look at Sloane as she spoke. "What she *needs* is for you to stop giving her the gratification of reacting whenever she speaks. Leave her to me."

Sloane grumbled wordlessly, but, to Taryn's surprise, he backed off.

Two mechanicks entered the room, carrying a new, glinting prosthetic arm. Taryn couldn't tear her eyes away from it. The arm was beautiful; the metal framework that protected the delicate inner workings was silver, while the clockwork itself was gleaming bronze. It was not nearly as realistic in shape as her original arm—there was no way this arm would pass for a real one, even hidden beneath a glove—

but Taryn hardly cared. She was just thrilled to have two working arms.

She held absolutely still as the mechanicks began to attach the clockwork to the gears protruding from her shoulder. They slipped on a new leather pad, nestling it snugly against her skin to keep the clockwork from chafing. The mechanicks worked speedily, attaching the new arm in minutes before they left her standing there, heart beating faster with excitement.

"Go on, biomaton. I know you are dying to see if it works," Harper urged.

Taryn flexed her new hand slowly, lifting it and turning it so the clockwork caught the light. Better, her hands were the same size, a luxury she hardly even remembered possessing.

"Do you like it?" Bellham questioned.

"Yes, sir," Taryn murmured, her voice filled with quiet joy. She knew her happiness was irrational, but she could not shake it. For something as simple as a working arm, she was content.

Until someone grabbed her shoulders from behind, and Taryn fell back into the reality of her situation with a jolt. Another assistant took her right arm and stretched it out so that the inside of her forearm faced up. Harper approached, holding a wicked looking quill pen with a sharp metal nib and a bottle of black ink that looked so thick it might have been machine oil. Taryn balked, trying to fight off the hands holding her in place, but their grips tightened and kept her steady. Harper dipped the quill into the ink and then placed the nib against the tender, pale skin on Taryn's exposed forearm.

"This is going to hurt, biomaton. Do try to keep still."

The nib sliced through Taryn's skin, embedding the thick black ink inside the cut. Taryn gritted her teeth, shocked by how much pain such a little thing caused. Her fists clenched and her entire body went rigid as she fought the urge to struggle against the assistants. Harper took her time, working slowly and methodically to prolong Taryn's discomfort. Finally, *finally* she finished and Taryn breathed a sigh of relief though her skin still burned. She forced her body to relax when Harper brushed a finger over her work. On Taryn's forearm were three small, black numbers, the skin around them blaring an angry red.

"743," Harper read coldly. "That shall be your tag as long as you are here, girl."

Taryn's mind immediately went numb. She could not understand what Dr. Harper was telling her, though it seemed simple enough. She began to panic, a numb sort of terror constricting her chest. It was becoming difficult to breathe.

Harper's eyes grew hard and sharp behind her spectacles. "Understood?"

No, I do not understand, Taryn wanted to say. *Are you taking my name? What is this number you have given me?*

But she did not say anything; she merely nodded as though she understood, as though she was already the quiet, mindless slave they wanted her to be.

The older of the gentlemen with Lord Bellham came nearer, his face curious and his eyes fixed on her forearm. "Will it not wash away or rub off?"

"The quill embeds the ink beneath her skin, though not as effectively as a true tattoo. The number will remain a month or so, and then wear away," Harper responded.

The gentleman looked fascinated. His eyes ran over Taryn's arm, down her body, and then back up to her face. His dark eyes met hers with a terrifying kind of hunger. "I could get good work out of you," he murmured, more to himself than to Taryn.

I would never *work for you.* She wanted more than anything to spit the words in this rich man's face, to tell him off as she had told off the boys at Grafton's when they insulted her. But she knew it would be incredibly stupid to run her mouth here, in front of everyone, so she simply held his stare with her own, daring him to say more.

"She is incredibly stubborn," the other gentleman said from where he stood beside Bellham. There was a tinge of amusement in his voice.

"She is an Erikkson," Bellham replied, as if that was an explanation.

"But she looks so…normal," the first gentleman said. He had a strong build and a stony, almost unreadable face. In contrast, the other younger gentleman had delicate features, soft chocolate eyes, and a mouth that concealed none of what he was thinking. Taryn was instantly reminded of Royal when she looked at him: the kind of reminder that gnawed at her ribcage. She loathed the man for that, for no other reason than that he reminded her of her best friend, the person she would never see again. The person she could never tell the truth about herself. "The other Erikksons—the reported ones, anyway—have unusual grafts. They are weaponized. But 743 looks like any other biomaton."

"Not quite. Come closer, Mr. Cody," Dr. Harper offered. The technicians holding Taryn tightened their grips as the younger man came closer. Taryn waited to see what they could tell her about herself before she chose to act. She knew so little about her creator that any information could help her in the future.

"You are not squeamish, I hope, Mr. Cody?" Harper asked, stepping behind Taryn.

Cody—who, close up, *still* looked so much like Royal it hurt—shook his head. "I hardly think I would be here if I was. Besides, I have dabbled in biomechanicks myself. No luck, I am afraid. Nothing like this one, at any rate."

Taryn's stomach lurched. *Dabbled in biomechanicks.* As

though biomatons were like clocks or windup toys, and it was permissible to tear them apart to see how they worked. How many children had died at this man's hands because he fancied himself a biomechanick and was too wealthy for anyone to contradict him?

"Ah, excellent. Then you will recognize this." Harper's hand caught Taryn's tangled red hair, forcing her head down as Cody came around behind Taryn, watching with fascination. "The control panel connects directly to her brain," Harper explained, as though lecturing. The knot of terror in Taryn's gut began to crawl its way into her throat. "You see? Emotion, pain, obedience, reward: all the proper dampers are here, set well within the requisite parameters. But here," Taryn felt a strange stirring in the back of her head, like a tickle *within* her consciousness. "Here are unlabeled controls, all on their lowest settings. I have only ever seen a control panel like this once before, and that was in Petrichor, Erikkson's masterpiece."

"Some say she was his greatest failure," Cody argued. His fingers rested on Taryn's neck, as though she was just some piece of furniture he could idly lean against. "What do the extra levers do?"

"Shall we find out?" Harper asked, a grin in her voice.

"Please—" Taryn tried to beg, but before she could even finish, there was a *click* in the back of her head. Blinding white pain flooded her skull. Taryn lost her ability to breathe, to think. The pain was similar to that which Bellham had inflicted upon her the day she arrived at the Black Castle, but this time it was so much worse. Taryn could do nothing but endure it. Even thinking was impossible in the face of such immense pain.

But a man's voice echoed in her head. *"Do not be afraid, little one, and do not give up. I shall watch over you, even if you no longer remember me. Just relax. I am here."*

Vaguely, she became aware of someone screaming, of her knees hitting the stone floor, of her inability to catch her breath. Taryn realized she must have passed out, that the man's voice in her head had been a hallucination, a side effect of the immense pain. Even as she awoke, the pain began to fade, seeping from her skull back into whatever dark corner it had come from. She stopped screaming, but remained doubled over and gasping for breath, the technicians still gripping her arms tightly. She shivered, soaked in a cold sweat while hot tears she couldn't remember crying streaked down her cheeks and dripped from her chin.

"What did you *do?*" Bellham yelled, angrier than Taryn had ever heard him. "What did you do to her?"

"It was only one lever! How could I have known?" Harper sounded panicked.

Lord Bellham crouched down in front of Taryn, his hands cupping her face and lifting her head up. He examined her with care, something almost akin to concern reflected in his colourless eyes. "Can you see me?" he asked gently.

Taryn's mouth had gone dry, her tongue thick in her mouth, but she managed to answer in a low voice. "Yes."

"What happened?"

Taryn felt her face twist. This was the first time anyone in this place had shown her kindness or concern, and though she understood Bellham's reaction was the concern of a salesman for his product, she still found tears coming to her eyes at the worry written across his face. "I do not know."

He studied her for a few more moments, those hawk-like eyes searching hers. "Can you stand?"

"I think so." The biomechanick assistants released Taryn's arms. Her new clockwork arm fell limp by her side, clanging against the stone floor. Taryn winced, and worry built in her chest. Had her clockwork been disabled? Had whatever Harper did to her brain make it so the arm no longer worked?

She focused all of her attention on it, her heart pounding. *Move. Please move.* She shut her eyes, focusing all her might on controlling her clockwork fingers. Ghosts of sensation prickled, shivers of imagined pain and discomfort running up shoulder, distracting her.

"Get up, girl. What is wrong with you?" Harper barked.

"Let her be, Harper," Lord Bellham said. "There is something wrong with her clockwork."

Taryn opened her eyes. She stared down at her beautiful new arm, trying to make herself believe it was not broken. It couldn't be. She could not bear to consider what it would mean if her arm was irreparably damaged. The immobile clockwork stared back at her, as though it was taunting her. Its gleaming surface meant nothing if she could not command it; her old, patchwork prosthetic was better than this shiny new one.

Her pinky twitched. Slowly, impossibly slowly, her clockwork fist clenched. The fingers moved in jerks and stops, as though the signals between her brain and the tips of her fingers were cutting in and out. At last, she managed to close her fingers and Taryn breathed a sigh of relief. Her hand worked. She *wasn't* broken. Her arm was not yet fully obedient to her commands, but it *was* moving, and her ghost arm no longer pained her. Taryn flexed her fist several times, until the movements were fluid once more, then raised herself to her feet.

"What happened?" Cody asked.

"I do not know," Lord Bellham answered. "Harper, I would like to examine her panel again later. But for now, I think it would be best to let the biomaton rest. Take her back to her cell, Sloane. Harper and I shall be by later to ensure the experiment with her panel did no lasting damage."

Sloane grabbed Taryn's arm, his meaty fingers digging into her flesh. "Let's go, biomaton."

CHAPTER SEVENTEEN

ACE STOOD AT THE RAIL OF THE QUARTERDECK AND WATCHED his crew move about the ship, working the lines, scrubbing the deck, and generally ensuring the *Dauntless* stayed airborne and efficient. The engines thrummed beneath his feet. They had struck some foul headwinds on the journey back to London—almost as if even the weather refused to allow them to abandon Taryn and Emmett without a fight—but they were finally nearing the end of their journey. They would reach London by morning. Ace had tried to forget the redheaded biomaton, had tried everything he could think of to keep himself from thinking about the place they had condemned her. But ignoring the loss of Emmett—with whom he had even shared a cabin—was impossible. Ace could not justify what had happened to his friend, and despite what he'd told Storm, Ace *did* feel that it was somehow his fault.

"You are just going to leave him in that place?"

Ace jumped, then turned to see Seraphim standing right behind him. "Do not sneak up on me like that!"

"If only you could see what you have condemned them to."

Seraphim blinked his strange green eyes at Ace slowly, like a cat, while his chiseled face remained expressionless.

"It was not I who left them there. Go bother Storm with your accusations." Ace turned away, the muscles in his jaw clenched tightly.

"You could have stopped it," Seraphim pressed. His large clockwork wings clicked as they adjusted to steady him against the wind. Half open as they were, the monstrous things truly made him look like some legendary avenging angel. "Their blood is on your hands."

Ace turned, glaring at the tall, powerful biomaton. "Watch what you say to me, Seraphim. Storm may have demoted me, but I am still your superior."

"You still do not understand. What you have done will affect every biomaton in England."

Ace scowled. "And why should I care? You are slaves. That is what you were designed for. And she was just another slave. We put her back where she belonged."

"Even you are not so blind as to believe that."

Ace studied the dark-skinned biomaton. "*What* is it that *you* know about her?"

Seraphim smiled darkly, revealing the silver fangs implanted between his bright white teeth. "You are afraid of me because I was built to be a weapon. But Miss Taryn is so much worse."

"What?"

"She was built for one thing: revolution."

Ace glared at Seraphim, stunned into silence. Revolution? This biomaton was speaking of *treason.* If Storm heard him speaking like this, she would have him hanged. And yet, his words made a strange kind of sense given what Ace already knew about Taryn and her creator. Taryn believed she was human. That was not just a defect of her construction. It *had* to be intentional. What if she'd been *built* to be different, to be disobedient? But they'd checked her brain. She was built correctly. Erikkson *was* suspected of treason, but Taryn was *built correctly.* It did not make sense.

"Lord Bellham checked her brain. She has all the proper dampers in place," Ace heard the words coming out of his mouth, but it felt like he was merely protesting because the ideas spinning through his head went against everything he understood about biomatons.

"Do you think Lord Erikkson would make it obvious that he built her illegally?" Seraphim questioned.

Ace frowned. "How do you know all of this?"

"That I cannot tell you."

"Curse it all, Seraphim, *why* are you telling *me* this?"

"Because I want you to truly consider what you did to her." Seraphim glided past Ace, the metal tips of his primary flight feathers scraping along the wood of the deck, the sound setting Ace's teeth on edge.

Ace had known Seraphim long enough to know he would get nothing else out of him. Seraphim was an enigma. He's been aboard the *Dauntless* for several years, and yet Ace knew next to nothing about him. Granted, Ace had never really taken the time to get to know him. The strange creature was a biomaton, and besides, there was the added trauma of his parents' assassination. Seraphim was a belonging, something that went with the ship like the grand engines below his feet, not someone to engage in conversation. At least, that was how Ace had seen him, until recently.

Ace chewed the inside of his lip. He knew he needed to report what Seraphim had said, but he didn't actually want to. Storm would arrest him and have him tortured until he gave up what he knew, or worse. And if it *was* true, if Taryn's dampers were wrong and that was why she seemed so different, Ace knew Storm would stop at nothing to verify it. They would vivisect Taryn's brain, or worse, kill her to make sure they could incriminate Erikkson. Ace already had enough blood on his hands.

But it was worse than that. *If* Taryn's humanity was still intact, if her creator had built her to *be human,* then Storm had condemned two people to slavery in that place. Ace couldn't stomach it any longer. His understanding of biomatons had been shattered by this tiny, redheaded girl from London. He wasn't sure what it meant, but he knew the winds were shifting. Something in the air was changing, and Ace dreaded where it would lead them all.

Sloane returned Taryn to her cell, throwing her through the door roughly. Taryn tripped on the uneven stones in the doorway and hit the floor on her knees, sending a painful *crack* echoing through the cell. The barred door slammed shut behind her and Sloane stomped away without a word. Taryn closed her eyes, fighting the pain and anger bubbling inside her. She was grateful Sloane had not taunted her, as she truly did not know how she would have reacted. She clenched her fists in her lap, rocking back and forth. The musty scent of the dungeon coated the back of her tongue. It tasted like defeat.

"Chérie? Que s'est-il passe? Qu'est-ce qui ne vas pas?" Emmett was by her side in an instant. "What happened? What is wrong?"

Taryn shook her head. She ran her new metal thumb over the number freshly etched into her forearm. It stung, more than she had expected it to, but the pain helped clear away the strange fog Harper's mistake had left in her head.

"Comment t'allez vous?" Emmett asked softly.

"I cannot bear this any longer," Taryn moaned.

"Chérie—"

"No, Emmett!" Her clockwork fist clenched around her

arm, her metal fingers so cold they seemed to burn against her skin. "I cannot bear it. They treat me like an animal—worse than an animal. Rebellion churns within me, Emmett, and the more I try to bury it, the more it rages. I cannot bear their abuses anymore."

Emmett touched her shoulder. "What do you mean?"

She shook her head. "I do not know where this—this *sedition* comes from—"

Everything froze up in her mind as the word passed her lips. *Sedition.* She had once been called by that name, and it meant more than just rebellious discontent. Her mind was filled with blurry images and old emotions, but also with a strange kind of hope that was freshly kindled within her. For the first time in her memory, she was proud to be a biomaton.

Taryn grabbed Emmett's hands. "I *remember.*" She hissed those two words as if they could free all the other memories locked up in her head.

"*Quoi?*"

Taryn closed her eyes tightly, trying to call up an image to go with the name. One cleared up briefly from the dancing colours and shapes in the back of her mind: herself, just after the changing, her hair cropped short, bandages covering most of her body, and the new, glittering clockwork arm resting in her lap. Strangely, Taryn's face broke into a smile. "*I* am Sedition."

"You are not making any sense, *belle.*"

"I am Sedition! Emmett, I *am* Sedition! I was built for—" *For what? For...* "For more than this. For more than slavery. More than subjugation."

"How do you know?"

"I *remember!*" She pressed her fingers to her temples. "I need to find Lord Erikkson."

"Who?"

"Master Erikkson. He saved me for a purpose. I need to

find him." A strange, astounding joy flooded her. There was joy in knowing she had a purpose.

"*Chérie*, we are trapped here. And even if we were free, you do not know where Erikkson is, or if he even remembers you. He built you a long time ago. And Taryn, he abandoned you. He did not—"

"*No.*" Her face fell. She knew Emmett was right, but she could not get the idea of Sedition out of her head. "I have to believe that is not true. I have to believe he is out there, waiting for me."

Emmett sighed and she read pity in his soft grey eyes. Taryn released his hands, ire flooding her. She shoved him away, stalking toward the bars of their cell. Her fists were clenched so tightly her nails cut into her palm.

"Do not pity me," she hissed. "I do not need your *pity.*" She spat the word; it tasted bitter on her tongue.

He stared at her, his face warped with pain. "I do not—"

"You do! I can see it in your eyes!"

"*Chérie...*" His voice was filled with confusion.

"Do not call me that!"

"Taryn, what is the matter?"

Her body shook like a leaf caught in a gale. She could not verbalize what was wrong. A dozen emotions boiled within her all at once, and it was impossible to sort them out. She ran her fingers over the numbers etched on her arm again. They ached at her touch.

"I am sorry," she murmured. She suddenly felt very weak, starved and exhausted. She sank to the floor, her body too heavy for her to hold up.

The silence stretched for a long moment, during which Emmett watched her rub her arm. "Your new arm is very beautiful, *chérie.* May I see it?"

She knew he was changing the subject, attempting to make

her feel better, but she nodded and held the arm out so he could examine it.

Emmett sat beside her, taking her arm in his hands.

"Do you like it?" he asked.

Taryn nodded, silent as she pondered the way it had shut down only minutes ago.

"*C'est trés belle, chérie.*"

"*Merci,* Emmett."

"It must be wonderful to have two hands again," he said tenderly.

She nodded, but there was no conviction behind it. She was still considering Sedition, still considering her purpose and her creator. She knew what she remembered was real, but how much of it was merely warped by the perspective of a child who did not understand her world? She had been reconstructed into a slave; that was undeniable. She had spent most of her life in hiding because of her creator and his machinations. How could he be a kind person and yet condemn a child to that kind of existence?

"You are thinking of your maker," Emmett said, releasing her arm as she nodded.

"*Chérie,* if this is important to you, I shall help you find him. We will get out of here and search until we do."

Taryn turned and studied Emmett, surprised. "I barely remember him. You may be right, Emmett. He made me a slave and then he left me alone to fend for myself in a world where I shall never be more than my clockwork parts. But *I* cannot give up until I know. There must be more to life than this. I must be built for more than this." She gestured, indicating the cell, her own arm, the dungeons, the castle in its entirety.

"*Oui,*" Emmett answered. "If it will help you understand, we will find him."

Taryn stared at Emmett. She wanted to say more, but she

could call no words to her lips. She could not even under-stand why Emmett even wanted to help her.

She opened her mouth, but her ears caught the echo of footsteps making their way down the stairs, and she instantly fell silent, trying to shrink into herself. *Please,* she prayed silently, *no more. They have done enough for one day. They cannot be back already.*

A figure appeared in the shadows near the stairs. Taryn breathed a sigh of relief. It wasn't Bellham, nor any of her other tormentors. This new figure carried a large metal pot in one hand, and a sack on his back. He shuffled slowly over to their cell, his old age clear in the stoop of his shoulders and the shaking of his hands. He stopped beside their cell and withdrew two wooden bowls from the sack hanging from his shoulders. Into each he slopped a helping of the grey sludge in his metal bucket, then slid the bowls between the bars. Having completed his task, he shuffled slowly to the next occupied cell.

Taryn and Emmett exchanged wary glances, then moved as one to the wooden bowls near the door. Taryn stuck one finger in the gruel, sampling it before she decided whether or not to consume it. The meal was cold and nearly tasteless, like oatmeal that had been overcooked and underseasoned. Three days earlier, Taryn might have refused the tasteless stuff, but her stomach was emptier than it had been in years, and she was not stupid enough to turn down a meal, no matter how unappetizing. Emmett seemed to silently agree, and they both gulped down the gruel as quickly as they could. It gummed up their throats and stuck in their mouths, but settled their growling stomachs somewhat, and for that Taryn was grateful.

She set her bowl on the floor and moved away, every strange emotion within her transforming into a single familiar one: exhaustion. "I am going to try to sleep. You should, too, if you can." She settled herself against the damp stone wall of their cell, but thoughts continued circulating in her mind. If only there was a way for them to escape this place. But she was afraid that Erikkson would need to come searching for her if they were to reunite.

The only way out of this place is in chains, or in a coffin. Sedition she might have been, but now she was Taryn, and she was tired. Still, she could not stop thinking that perhaps if she found Erikkson, she would finally understand. Her questions would be answered. If they could just escape...

CHAPTER EIGHTEEN

Taryn did not sleep, though her body begged for it, though her mind longed for the release slumber would bring. Instead, she lay awake, her mind dancing with half-forgotten memories. She thought of Royal, of the first time they met, when she kept filthy linen bandages over her arm to keep her secret hidden. He had come right up to her and offered to be her friend. Not only that—he had taken her home, had given her a meal, a bath, and a clean frock—and more than just the material items, he had provided her with the warmth of being cared for.

And what had Taryn given him in return for his kindness? Lies, nothing but lies, and all because she wanted so badly to keep basking in that warmth, that immense joy of being *wanted*. Perhaps she should have told him what she was that very first day. Perhaps she should have removed her linen bandages and shown him her arm. Perhaps she could have worked for the Stokkers—she could think of far worse masters than Lord Stokker and, eventually, Royal. She would not have had the same life; she would have been property, uneducated. But no, that wasn't entirely the case.

Master Erikkson *had* educated her. She knew how to read and write before the streets, though she could not remember learning. *Who educates his biomatons?* And her skill with mechanicks: had that been taught to her as well, or had she taught herself those skills to survive? Her past was so blurry she no longer knew what was real and what was constructed.

Taryn heard footsteps. Dr. Harper and Lord Bellham approached, their shadows thrown by the lamplight, becoming distorted, monstrous apparitions. Taryn could tell from Emmett's breathing that he had fallen asleep. She got up quietly and went to the bars of their cell, not wanting to disturb him.

Filling her green eyes with all the venom she felt for these people, she watched as Bellham unlocked the cell door. Taryn stepped out before he could order her to, her hands in tight fists by her sides. Inside, she was dreading this, dreading that they could get inside her brain and change it without her permission. She was terrified she would be broken forever, or worse, that whatever they did would kill whatever it was within her that made her want to rebel, and her mind would shut down for good, leaving her an empty shell, good for nothing more than following orders.

"Come, girl." Bellham took her arm, though his touch was not unkindly. "Do not be afraid. I merely want to ensure Harper's little indiscretion this morning did no lasting damage."

He led her out of the dungeon, through the part of the castle Taryn recognized from her first day, a day that already felt like a lifetime ago. The whole place had a vaguely gothic feel, which reminded Taryn of the ghost stories she had read late at night in her boarding school dorm room. Gooseflesh rose on the back of her neck. She wondered if those halls could be haunted with the lost souls of all the children who'd been turned to biomatons. She didn't believe in ghosts, but a little shudder of dread ran down her spine with the thought.

As the three of them moved through the dimly lit halls, they passed several burly men, pacing up and down. The men carried rifles and nightsticks, and eyed Taryn coldly as she passed. These men were night guards, she realized, though whether they were there to ensure their merchandise was not stolen or to keep it from escaping she could not say. Taryn began to understand that there really was no escaping this place—not alive and whole, anyways. There was no other way to leave the Black Castle, not once it had swallowed you.

They entered the study, and Bellham gestured to Dr. Harper, who began to turn the gas lamps up until the room blazed with light. The entire time, Bellham didn't take his eyes off Taryn.

"Have you had any more trouble with your graft?" he asked her.

Taryn shook her head, but there was an unfamiliar emotion boiling in her gut. She prayed they would not keep her long.

"And no more pain?" he asked shrewdly.

"No," Taryn answered. The new emotion lashed about like a living thing, fighting to rise from her gut even as she swallowed it down.

Bellham handed her a small puzzle box: nothing difficult, but with many small pieces that moved and slid and turned. Taryn had seen such things before. They were popular among the upper class, and often held sweets or trinkets, even small pieces of jewelry, to be given as gifts. It was generally considered amusing to watching a friend or relation work hard to solve the box so that they might reach the prize within.

"Solve this for me," Bellham commanded. Taryn took the box in her left hand, beginning to fiddle with the panels with her right. "With your left hand."

Taryn scowled, but transferred the box to her right hand so she could work it with her left. She understood the task now; Bellham was assessing her fine motor movement. If her clockwork was damaged in any way, it would be impossible for her to perform the precise movements required to solve the box.

Her clockwork moved a little sluggishly at first, but soon enough it responded to her mental commands at the speed of thought. A strange feeling swelled within her as she worked the little box; hatred for this shiny new prosthetic formed in her throat. This was not her arm. It was an impostor, a false friend, no more a part of her than a tool, and she detested it, even as she demonstrated its abilities. She tried to tell herself that it was better than nothing, better than being a one-armed freak, but the thought tasted bitter in the back of her throat. This wasn't her arm, and the strange, new, violent Taryn inside her wanted to tear the limb off and destroy it. It was as if someone had attached a dead limb to her shoulder—it was no more hers than the limb of a corpse would be.

Taryn solved the puzzle box with one last shift of the panels, and it opened like a flower. A small sweet lay within the hidden compartment, wrapped in brown butcher's paper. Taryn just held the box out to Lord Bellham, expressionless.

"You may eat it, 743. You have earned it." He spoke to her as one would speak to a child.

Taryn glowered, but she supposed this was yet another test, and took the sweet from the box. It was a small, hard candy, snow white inside its brown paper. It tasted of peppermint; peppermint and something sultry coating the back of her tongue.

Both Bellham and Harper watched her intently. Taryn wondered at the tumultuous emotions that roiled through her —anger and hatred and vitriol worse than any she could remember feeling. She never knew she had the capacity to feel anything this deeply, and she certainly had never visualized snapping anyone's neck as precisely as she had Harper's. She felt boiled down to her very essence, her very being, and that being was a predator tired of being treated like prey. She wanted to kill, kill until there was no one standing between her and freedom.

Taryn realized she was clenching her right fist so hard her nails had cut into her palm. She forced herself to swallow all that violence roiling inside her and focus on the calm forming just behind her eyes. The calm tasted of peppermint.

"What do you think, Dr. Harper?" Bellham did not seem to notice Taryn's distraction. "Do you see any abnormalities?"

"No, sir. She appears in working condition."

Yes, except she should like to kill you. Taryn again focused on the peppermint calm, letting it flood her mind.

"I agree. Now, I believe we ought to allow 743 to rest," Bellham said, taking her arm. "It should not take long for our little reward to perform its work."

Taryn started, trying to pull away from him. *They drugged me. That is what is wrong. They drugged me.*

"Now, girl, it will not harm you. It is only something to help you sleep. You will need your rest after Dr. Harper's little indiscretion."

They drugged me, Taryn repeated silently, but already the peppermint calm had taken over her mind. The predator within, only minutes ago so eager to escape, now lay dormant and still. She had returned to being poor, meek Taryn, and she could do nothing as Bellham led her back to her cell.

CHAPTER NINETEEN

Taryn soon became aware of the sounds of a struggle, of yelling and cursing, and the smack of fist against flesh. She almost believed it was a dream, a nightmare induced by the drugs she had been slipped the night before to make her sleep. Then, the slam of the cell door burst through her foggy mind, and Taryn's eyes snapped open. Squinting against the torchlight, she could just discern Emmett struggling against four men outside the cell. His wrists were chained behind his back and his lip was split, blood trickling down his chin as his dirty blond hair fell over his eyes.

Taryn forced herself to her feet, racing to the bars of her cell and shoving her hands between them to reach for him. "No, please! Emmett!"

One man, who she recognized from their first day there, had tired of Emmett's struggling. He slammed a meaty hand into Emmett's stomach, causing him to double over, spluttering.

"Stop it! Stop it!" Taryn screamed.

The man turned and his black eyes filled with a burning hatred, the kind Taryn recognized all too well. "Do not worry, biomaton," he told her, chuckling. "We are only taking him to be changed like you. He will be back soon enough."

Taryn reached for Emmett desperately. "Let me go with him, please—"

Emmett's grey eyes met hers, and there was immense sorrow there, as if *he* were the one who had to be sorry, and not her. "Let me go, Taryn," he said tenderly. "It will be all right."

"Please," she begged once more, staring at their captors. "Please do not do this."

The plea fell upon deaf ears. The men dragged Emmett away, and Taryn could do nothing but watch helplessly. The sour taste of guilt coated her tongue and she pressed her forehead against the bars as new, hot tears streamed down her cheeks. She couldn't bear to imagine what they would do to him. Would they steal his love as they had stolen hers? Would they make him an empty shell of the man he was now? *Oh, please. Protect him. Let them be merciful.*

She understood now that her own humanity had been left mostly intact as a part of the terrible purpose she'd been created for. But Emmett had no such safeguard. These people were cruel. They did not care if they damaged Emmett, so long as he obeyed them. Taryn feared she would not recognize him when they were done, and that was entirely her fault.

"Do spare us the crocodile tears," a lazy woman's voice interrupted Taryn's thoughts. Taryn lifted her sticky lashes to see a woman standing outside her cell. She wore her dark hair in a tight bun, and her high-collared dress was black. The hem of her crinoline swept against the stone floor, just beyond where Taryn could reach if she stuck a hand through the bars. Her arms were crossed, her hawk-like face glaring down at Taryn. She reminded Taryn of the severe headmistress at the finishing school she had attended. "You and I both know you cannot care any more for him than I do. Now, turn about so I can get a good look at you."

Taryn just stared at the woman, taken aback as the woman frowned back at her. "I was truly hoping we could do this without any of Bellham's enforcers. I do so hate violence, and I feel it is an insult to your intelligence to have them constantly manhandling you. Now, it is not so hard. All I am asking is for you to turn about."

Bewildered, Taryn did as she was told. The woman studied her intently. "Yes, they did mention you were a pretty slip of a thing. I do believe Lord Bellham's assessment is correct." She did not seem to be addressing Taryn so much as thinking out loud.

The woman unlocked the cell door. "Come along, biomaton. It is time you met with Dr. Finch, our expert."

Taryn wondered at the woman's difference to all her other tormentors. She did not have the strength to hope she would find compassion; she merely wondered what new kind of torment this woman had in store.

She stepped from the cell, chewing the inside of her lip. The woman barely spared her a glance as she led her out of the dungeon and back into the rich wing of the castle. Taryn was beginning to recognize certain paths through the castle, though most of the huge building felt more like a labyrinth. It was a city in itself, she realized. One could live out their life here and still not see everything.

This time, she was brought to a sunroom on the third floor of the castle. The walls were inlaid with many massive windows, and Taryn found herself blinking against the piercing grey daylight that flooded the room—the first daylight she'd seen in days.

Slowly, her stinging eyes adjusted to the light, and Taryn could gaze about the room to take everything in. It was well-furnished; the furniture upholstered in pale whites, creams, and pastels that magnified the brightness filtering through the window panes. An elegant harpsichord took up one corner of the room, sitting with its face open to her. Nearby, there was a man sitting in an armchair—an ancient man, his face withered and covered in wrinkles. His gnarled hands rested upon the head of a black cane. He gazed at her with cloudy, cataract-filled eyes.

"Is this the Erikkson, Lady Trace?" he questioned, his voice surprisingly clear and deep.

"Yes, Dr. Finch. Lord Bellham will be along shortly. He is just overseeing the changing of the boy who arrived with her."

The old man—Finch—harrumphed in an irritated sort of way. "Well, come closer, girl. Let me have a good look at you. My eyes are not what they once were."

Taryn wanted to refuse, to defy this old man. Oh, how easy it would be to snap his neck, to remove what little life he had left... But she remembered herself, breathing steadily. She stepped forward until she stood just a few steps away from him. She glowered down at the small, frail old man.

"Mm," he said. His pink tongue ran over his dry parchment lips, and Taryn found herself so disgusted she could barely keep herself from attempting escape. She clenched her fists, surprised at her own reaction.

Bellham entered the room then. "I apologize for my delay, Dr. Finch," he said, but Taryn had already lunged toward him.

"Where is Emmett? What have you done with him?"

Two burly men she hadn't noticed before caught her arms, keeping her from attacking Bellham.

He smirked at her. "I should have thought I made that abundantly clear."

Taryn struggled against the men holding her. They were biomatons, she realized with a shock. Biomaton guards, loyal to Bellham alone. She wondered if they could even think for themselves, or if they were little more than glorified animals.

The woman who had brought her to the room watched the confrontation with a strange expression creasing her otherwise smooth forehead. "She is attached to that boy. How can that be?"

"She is Erikkson's masterpiece," Finch replied.

Bellham scoffed. "This slip of a thing? Erikkson's failure, more likely. She is hardly an Erikkson at all, if you compare her to Petrichor."

"Most of her clockwork is not visible, but she is just as altered as any of Erikkson's pieces," Finch responded. He gestured with one gnarled, crooked finger. "Bring her over here."

The guards dragged Taryn across the room, despite her struggling, as if they did not even notice. Finch lifted her skirt with his cane, just enough to reveal her bare feet and calves. "You see the way she stands? Her feet point slightly outward; she naturally keeps her weight on the balls of her feet. Her legs most certainly have been altered. I would guess she can run faster and longer than any human. I noticed it as soon as she stepped into the room. Truly, it is incredible she hid herself as long as she did. She does not even move like a human being. Had I visited that so-called school of hers, I should have spotted her in a moment."

Taryn found hot anger igniting in her veins. He had no right to speak of her that way! And beneath the anger was incredulity. He was lying—only her arm was clockwork. Erikkson hadn't changed her completely. She wasn't like Seraphim. She wasn't a weapon.

But what if she was? What if that was Sedition's terrible purpose, the purpose Taryn could not even remember? What if he *had* built her to be a weapon?

The woman—Lady Trace—frowned. "You are saying Erikkson altered her entirely?"

"Yes. She is Erikkson's masterpiece: a biomaton who appears nearly human, yet is as far from human as she can be."

"Can she be trained?" Bellham questioned, and Taryn bristled.

"Any biomaton can be broken, if you are willing to take the time with them," Dr. Finch answered. "But with this girl, I believe the best course of action is using her dampers. It is likely Erikkson imprinted himself upon her, programmed her to obey his orders alone. A combination of force and her dampers should fix her rebellious streak."

Taryn glared at Finch. He spoke as if she could not even understand him, and if she were not held back by the guards, she knew she would have leapt at him. She was shaking with anger, and the guards had to feel her trembling where they grasped her, but she guessed they would take it for fear. Her jaw clenched so tightly it ached.

"Nonsense. Look at her. She is shaking like a child. I am sure I can get her to obey without her dampers," Lady Trace answered, rolling her eyes.

"I should like to see that," Bellham replied.

"It is only your handling of her which makes her act out," Lady Trace said haughtily. "Release her."

The guards let go of Taryn and stepped back, leaving her unfettered in the centre of the parlour. She met Lady Trace's eyes, her head held high. "I want to see my friend."

The woman just smirked. "You will only speak when spoken to, biomaton."

Taryn swore at her in response.

A girl entered the room then, a slight, pretty young biomaton carrying a tea service tray. Lady Trace brightened at the girl's entrance. "Leave the things upon the table there," she ordered, indicating a coffee table in the centre of the room. The girl did as she was told, and as she turned, Taryn caught a glimpse of her gleaming copper control panel under her cropped hair.

"Serve us, 743."

Fury built inside Taryn once more. Everything within her urged her to refuse this woman. "I want to see Emmett," she repeated.

"Serve us first. Then you may see your friend."

Taryn considered it, really *considered it.* She even stepped over to the tea tray, aware of all the eyes on her. She lifted the elegant hand-painted china teapot, an item they thought was worth more than she was. So, they wanted to see her rebellious side? Taryn would give them what they wanted. She lifted her eyes and locked them with Lady Trace's narrowed ones. Everyone in the room was waiting, breath held as they waited to see what she would do. The teapot slipped from Taryn's fingers, shattering at her feet in what seemed like slow motion. Taryn allowed herself a dumb, lopsided smirk.

Lady Trace slapped Taryn hard across the face, but Taryn barely felt it. She just stood there in the widening puddle of hot tea, her bare toes scalded, a smile of triumph and defiance on her face.

"Stupid girl!" Lady Trace cried. "Stupid, clumsy girl!"

"That was neither clumsiness nor stupidity," Finch cackled from where he sat, observing the chaos. "That was a calculated act of defiance."

"But her dampers ought to prevent her from any kind of directly seditious act!"

Taryn nearly laughed aloud at the woman's poor choice of words. "I *am* Sedition," she crowed with pride, the teapot in shards at her feet. Tea was seeping into the elegant rug, the stone floor. "And I shall be your downfall."

Bellham's lip curled in disgust. "*Now* do you see why we must break her? This cannot be accepted. You have the authority to use whatever means are necessary, Lady Trace."

The woman came as close to looking pleased as Taryn suspected she was capable: a twitch at the corner of her mouth, a wicked gleam in her eye.

"With pleasure." She pointed to the broken teapot. "Clean it up, girl. Now."

Taryn merely stared at her. She had progressed beyond reckless now, her actions so insane as to be considered nearly suicidal. She hadn't the faintest idea where all this bravery came from. It was as if a new Taryn had awoken with her memories, and now she would not be denied.

"No."

Lady Trace blanched. Fury emanated from her. "Clean up this mess. And if you speak so flippantly to me again, I shall not hesitate to have your tongue cut out. I am sure it shall not affect your price."

Taryn's bravado began to drain out of her at the threat of damage that could not be undone. She clamped her teeth around her tongue, and did not speak.

"Until she cleans this up, she may stand here," Bellham growled, "and when she *has* cleaned it up, return her to her cell. I think it is time she understands the consequences of her actions on the boy she pretends to care so much about."

As he spun about and left the room, Taryn felt fear prickle over the back of her neck, her cheeks growing hot as she understood what he meant. Emmett had been hurt. Because of her. Was he dead? Was he unrecognizably changed? She couldn't bear the thoughts that flickered through her mind. Her fault, this was her fault. Without a word, Taryn bent down and began to pick up shards of the shattered teapot.

"Fascinating," Finch observed, as though she was an animal, incapable of understanding him. "She is motivated by the pain of another. What kind of programming results in that?"

Taryn's fist clenched involuntarily at his words. She jerked, pain ripping up her arm. The shard she was holding gleamed with fresh blood. Taryn bit her tongue between her teeth, knowing if she spoke now they would never let her see Emmett again. She had to stay silent, for his sake. She continued to pick up the pieces of her shortlived rebellion, blood dripping down her palm and wrist. She did not bother to clean it up as it spattered upon the stone floor. If it stained, at least she would have left some permanent mark of defiance upon the world.

CHAPTER TWENTY

Taryn's hand was bandaged before she was returned to her cell, but Lady Trace could not (or would not) do anything for her scalded feet. Every step she took on the cold, rough stone stung. The musty smell of rot and mildew filled her nose, an almost familiar smell at this point in her stay at the Black Castle. Harper and Bellham were just leaving the cell as Taryn approached. They passed without a glance at her, muttering in low voices.

"I told you it would not work," Harper said as she passed. "Now we have wasted time and money. He is useless."

"Perhaps we could..." Bellham began before they were out of earshot.

Goosebumps rose on Taryn's arm as she was shoved into her cell. The door slammed behind her, but she just stood there, shaking, her eyes locked on a figure hunched in the far corner. Could this possibly be the same Emmett they'd taken away this morning?

"Emmett?" Taryn asked softly, her voice shattering the horrible silence.

He lifted his head but did not turn toward her; he faced the far wall, his head cocked to the right. *"Chérie?* Is that you?" There was something terrifyingly childlike in his voice.

"Yes. Emmett, what have they done to you?" She took a single step toward him.

He swung a hand back, his palm facing her in supplication, as though to hold her back. "Stay where you are!" His voice cracked like ice breaking in a spring thaw. Taryn froze, surprised by the raw emotion she heard. "Do not come any closer, *chérie,* I beg of you."

"Emmett—" She could hardly find it within herself to say anything more. She dreaded to see what they'd done to him. What could be so bad he would not want her to come closer? Why would Harper call him useless? Abject horror mixed with sorrow and fury churned in her gut, a toxic magma of emotion. She had to know, even as her heart threatened to beat out of her ribcage at the sight of his hunched frame. "Please," she whispered.

"Non," he moaned, visibly shuddering. He drew his hand back and pressed it over his face. It was too dim in that back corner to see if his other one had been changed to clockwork. *"Non, chérie,* you must not see me this way. They have done it to break you."

"What did they do?" She took another step toward him, but then froze. Did she truly want to see? No, she had to know, if only to keep them from gaining control over her. "Tell me, Emmett. Please."

He was silent for so long that she could hear the click of her own clockwork and the thunder of blood in her ears. Emmett shifted, moving like one who had not moved in a thousand years, and pressed his hands against the back wall and the bars, obviously needing the support. Then, he turned his face toward her.

Taryn's knees buckled beneath her. She slammed to the floor, all her air escaping in one rush. She could not breathe, and try as she might, she could not force herself to look away. They had taken Emmett's eyes.

In his eye sockets were two orbs of glass surrounding clockwork within. The mechanicks had used silver cogs in an awful mockery of Emmett's stormy grey irises, and behind them copper ones shone, glinting against the torchlight. The lids of his eyes were swollen and red-rimmed, but Taryn did not think it was only from the cruel surgery. He had been crying. Nausea washed over her in waves, and she could barely find her own voice. "Oh, Emmett."

"This graft is for your benefit," he said, his voice cracking again. "They have done this to break your heart."

Taryn felt a strange scoff rise in her throat. "And yet they know I do not have one."

And as the words left her lips, she *knew* that was true. She should have felt compassion for Emmett, or at the very least *sorry*. But what she felt was disgust at the cruel nature of his graft, anger at herself and their captors for how they had ruined this boy who was nothing but kind. And hatred. She felt so much hatred for what they had done. But she felt no compassion toward the man she'd led to slaughter. There was no love inside her heart, and there never would be.

"*Non!*" Emmett exclaimed. He reached toward her with trembling hands. "*Non,* Taryn, that is not true."

She watched him, disgust twisting like a knife in her gut as his hands groped blindly through the air between them. "It is true, Emmett," she answered flatly.

"*Non.*" Here he was, blinded, and *still* all he cared for was her self-esteem. Whatever else they had done to him, they had not removed his love. Silently, Taryn thanked heaven for that. She caught his outstretched hands in her own.

"I heard them speaking, *chérie.* They said you are more human than any biomaton they have ever seen. That is why they hate you so." He tenderly ran his fingers over her knuckles. "No slave driver desires to see his property acting human."

Taryn didn't reply. It was too much, all of it, and though she appreciated Emmett's attempts to cheer her up, it did not change the fact that there was no going back for him now.

He fingered the bandage on her hand, clearly bothered by her silence. "How did you hurt your hand, *belle*?"

The tender nickname was like another knife in her gut. This was all her fault. She could not deny that. Was Emmett's sight worth a few impudent words, her insistence of being human (which she herself did not even believe any longer), and a broken teapot? Had her trade been a commendable one? Anger mounted within her, and she knew the answer was *no*. She began to understand that she would have been better off without him, would have had more agency to act against these people had he not been there to become their leverage against her. She felt sick.

"I broke the teapot they asked me to serve them with," Taryn replied, grinding the words out between her teeth. "I cut my hand cleaning it up."

He focused so intently on her voice. She could see it in the concentration in his face, the way he turned his head and cocked his ear slightly toward her, as if by sheer force of will he could see again. Taryn found a wellspring of hatred opening in her chest, metastasizing into an ugly web that she could not untangle.

"I will make them pay for what they have done to you. I swear, I shall make them pay."

"*Non*," Emmett tried to interrupt, but she would not heed him.

"I do not care what they do to me." And it was true. "But I shall *not* let this stand. They shall not go unpunished."

Emmett touched her cheeks tenderly, as if trying to soothe

away her anger. "Hush, *belle,* do not say such things. They will only hurt you more."

She shoved his hands away and stood to pace the length of their tiny cell. "Did you not hear me, Emmett? I *do not care.* Let them do what they like to me after I crush their skulls for this! Then we shall see if they call me a pretty little *thing!*" She was aware that her words were utterly irrational, but she was too lost in the violent ideas swimming through her head to pay it much attention.

Emmett sat where she left him, his hands reaching out, searching the air for her. She stopped pacing to watch him, disgusted somehow by the *thing* he'd been reduced to.

"Taryn—" his voice broke, a hiccupping sob of fear shaking his shoulders. *"Taryn,"* he begged. Tears slid from his red, swollen eyes. He looked so small and frail there, reaching for her.

A tsunami of guilt and shame washed over her then, dragging her back from whatever temporary madness had engulfed her. What was she thinking? Here was her friend, her *last* friend in the world, crying, injured and broken, and she was speaking of crushing skulls? There was something seriously wrong with her, and she did not think it was just her missing capacity for love. She forced herself to return to him, to sit beside him and wrap her arms around him, praying her actions would teach her the proper way to feel.

Emmett buried his face in her shoulder, trembling like a frightened child. His hands grasped handfuls of her frock, her hair. *"Ne me quitte pas,"* he whispered to her. His weeping had stopped upon her return, but he still shook with dry sobs. *"S'il vous plaît, ne me quitte pas."*

She understood then, between her rusty finishing school French and her half-intact humanity. She was his world now. Without her, he was adrift, alone in the unending darkness. Taryn understood, but she did not know what to do. She could not hold him forever. Their captors would come for her tomorrow and she would have to leave him… But he understood that, too. He was asking Taryn to be *here,* to be present with him. He was asking her not to retreat into her own head, where she now knew insanity lurked.

"I am not leaving," Taryn answered. This was her fault, after all. The least she could do was truly feel what she'd condemned him to. She studied his face, his blank, empty eyes as he wiped his tears away with the backs of his hands. "Does it hurt at all?"

Emmett took a deep, shuddering breath. "Not badly. *Ce n'est pas grave.*" One trembling hand rose to his cheek, as if he was afraid to touch his own face. Hesitantly, he ran long, thick sailor's fingers over his swollen brow. "What—what does it look like?"

She took his hand and pulled it away from his face. "They took your eyes and replaced them with glass and clockwork." The words emerged strangled and tight from her lips. "It—it is—" She could not even find the words to describe it to him. Not only was the graft horrifying, it was arrogant. It blatantly flaunted the Black Castle's power, said that they could take Emmett, a strong sailor, a human being, and turn him into *this.* A biomaton, and not even a *useful* biomaton, but instead one built purely to teach one single, defiant girl how helpless she really was. It was cruelty beyond any Taryn had ever experienced. She did not dare express it to Emmett. It would only hurt him, at best. At worst, it would make him hate her as much as she hated herself.

"*Chérie,* I am sorry," Emmett said softly.

"What? What have you to be sorry for?"

"For breaking your heart."

Taryn pushed him to arm's length, angry again. But she did not know if she was angry with Emmett or with herself or with the whole bloody world they lived in. "This is not your fault, Emmett." She bit the words off, one by one. "The *last* person to blame is you. We shall figure something out."

"Taryn," he choked her name out between gritted teeth, "I am *blind.* That is not something to figure out. This is permanent, *chérie.* Permanent." His voice wavered. "I am a biomaton now. A broken biomaton. There is no future for me." His hands drew away from her, clenched into fists in his lap.

"No," she hissed, refusing to let his words penetrate her mind, even for a moment. "*No!* We can fix this."

"There is no fix, Taryn! *Je ne peux pas voir.* There is no fixing this."

She just sat where she was, stunned, staring at him in the dim torchlight. Tears traced tracks down his dirty, swollen cheeks and she finally understood that this was what she had inflicted upon him: a world of infinite darkness and misery. She should have pushed him away from the very beginning, but she had only thought of herself, her own loneliness. And where had all her selfishness led? Here. This broken, weeping boy—not much older than she—who sat beside her without his sight. Because of her.

Taryn sighed, reached out, and tenderly touched one of his white-knuckled fists. "I am sorry, Emmett." It was sincere, or as sincere a *sorry* as a biomaton could utter.

Emmett turned and buried his face in her shoulder again, clinging to her as if she was the one rock left in the middle of a vast ocean. Taryn let him, but she did not allow herself to take comfort from the human contact. She no longer deserved it.

CHAPTER TWENTY-ONE

Ace stood on the deck of the *Dauntless*, staring out at
the rooftops of London. From this high up, one could almost
forget the smells and the dirt and the fog so thick you could
slice through it with a knife. From up here, the sprawling city
seemed almost—*almost*—beautiful.

They had arrived hours ago and moored the airship in the
shipyard amidst countless others. The majority of the crew
had already scuttled down the rope ladder to make the most
of their twenty-four hours of shore leave. Ace knew they
would sample all the licentiousness London had to offer
before returning, intoxicated more by the city itself than by
any drink or narcotic. He had not chosen to join them, but
watched them go as he paced the deck until he'd practically
worn a groove in the old, weathered wood with his boots. His
mind was filled with thoughts of Emmett, who should have
been there, but was instead trapped in a dungeon, undergoing
who knew what torture.

"Whatever is the matter, brother dear?" Storm's teasing
voice broke his meditative gaze over the city. "I thought you
liked London best out of all the places we have been."

"I cannot stand by and let this continue," Ace answered, his voice low and dark. He turned to see her standing behind him, arms crossed, a smirk on her lips.

"Let what continue?"

"Do *not* play innocent with me, Storm. It does not suit you." He spat the words at her, each one an accusation for all the crimes she would never have to account for.

"Stop moping, Ace. It is too late to change anything."

"No." He took a step, attempting to move past her. "I am going back there for them, regardless of what you say."

"You are going to rescue a biomaton? Even after what her kind did to our family?"

Ace leveled a glare at her. "Your precious sob story is useless on me. You and I know all too well why that biomaton assassin came after our parents."

She grinned at him, and the madness in her eyes sent shivers down his spine. "Then you know that my loyalty is first and only to my queen and my country." He tried to walk away, but she caught his right wrist in her gauntleted hand, squeezing so hard that the sharp points of her armoured fingers dug into his skin. "And you, dear brother, have an interesting decision to make."

"What decision?" he spat, trying to tear his wrist from her grasp though her iron fist was like a vise about his arm.

She twisted his wrist so his inner arm faced up, revealing the crossed cutlasses and clockwork brand he'd been marked with so long ago. Ace's heart turned to lead.

"The only reason you are not wanted by the Crown is this mark. You are the property of Her Majesty's Navy just as much as your little friends are property of the Black Castle. You know this; we all bear this mark to prove our loyalty. Without it—" she squeezed his wrist so tightly that blood began to well from the places where her fingers dug into his flesh— "you are just another pirate."

"And you are willing to report me?" he snapped, too angry to notice the pain; the fingertips of his right hand were beginning to buzz with the loss of circulation. "You are willing to destroy the mark and make me a pirate?"

"I will do what I must," she answered, malice glinting in her eyes.

"Very well. I have made my decision. Do what you must. If that means condemming me to a life on the run, so be it," he answered, calling her bluff and never breaking eye contact with her.

Her head snapped up, her eyes wide with surprise. The breeze caught her tangled brown hair, tugging it over her shoulders. "And what will you do when you cannot save them? Where will you go when you are being hunted down?"

Ace could practically see the cracks in her armour now, broadening as he held her gaze.

"Will you let me go? Or must I fight you first?"

"You always were too much like our parents," she said quietly, her voice full of venom. She released him, and he thought he saw her hand tremble for the merest of moments. "Go. But know that I must report that you have gone rogue. It is my duty."

Ace nodded. "So be it."

He walked toward the rail, not even allowing his eyes to rove about the beloved ship he was leaving, perhaps for good. He loved being a privateer, loved the wind in his face and the snap of the rigging against the balloon above him. He loved the thrum of the engine beneath his feet and the taste of the thin air. He loved to ride atop the balloon on clear days; it made him feel as though he were flying. Best of all, he loved the thrill of a fight, his pistols singing in his palms, his heart beating too fast against his ribcage, his breathing shallow and sharp. And he was giving it all up, but for what? A friend who might not even be alive, and a pretty girl who was not even human. Some sailor he had turned out to be.

"Ace!"

He stopped, but did not turn, half afraid she would manipulate him into staying as she had so many times before.

"You will not like what you find there," she said, almost pityingly.

"It does not matter whether I like it," he replied. "What matters is that I go back anyway."

Taryn woke with a start. Her heart pounded, and unseen terrors lurked in the back of her mind. She sat up gingerly, her body aching in protest from being forced to sleep upon the hard stones for so many nights. Beside her, Emmett lay curled, his fingers tangled around her clockwork hand. The awful swelling of his brow had gone down somewhat, and if she did not pay attention to the small, neat rows of stitches on his eyelids, she could almost believe it had been a nightmare. Almost. She pulled her clockwork prosthetic from his grasp with care, doing her best not to disturb him. He stirred in his sleep, a quiet whimper rising from his throat, and Taryn rubbed her face with her hands.

Sleep had not settled the strange mix of emotions within her. Chewing the inside of her lip, Taryn tried to steady herself. Why had Erikkson bothered to leave any emotions in her at all? It was not a blessing; it was no help to *her* to feel. In fact, it stood in her way. It gave her pause when she should be acting on instinct—like now. Staring down at Emmett, her throat constricted with the noose of guilt that was trying to strangle her.

Emmett stirred, his eyes blinking open—those horrible

dead glass eyes staring up at nothing. His breathing quickened. "Taryn?"

"I am right here," she answered, her voice too flat, even to her own ears.

Emmett reached out and touched her elbow. Taryn's stomach twisted into knots. There, on the inside of his wrist, the numbers *744* were written in the same careful hand as her own mark.

"How did you sleep?" Taryn questioned, more to fill the silence than to begin a conversation. The air hung heavy with nightmares. She had no doubt he had slept as fitfully as she.

A hint of a smile touched his lips as he cocked his head toward her. "In my dreams, I can still see. So even nightmares are better than this place."

A heaviness settled over Taryn's heart at his words. She did not know how to answer him, for she had no words of comfort to offer. And anything she attempted to invent would seem bland, emotionless.

Taryn ran her right hand through her copper hair. It was tangled and fell into her eyes. With a sigh, she lifted her left hand and ran it through as well in an attempt to tame the wild mane. Her clockwork fingers jolted to a halt, tangled in knots of her hair. Pain flared along her scalp and Taryn swore in frustration.

"What is the matter?" Emmett questioned at once.

Taryn blinked away the tears burning in her eyes. "It is this bloody new prosthetic. My other one never caught in my hair. The casing was too fine. But this," she growled, yanking it against her hair, knowing it would only make it worse. "I hate it!"

"Hush," Emmett soothed, drawing nearer. "You do not mean that." His hands reached out cautiously. "May I help?"

Taryn rubbed her cheek with the fingers of her right hand. "If you like."

Emmett's nimble sailor's fingers began to work around her prosthetic, ever so carefully untangling the worst knots before sliding her clockwork fingers free, one by one. Taryn felt foolish. She could have done it herself, except… Except she couldn't. Not with this burning furnace of fury inside her. In her impatience, she would have torn her own hair out.

Emmett freed her hand, but did not stop combing his fingers through her hair, smoothing the mess and untangling the knots. He did it all by touch alone, and Taryn knew then, almost instinctively, that hers was not the first head of hair that Emmett had cared for. He began to braid her copper locks, careful not to let the ends tangle.

"Where did you learn to do that?" Taryn asked, her own hands settled in her lap. It was perhaps the first time she could ever remember allowing someone else to do her hair. Always before, she had been hyperaware of the small metal plate hidden on the back of her skull. No matter how many ladies' maids or fellow schoolgirls begged her to allow them to style her hair, Taryn could never consent. It would have meant revealing her secret.

"Home," Emmett answered. "*En France. Ma petite sœur,* Amelie, would let me play with her hair." Taryn could hear him smiling as he talked about his little sister. "She had the most beautiful golden hair. She was tiny and perfect, and I loved her more than anything." Emmett fell silent for a long moment, still methodically braiding Taryn's hair. "She was only thirteen when I joined the Navy. I sent back all I earned. At *Noël* I was given two weeks of leave. I went home to see *ma* Amelie, *ma petite, mais…*" He halted mid-sentence. Taryn waited. "She was not there. *Mère* said she took ill and passed that autumn. I—I never returned."

Taryn nodded wordlessly. It seemed everyone had lost someone.

Emmett kept speaking, as if once the floodgates were

open, nothing could stop the rush of words. "When they took me yesterday, I thought perhaps I would finally see her again. *Mais non,* the Creator is not finished with me yet." He finished her braid and Taryn turned in time to watch as his hands flew up to his face, covering his eyes. He muttered into his palms, more to himself than to her. "*Je veux mourir. Ensuite, je vais la revoir.*"

Taryn did not know what to say. Since they had left the *Dauntless,* she had seen a completely different side of Emmett, and now she understood. This protective nature began with Amelie.

"How did you come to be aboard the *Dauntless* if you were flying for France?" Taryn asked.

"I was—" He stopped, head cocked, cheeks going pale.

"What is it?" Without conscious effort, Taryn dropped her voice to a whisper.

"Someone is coming. Many someones."

Taryn rose, listening hard. She could just make out the echo of voices and the tromp of boots over the usual sounds of the dungeon: dripping water and rasping chains, and the occasional distant moan of someone in agony. But Emmett had been right. Someone was coming. Taryn's frame grew taut, like piano wire drawn tight beneath her skin. Without fully knowing what she was doing, she positioned herself between Emmett and the door, and waited.

One face came into the light, then another, then two more: all malevolent, dirty and grinning, drunk on the power they held over the helpless biomatons. Taryn recognized Sloane and two others whose names she did not know. There were six of them in all outside the cell, just staring back at her. Ire burned in Taryn's throat.

"*Qui est là?*" Emmett asked. He stood just behind her, his coarse sailor's fingers wrapped around her right wrist.

"*C'est six—*" Taryn struggled with the half-forgotten words.

Finishing school felt like lifetimes ago. *"Six hommes."* Six men. *Six men here for who knows what nefarious purpose.*

Emmett's fingers tightened around her wrist.

"Bring them out here," Sloane commanded.

The cell door banged open. Three sets of heavy boots tromped toward them. Beside Taryn, Emmett flinched. She pressed herself closer to him, her stance widening as she tried to clench her fist, ready to swing, but the arm was not hers and did not respond. Taryn cursed the new clockwork. The men grabbed them both, pulling them apart. Emmett's fingers scrabbled for purchase across her arm, leaving long scratches in his attempt to stay with her.

"Come on, freak." The man who'd grabbed her reeked of alcohol and had a thick cockney accent. "Step outside."

He dragged her from the cell, her clockwork arm twisted behind her back. The others followed with Emmett, who turned his head frantically in search of some clue as to what was going on. The six men assembled themselves in a rough circle between the cells, with Taryn and Emmett each held hostage on opposite sides, facing each other.

"Looks like the operation did not go exactly as planned. Shall we see what this new biomaton can do?" Sloane gave Taryn a pointed, gloating look.

"Leave him alone!" she screamed, fighting against the man holding her. "You leave him alone!"

"Very well."

They shoved Emmett into the centre of the ring, leaving him isolated. One man, a dark-skinned figure wearing one gold earring, reached out and tapped Emmett's ear once, twice. The third time, Emmett caught his wrist, spun, and parried with a quick strike of his arm. The man ducked, and landed a solid blow to Emmett's ribs. As Emmett doubled over, Taryn felt sick, having worked out the meaning behind the exchange. Emmett's one ability, the thing he was better at than anyone else, was fighting. Taryn remembered when he'd told her he could read opponents like a book. No longer. Their one last smouldering ember of hope for escape was irrevocably quenched. Emmett could fight no one in this condition.

"Go on, boy," Sloane said in a teasing voice. "Find your pretty little biomaton, and we shall let her stay with you."

"Emmett—" Taryn began, but a meaty hand slapped over her mouth, filthy and foul-smelling. The man passed her along to another, her arm still twisted behind her back and her jaw clamped shut. She watched helplessly as Emmett took a few, hesitant steps toward the place she had been standing only moments ago.

"You will have to do better than that!" a man crowed across the circle. He had a mermaid tattoo on one forearm.

Emmett turned toward him, pausing, listening *so* intently.

No! Taryn tried to scream, but only a muffled whimper emerged from her throat. She could sense the fury, fury like she'd never known building within her, threatening to explode at any moment.

The man holding her passed her to Sloane just as Emmett turned her way.

"Taryn," Emmett whispered. There was abject terror in his voice.

She struggled again, trying to gain some purchase against the massive man holding her. *Do not do this, Emmett. Do not play their game. If you stay still, they will lose interest. They will move on.*

"Stay quiet, girl," Sloane murmured, his face close enough to her ear that she could feel his fetid breath on her neck. "Or we shall do more than just tease him."

Taryn stilled her frantic struggling, though she was so full of hatred and anger she was trembling. Her whole body shook with the effort of containing all that violence inside.

"Come on, boy! Find her!"

Someone spat at Emmett. Another mimicked Taryn's whimpering, a pathetic animal sound. Emmett stumbled first in one direction, then another, utterly lost, utterly helpless. At last, he stopped moving completely, standing at the centre of the ring, head hanging. They had defeated him. He was done playing their game. Taryn couldn't tell for certain, but she thought he might have been crying.

"Do not give up!" the man with the mermaid tattoo called in mockery. "Can you not see her waiting for you?"

Something within Taryn snapped. She clawed at Sloane, shaking him off. She slammed her head back, ramming her skull into the man's jaw as hard as she could.

"Stop it! Stop it!" The words were more animal than human, guttural and utterly out of control. She wrested herself from Sloane's grip and lunged toward Emmett, placing herself between him and his tormentors as she panted for breath. "Just leave him alone!"

Emmett grabbed fistfuls of the back of her frock, hanging onto her as if she were a life preserver and he a drowning sailor. Silence reigned all around the circle, and blood dripped down Sloane's chin; he bore several claw marks on his forearms and looked furious.

Taryn could hardly believe—or understand—how she'd done all that, but she glared around the circle with all the confidence she could muster. "What is it you want from us?"

Six hard pairs of eyes stared at her. "Dr. Harper wants to see the boy," Sloane growled, wiping the blood from his lip. There was murder in his eyes.

"I am staying with him. We will go together, or not at all," Taryn replied fiercely, her wide, defiant eyes on Sloane alone.

Sloane spat, and blood spattered the stone at his feet. "Fine. We will find out what punishment Harper deems worthy of this *freak*."

Taryn had never heard the word spoken with such vehemence. She held her head high as they were shoved forward and kept Emmett close, bristling when anyone neared him. He'd stopped shaking, but she could tell he was still terrified. Fury pumped through her veins, preparing her for a fight. Let them try to take him from her. Let them *try*. Every step brought her closer to exploding, to risking her own life in order to destroy as many of these cruel people as possible. But every step brought her closer to Harper, too, and to whatever consequences awaited them.

"How *long* does it take to bring two biomatons from the dungeon?" Harper fumed when they finally reached her lab.

"The Erikkson is infuriatingly uncooperative," Sloane growled. "She attacked me."

Taryn spat a curse at the lie, though she was sure it only made her look worse in Harper's eyes.

"I have had just about enough of this Erikkson. We have enough business to attend to without a viper of a biomaton to train." Harper's cold eyes studied Taryn, the lamplight glinting off her spectacles. "This ends today.

"But first, let me see the boy." Harper moved toward them, and Taryn placed herself between the biomechanick and Emmett. Harper scowled. "Will someone *please* make this creature behave?"

Sloane grabbed Taryn's shoulders, yanking her away from Emmett. Taryn fought him like a caged tiger, struggling with all her might. She managed to elbow him in the gut before he caught her wrists and twisted her arms behind her back. "Johnston!" Sloane yelled. The man with the mermaid tattoo secured her wrists with a length of chain he carried on his belt as Taryn panted wildly.

"Come here, 744." Harper touched Emmett's shoulder. "Let us see how your grafts look today."

Emmett shuffled behind her to the metal table, and Harper

helped him sit on the edge of it. He flinched as her slender fingers touched his swollen brow bone.

"Do not touch him!" Taryn screamed, struggling against the men that held her back.

"Someone *please* shut her up," Harper huffed. She didn't even turn and look at Taryn before Sloane slapped his hand over her mouth.

But she was sick of being silenced. She bit down viciously on the thick muscle of Sloane's palm until she tasted blood. Sloane cursed, yanking his hand away. Taryn bared her teeth, daring anyone else to try it, to touch her again. A rough band of cloth wrapped across her mouth from behind and Johnston pulled it tight, gagging her. Taryn tried to fight it, shaking her head, but he had knotted it so tightly that the rough cloth cut into the edges of her mouth.

Emmett's head turned in her direction, hearing the struggle. "Taryn?"

"743 is fine," Harper soothed. Her fingers forced Emmett's face back toward her and she studied him carefully, shaking her head from time to time. "There is nothing to be done now. We will add the control panel in a fortnight, to ensure there are no complications. But once again, Bellham's designs have proved disappointingly problematic." Harper's lip twisted and she turned to Taryn. "Now, let me see what is to be done about your behaviour."

Her eyes flickered to the men behind Taryn. "Hold her."

Their grips tightened instantly, keeping Taryn more or less still despite her best efforts. Harper moved behind Taryn and deftly manipulated the tiny control panel on the back of her head. Taryn froze, bracing herself for the pain. As she readied herself for it to come and consume her, she made a silent promise that this time, she would not scream. She would not give Harper the satisfaction.

But no pain came. Instead, something clicked at the back

of her mind. A strange, cold numbness began at the top of her head and ran down her body, through her veins like ice water, quenching the furnace of hatred that burned inside her as it went. It was a pleasant sensation, a soothing numbness that took over, relaxing her until she no longer remembered why she had been angry in the first place. Her heart was enclosed in an icy fist. Harper stepped back into Taryn's line of sight, staring at her with a smile that should have made Taryn's stomach boil.

Instead, Taryn felt nothing at all.

"You may remove the gag now. She will not be any trouble."

The gag slipped away, and though she meant to scream obscenities at them, she did nothing. No words leapt to her lips. Johnston chuckled. "I will never get used to that." He slapped the side of her head, but Taryn barely noticed. It was as though she'd withdrawn deep, deep inside herself, so deep that she no longer cared what happened to her body.

"Take 744 to the training ground. And 743 may go to be inspected by Lady Trace," Harper said dismissively as she turned away from them.

Sloane grabbed Taryn by the back of the neck and led her from the room, as docile as the biomatons she had sworn never to become.

CHAPTER TWENTY-TWO

Taryn stood before Lady Trace, lost in a pleasant white fog, retreated so deeply within her own mind that she did not hear the woman speaking. Vaguely, she knew this was bad—this was something she *did not want*—but she could barely hold the thought in her conscious mind. It kept slipping through her fingers like sand.

Lady Trace ordered Taryn about and Taryn obeyed, not minding the menial tasks as she once would have. She said, "Yes, madam," or, "Yes, my lady," when it was called for, her tongue too heavy to pronounce any other words. She floated in a haze of happy ignorance, and even the niggling sensation at the back of her mind that something was very wrong did not faze her. She was happy to serve, to be spoken to civilly, and to not be treated like a freak. Best of all, as long as she did as she was told, no one struck her. She began to understand why the others obeyed without complaint.

After hours of simple tasks—serve the tea, 743; wash the dishes, 743; dress me, 743—she was sent to a new, unfamiliar section of the castle. These were the biomaton quarters, the same accommodations that Harper had promised her that first day in exchange for her obedience. The rooms had cots lined up in rows, twenty or thirty to a chamber. The biomatons were segregated: males in one dorm, females in another. Taryn was led into a room full of other biomaton girls, where about two-thirds of the thirty beds available were occupied. She was pointed to a cot of her own and left alone. She sat on the cot, feeling her mind begin to shut down completely now that she was not actively obeying orders.

Taryn barely noticed the other girls as they wandered in and out of the room, going about their duties. She was lost deep inside the cool white fog that filled her mind. In a moment of semi-lucidity, she wondered what Harper had done to her mind to make her like this. Would it wear off, or would she be permanently trapped inside her own mind, barely conscious, good for nothing more than following orders? Perhaps this was better. Perhaps this would be easier than existing as a free creature in her mind but a slave by law.

Time seemed fluid in this new state of mind. She sometimes slept dreamlessly, and other times just sat, eyes open, aware of nothing at all. Hours passed like seconds, or dragged for an eternity. At times, she felt herself nearing the surface... And then she would slip away again. Sometimes she could not remember her own name, and the number etched into her arm became her only identifying appellation.

Only once did Taryn dream in the whole of that miserable night, and then she dreamt of being free and human, in full control of her mind and body. In her dream, she belonged to no one. No one could touch her. It was the closest to being free that she'd felt in weeks. When Taryn awoke, the white fog that crowded her mind and kept her captive was more confining than any chains. She would have mourned her loss of agency, if she could have found enough emotion in her to do so.

Lady Trace came for her early the next morning, and

Taryn tailed the woman obediently, locked so deeply within herself she could not keep from following the woman as a loyal cur follows its abusive master. Taryn did not even see the halls they traveled, just the sweep of the woman's skirts ahead of her, leading her along. Everything else was drowned in a tunnel of white fog. It was as though she had been supplied with mental blinders that hid all but the most important thing—her master—from view.

Someone grabbed the back of Taryn's dress to stop her, and pulled her hair. She halted, and waited. Waited for the blow she knew was coming. Instead, firm hands turned her around by her shoulders. Taryn did not even raise her head. She kept her eyes down, her face expressionless. Her mind still doggedly followed Lady Trace.

"Come now, girl. Where did all that fire go?" A hand struck the side of her head. Taryn did not flinch. The defiant Taryn stuffed deep inside roused a little, lifted her head angrily at the abuse, but the emotion was as difficult to grasp as a wet bar of soap.

"Go on, boy, since you cannot stop asking about her," the man spat. Taryn thought she recognized Sloane's voice, though it meant nothing to her.

Someone was shoved in front of Taryn, someone small and wiry, someone who moved his head in a strange, jerking way. His shaking hands reached out and hesitantly brushed her face. His touch was gentle and kind, not the possessive, firm touches she was becoming accustomed to. His fingers touched her cheeks tenderly, like the flutter of butterfly's wings. "Taryn?" he whispered.

The fog cleared, if only for a moment, and Taryn recognized Emmett. His clockwork eyes were red-rimmed with dark, heavy bags beneath them. His hair, which he had kept so carefully combed even when they'd first arrived here, was disheveled and hung in dirty, limp curls over his forehead.

Fine sailor's clothes had been reduced to little more than filthy rags draped across his narrow frame, and across his forearms were thick, red welts—yet he touched her with such gentleness. She felt the first real emotion she'd had in more than a day stir inside her: fury toward the people who had done this to him.

But Taryn's tongue was still made of lead. The fog had cleared somewhat, but she could still feel its grasp on her mind. So she performed the one act of defiance she could still muster; she lifted her heavy arms and clasped onto his wrists with a grip that spoke all the things she could not say.

His expression twisted to one of pain. "Oh, *belle*. What have they done to you?"

I do not know, Emmett, she thought, but could not say. *I do not know, and I am terrified.*

Terror. Now that was an emotion, something to hold on to. She struggled to keep it inside, to taste it and feel it more than any emotion she ever had before. But even terror was not strong enough. It slid right past her as a new wave of calm turned her bones to ice. She could sense herself falling back into the depths of her own mind, and there was nothing she could do to stop it.

"743!" Lady Trace's command rang out, clear and precise. "Do not make me call you again."

Taryn watched her own hands drop to her sides, helpless as she turned to Lady Trace. Emmett grabbed her wrist desperately.

"*Non! Ne me quitte pas,* Taryn! You promised me! *Tu m'avais promis!*"

The words cut Taryn to the core. Sloane yanked Emmett away from Taryn, apologizing to Lady Trace for the delay. "I do not believe he will bother her anymore," he said with an ugly smile.

Lady Trace spat a cutting remark Emmett's way, a remark

Taryn did not hear over the roaring in her ears. And then she was led away, all while Emmett continued screaming her name. "Taryn! *Non!* Taryn! *Levez-vous! Réveillez-vous!*

"Wake up!"

"Did she seem to recognize him?"

All of a sudden, Taryn found herself listening to the conversation Lord Bellham and Lady Trace were having as she obediently performed tasks—simultaneously shining a silver set and serving them afternoon tea—as she was directed. This sudden, momentary clarity seemed to happen when she least expected it; she would be lost in a dense fog, so thick she was unaware of her environs, and then it would part just enough to allow her to listen, though the part of Taryn that paid attention was locked away so completely she could do nothing about what she overheard.

"Not that I could see," Lady Trace replied. Taryn supposed they were talking about her run-in with Emmett earlier, but she had missed the beginning of the conversation and could not be sure. "Her programming is impressive. Some of the best I have seen, certainly. It is unfortunate she was so rebellious at the beginning. An obedient biomaton with fewer activated dampers would fetch a high price, especially when we can attach a name like Erikkson's to her."

"There are still plenty of collectors interested in her, with or without her dampers," Bellham replied, sipping at his tea. Taryn sensed him watching her, but the knowledge did not bother her. She took in all their words with little emotion.

"How is 744's training coming along?" Lady Trace asked.

Taryn heard the *clink* of a cup being set in its saucer. "He is learning. I believe with enough training he will be a useful tool to have around, though he may require a companion his entire life. I will be glad when we can reprogram him as well. He constantly asks after 743."

"What a shame his graft did not work properly."

"Yes, well, we cannot all be Erikkson," Lord Bellham sighed. "743, more tea, please."

Taryn rose from her perch, feeling her mind begin to try and fight, really *fight* against her programming for the first time. Even as she poured Bellham another cup of tea, she was mentally hurling herself at the white wall that blocked her emotions and her free will. She had not been designed to be a mindless slave. She needed to wake up.

"Tomorrow morning, make sure 743 is made ready. I have a handful of prospective buyers coming to examine her." His skeletal fingers reached out and tugged at a lock of Taryn's long, tangled copper hair. His lip curled. "Make sure she gets a bath, and this hair is washed. We want her looking her best."

Within her muddled thoughts, Taryn found the hatred she harboured for him and grounded herself in it, only to find it draining away, replaced by that comfortable numbness she'd become far too familiar with. As she returned to the silver set and the polishing tools, she searched for something, any emotion that would not slip through her fingers. She was battling her own brain, and part of her begged to give up. She wanted so badly to lie down and surrender. She was so very tired of fighting.

Yet she knew she could not submit to that fog. To submit would be tantamount to accepting that she was nothing more than what society said she was. To give up now would be to invalidate Sedition, to invalidate the very reason she had been created. And that one thing rankled her more than anything else. She could not allow herself to die. Not here. Not this way.

An image of Emmett came to her then, the Emmett she had met only moments—or was it hours?—before. She felt again the anger and the hatred flow through her, though it was weak, suppressed by the urge to obedience that filled her head. Emmett had followed her all the way here. He had given up his autonomy and his sight for a girl he barely knew; and even now, blind as he was, he could do nothing but ask for her. Taryn wondered at his selflessness. Could she abandon him to this life? With this fog clouding her mind, what other choice did she have? Even as she fought her internal battles, her hands mechanically polished silver.

"Have you notified Erikkson that we have her?" Lady Trace's voice came into focus once more. The hidden Taryn began to listen so intently that even her autonomous hands paused for the briefest of seconds. "The law says you must give him the opportunity to claim her before you sell her."

Erikkson is alive? Taryn felt dizzy. Not even the white fog could suppress all of the elation she felt. But of *course* he was alive. Hadn't that been why she was brought here in the first place? Storm wanted to charge Erikkson with treason... Taryn's gut sank when she realized how close Storm had been to the truth. Taryn could remember little, but she knew she had been built for some great and terrible purpose. She had *not* been built to be a slave.

"Why should I notify him? Surely, he will not remember a tiny, redheaded girl he abandoned years ago," Lord Bellham scoffed. "It was probably her disobedience that caused him to cast her out in the first place. He has a reputation for throwing broken playthings away."

No! Taryn's hands paused in polishing the silver spoon. The real Taryn stirred as anger at Bellham's words flowed beneath her skin, barely suppressed. He was wrong, utterly wrong, and he had no right to talk about Erikkson that way!

Taryn forced herself to take advantage of the icy calm that wrapped itself about her mind, keeping her from holding on to her anger, and tried to think logically. What did she truly know about Erikkson? She knew nothing more than the blind devotion she felt—a blind devotion that could be mere programming. What Bellham said about Erikkson could be true. Worse, all she felt she knew could be a lie. She could not remember much, just a few fragments of memory and the feeling that she was meant for more.

"Have you ever met him?" Lady Trace's voice grew lower, more excited.

"I did once, long ago. He was very young, and very strange. We attended the same party—before he became famous, of course. He was just beginning in his biomechanickal experiments. I believe that night was the last time he was seen attending that sort of public event. He has become quite the recluse. Even if I did inform him we had his—what was the girl's name? Tracy? Tess? Something along those lines: I never can recall what they title themselves. Regardless, even if I did inform him we had her here, I doubt he would leave his solitude just to come fetch her."

Taryn lost the thread of the conversation after that. The day passed in a daze, a flurry of colours and commands, and before she truly knew what was happening, she was back in the biomaton quarters. Taryn curled up on her narrow cot and closed her eyes. All she wanted was to sleep, to escape this cold, lonely existence in her dreams. There, she was free and whole.

It did not take long for her to fall asleep.

CHAPTER TWENTY-THREE

TARYN WOKE WITH A START IN THE MIDDLE OF THE NIGHT. SHE sat up, blinking, waiting for the white fog to fade from her eyes. She knew immediately that something was wrong. People shouted in the hall, feet pounded along the floor. A ripple of murmurs started as the other biomatons stirred, the commotion disturbing all but the deepest of sleepers.

Taryn squinted as her eyes adjusted. Light filtered in from the hall to her right, and dim, silvery moonlight came through the narrow windows to her left, but it was still dark in the room, everything washed in shadow. Without fully knowing why, Taryn rose and stood at the end of her cot. Her bare toes curled against the cold stone floor as she focused on the door-way, listening to the chaos beyond. The white fog that kept her mind in check had faded to a pleasant glow at the edges of her vision, keeping her utterly calm despite the commotion.

A man raced through the door and stopped, glaring at the girls in their beds. He was bare-chested and barefoot, his head shaved so close to his scalp that in the dark he appeared bald. Despite the shadows, Taryn could see there was a wildness in his eyes and his movements; his head jerked from side to side as he scanned the room. Something was not right about this man.

He turned, and his forearms reflected the silvery moonlight filtering in through the window. Taryn caught her breath; his forearms and hands were made entirely of clockwork. He was a biomaton.

A pair of burly night guards appeared in the doorway, calling out to the biomaton girls, most of whom were stunned and still at the appearance of this new man. "Do not go near him! He is armed and dangerous. Just give us space, and we shall stop him."

The biomaton seemed to panic, his eyes rolling wildly in his head as he backed away from the guards in the doorway, moving closer to Taryn with a piece of sharp metal held in one hand like a knife. The white fog that clouded her mind was beginning to move in again, narrowing her vision and blocking out the fear and excitement in exchange for the calm that came with following a direct order. She barely noticed the guards making their way slowly up the aisle between the rows of cots, toward the crazed biomaton.

A girl in the bed beside Taryn's stumbled to her feet and into the aisle. Taryn watched numbly as the biomaton man turned toward her, locking eyes with this new girl in his path.

"Get out of the way! Stay back!" one of the night guards cried, but the girl didn't seem to hear. Her eyes bore the glassy, empty stare of an obedient biomaton, oblivious to the danger. The crazed man lunged forward, closing the distance between himself and the girl. The metal shard in his hand gleamed in the moonlight.

Before she really understood what she was doing, Taryn leapt into the aisle. She placed herself firmly between the man and the girl, taking up a fighting stance. Her body moved of its own accord, separate from her mind, which was screaming at her to get out of the way. Had she gone completely insane?

Was living as a human automaton so bad that even her body would rather commit suicide than continue living this way?

The thoughts flashing through her mind were driven out as soon as the man attacked. Taryn countered him as easily as if he'd been moving in slow motion. She caught his wrist as he thrust the metal shard at her and twisted it backwards, forcing him to drop the weapon. It clattered to the floor, the sound ringing in her ears. *What am I doing?* she wondered, losing herself momentarily at the sight of the jagged metal glimmering in the moonlight on the stone floor.

A moment was all it took. The white fog clouded her mind once more, and the mad biomaton saw his chance. He drove a metal fist straight into her temple.

A burst of light spun across Taryn's vision as she crumpled under the weight of the blow. The white fog coalesced into a solid wall and shattered, shooting nearly tangible shards of debilitating calm through her mind. Taryn blinked, the pain momentarily disorienting her. When she raised her head, the biomaton was standing over her, his face expressionless save for the insane look in his eyes. Taryn raised her hands, sheer terror running through her as adrenaline pumped into her body like liquid fire, lighting every limb up like a firework. Her left hand tingled with phantom feeling, itching to return the blow that had knocked her down. She shoved her hair from her face and stood, fists raised.

The biomaton threw another punch at her, but Taryn was ready this time and blocked it with a forearm, then countered with a blow of her own. Her solid punch did not even faze the larger biomaton. He moved forward, his metal hands cutting through her defenses despite her attempts to keep him back. He got a fist around her throat, strong fingers locking down on her windpipe and cutting off her air supply. Taryn struck at him, struggling, but it only took seconds for her to realize she could not win this battle. He wrapped a second hand around her throat, and Taryn's legs went weak. She stumbled, falling to her knees while her vision dimmed and she struggled to breathe. She pried weakly at the metal fingers, but could not loosen their grip around her throat.

"Do not come any closer," the biomaton rasped in a hoarse half-whisper, speaking to the night guards just steps behind him. "Or I will snap her neck in two."

The guards halted. Taryn's vision darkened to a mere pinprick of light and her right hand slipped from the man's prosthetic, falling limp at her side. Her fingers brushed the cold stone floor, and something else: the sharp metal shard her assailant had dropped.

Something vital snapped inside her, as audibly as a bone breaking under a hard blow. Taryn did not hesitate to wrap her sluggish fingers around the cold metal. With every ounce of strength she could muster, she brought her arm around and drove the metal shard into the man's shoulder.

He released her immediately, crying out in pain as he stumbled backwards, clutching at the metal shard. It protruded from the space just above his collarbone, already bleeding profusely. He backed right into the hands of the guards, and they cuffed his hands behind his back and turned him toward the door. Taryn slumped to the floor, coughing and struggling to catch her breath. Her entire body shook as the adrenaline that had kept her upright leeched from her bones. One of the more aware biomatons ran over to her, but Taryn did not even notice her.

A guard came back to Taryn. "You. Girl. Get up. Come with us."

Dimly, she was aware that the numbing white fog had not returned. She'd somehow broken through the programming that kept her locked away. Had it been the fear? Or perhaps the blow to her temple? She supposed it must have been, but she was still too stunned to even fully understand what had just occurred.

"Did you hear me?" the guard repeated.

Taryn tried to nod, tried to force her shaking legs to hold her weight, but she found she could not muster the strength to stand. Breathing alone was as difficult as turning water into oxygen. The biomaton girl who had run over to help gripped Taryn's upper arm and helped her rise. The night guard then took Taryn by the shoulder. "Everyone back to bed," he said curtly as he led her from the room.

As her breath returned, Taryn found she could think more clearly. She hadn't any idea where the guards would take her and the crazed biomaton who walked ahead of her. Some of his blood had sprayed on her when she stabbed him; her right forearm and the linen bandage on her right hand were spattered with crimson. The sight should have bothered her, but she just stared numbly at it. It was too bright to be real blood; the colour was wrong.

She kept her head down, eyes on her feet, and prayed they would believe she was still under their control. But she knew the strange fighting instinct that had taken over her body and mind for those few moments was not something she should know, and certainly not something a person would want their otherwise perfectly programmed biomaton to know. The whole point of shutting her mind down so completely was to make sure she could not fight back; whatever had just happened, it wasn't normal. But perhaps, if she pretended to be docile, they would not punish her too much...

She *had* to pretend, she decided. Any signs she'd broken through her programming would at best land her back in the same mindless predicament she'd been in the last couple of days. At worst, she'd find herself in those terrifying fighting rings Harper had threatened her with. Taryn could not imagine being forced to fight. No. She would act like the good, obedient biomaton she was supposed to be.

"We finally caught him in girls' dormitory number three," the first guard announced, shoving the bare-chested biomaton into Harper's laboratory. For the first time, Taryn noted that the metal control panel on the back of the man's head hung open, swinging as he jerked his head back and forth. Taryn suddenly understood why he had gone insane, or at least, she thought she did. "He attacked this one before we could apprehend him."

The guard who had led Taryn along pushed her forward to stand beside the man who'd attacked her. The man *she* had also attacked. Taryn stared at the stone floor, allowing her eyes to glaze over. The stone right in front of her had been worn smooth with the tread of so many shoes. She was aware of Harper's shrewd gaze on them both.

"Biomaton 743. I should have guessed. The girl is more trouble than she is worth," Harper hissed with disdain. "But what happened to 431? He was not damaged when he escaped."

Taryn's guard spoke up. Despite everything, she thought he had a kind voice. She wondered what compelled him to work for a place like the Black Castle. "She leapt between him and another biomaton. She seems to have some kind of battle training, perhaps a kind of sub-network built into her programming. I have never seen a biomaton fight like that outside the ring."

Taryn swallowed hard and bit down on the edge of her tongue to keep herself from reacting to the man's words. Still, she was more terrified of her own mind in that moment than she'd ever been before.

"And she managed to do *this* to a biomaton trained for the ring?" Harper questioned. She moved over to the crazed biomaton, studying the wound left by the metal shard.

"Yes, ma'am. I believe he would have killed her if she had not acted."

Taryn watched out of the corner of her eye as Harper's expression changed to one of curiosity. "Very interesting." She ran a hand through her hair, which was coming loose from its tight bun. "Well, 431's break has not been entirely unproductive, it seems. It *is* too bad he could not handle the mental strain. Take him away, Mr. Stollen. You know how to dispose of him."

The crazed biomaton—431, though Taryn hated to refer to him with only a number—seemed to understand exactly what Harper's veiled threat entailed. His head jerked up. "No, please—"

"Terminate him immediately, Mr. Stollen. He killed two other biomatons and a guard tonight. He has become a liability."

The guard dragged the biomaton from the room; the man struggled the whole way, yelling wordlessly. The door closed, effectively quieting him. Taryn's heart was lodged in her throat. Her guard stood just behind her, one hand on her shoulder while Harper considered her.

"And as for you, 743..." Harper removed her spectacles and began polishing the lenses with a handkerchief. "What *am* I to do with you?"

Taryn did not move. She hardly dared to breathe. She kept her eyes glossy and unfocused, waiting. *Please, please believe I am still the obedient slave you want me to be.*

"I suppose I ought to examine her dampers once more. It is possible there is something wrong with her programming. It should not allow for such a thing." Harper stepped behind Taryn, lifting her hair while Taryn kept perfectly still. The plate in her head clicked open, and Harper hummed a little to herself. "Then again, she *is* an Erikkson."

"Pardon my asking, but I am new here," the guard interrupted Harper's monologue. "What was wrong with that other biomaton?"

Harper did not let go of Taryn as she answered. "Occasionally, a biomaton's mind is not strong enough to endure the strain of the programming. 431 was to be trained as a footman. Unfortunately, his previous master had used him in the fighting rings and neglected to inform us of that little fact when he sold him to us. The more restrictive dampers did not agree with him, and he snapped."

Taryn inwardly grimaced at the matter-of-fact way Harper discussed the biomaton's plight, as though it was just a broken toy and not a man's mind. Each time she thought she had glimpsed the very depths of human cruelty, the Black Castle proved her wrong.

"And yet, *this* biomaton is the one that continues to surprise me. Her controls have not changed. She should not have been able to do what you say..." Harper paused. "What did you say your name was?"

"Stark, ma'am."

"Well, Mr. Stark, by all accounts, this biomaton should have obeyed every word you said. I do not understand it."

Taryn felt her heart lift a little. Whatever was hidden behind that little metal panel on the back of her skull was lying in her favour. As long as she kept up the charade, Harper would never have to know the difference. She could keep her mind free and unfettered. She closed her eyes for a moment in gratitude.

"You said she was an Erikkson, ma'am?" Stark asked cautiously. "Could it be a part of her programming? I do not know much about biomatons, but I do know Erikkson is the man who created the clockwork assassin, Petrichor."

"You may be on to something," Harper allowed, but Taryn could hear a bitter note in her voice as she clicked Taryn's control panel closed. "Not a word to Lord Bellham about any of this, understood? He has a few prospective buyers attending tomorrow and he needn't worry about something going wrong. I will examine her more thoroughly when the buyers have gone."

"Yes, ma'am."

"Return her to the dormitory. She ought to rest after an encounter like that. If you notice any more abnormalities, report to me immediately."

"Yes, ma'am," Stark replied. He took Taryn by her shoulder again, steering her to the doors, but his touch was almost gentle compared to the way some of the other guards handled her. "Come now, biomaton. It is time to go back to bed. You are no longer in any danger."

Taryn allowed herself the tiniest of smiles. She'd found one kind person in this cruel hell, and it lifted her spirits somewhat. But what really brightened her outlook was the fact that when she arrived at her dorm, she would be free, unfettered, and in control of her mind once more. It was her last chance—her *only* chance—to attempt an escape. Tonight was the night. She just had to have enough patience to bide her time until she was left alone and the castle had settled down.

Taryn folded herself up on her cot when they reached the dormitory. The adrenaline had evaporated, leaving her feeling empty and spent. She was so exhausted it was difficult to think.

But she had to think, if she was going to try escaping. She would wait until she was certain most of the castle was asleep, perhaps two or three hours from now. Then, she would sneak past the guards. She would find her way down to the dungeons and free Emmett. The keys could be troublesome, but if she came across a guard who had fallen asleep, she could steal his. And from there, all she had to do was leave with Emmett at her side. They could steal a horse or escape across the moors on foot. She did not care; either way, they would be free.

It was a suicidal plan, nigh impossible. But despite that, she had to try. If for no other reason than to be able to say she had. All she had to do was wait.

She lay back on her cot, pulling the single, coarse woolen blanket up to her shoulders to ward off the castle's chill. Taryn closed her eyes. She would wait. In the meantime, she would rehearse her movements in her head. Yes, she could wait...

CHAPTER TWENTY-FOUR

"Get up, 743! We have one hour before you are to be presented!"

Taryn blinked her eyes open blearily, confused. Surely, it could not be morning already. She had just closed her eyes for a moment. She was still biding her time, waiting to make her escape.

"What is wrong with you, girl?"

Lady Trace grabbed Taryn's arm and forced her upright, and Taryn instantly understood that she had fallen asleep. It was morning, and she had missed her one opportunity for escape. She almost cursed aloud before remembering Lady Trace still thought she was programmed to obey. That was the one advantage she still had. She could not give that away.

Taryn rose and followed Lady Trace, who seemed flustered and overworked. It seemed Bellham had not given her enough time to clean Taryn up. "An hour? Hah! I should have liked three to spend on those red locks alone!"

She practically shoved Taryn into a room filled with gowns and beautification tools, all the things Taryn recognized from her days in finishing school: jars of expensive

French cosmetics, pots of perfume, brushes, hair pins, and soaps stood on shelves along the walls, lined up like fresh-smelling soldiers. The plush Persian carpet covering a portion of the stone floor was like a balm to Taryn's bare feet. In the middle of the room, a copper tub was already filled with steaming water. The humid air smelled of lavender. Three biomaton girls stood to one side, waiting. *Waiting for me.*

"Well, what are you waiting for? Into the bath with you."

Lady Trace unlaced Taryn's bodice while the other girls assisted, and they led Taryn over to the tub, pulling a silk screen between it and the door to protect Taryn's modesty. Though she wanted nothing more than to scream and attack them until they all left her alone, Taryn used every last ounce of her willpower to sit and allow the biomaton girls to scrub the grime from her body. Lady Trace herself washed Taryn's hair in a separate basin of water, carefully smoothing the tangles away as she worked. Taryn refused to allow herself to appreciate how good the hot water felt against her skin.

When Lady Trace was satisfied with Taryn's newly scrubbed appearance, they raised her from the tub, dried her with a fluffy towel, and dressed her. The new frock was not as thin as the one she'd worn before, but it was dull grey in colour, and the most basic of shapes. The only unusual aspect of the gown was the missing left sleeve, allowing it to reveal her full clockwork arm from shoulder to fingers. So, they did not use glitter and finery to sell their biomatons. She wondered how she would be marketed wearing this drab dress. Not as a beautiful thing, a showpiece to be displayed... Or perhaps her clockwork *was* the showpiece all on its own.

Taryn realized with a sickening in the pit of her stomach that this was the day that decided her fate. She briefly wished she had never broken her programming. At least then she would not have to run this gauntlet, fully aware of her shame.

The girls pulled Taryn's hair into an elaborate updo,

creating layers of curls that wound in and out of a bun high on the back of her head. It was an elegant hairstyle, one Taryn could never have risked in her former life because it would have revealed the metal plate on the back of her head. One girl applied a touch of rouge to Taryn's lips, while a second polished Taryn's prosthetic, and the third trimmed and filed her nails. Taryn bore it all like a statue, feeling as if she'd lost something vital within herself. Whatever spark had kept her fighting had finally died. This was all that was left for her. There were no other paths to take. All other doors were closed.

Finally, Lady Trace deemed Taryn ready. She took her from the room, into the finer part of the castle, and then down a red velvet carpeted hall Taryn did not recognize. Lady Trace paused outside a thick oak door, eyeing Taryn once more before fixing a stray copper hair with two fingers. "Make me proud, biomaton," she muttered, and it sounded like something she repeated every time she prepared for a sale. She pushed the door open.

Taryn found herself at the center of attention in a very strange sitting room. There were chairs arranged in a rough semicircle around a large central space with no furniture. Windows inlaid in the far wall let in natural light, and bookshelves stood against the walls adjacent. The room was roughly hexagonal in shape and done up in dark reds from the walls to the draperies, and all of the chairs were upholstered in black leather. The light provided by both the windows and the fireplace on her left offset the dark décor and filled the room with warm golden light. Across the room and slightly to her right, there was a solid wood mahogany desk.

Six people were present, three she recognized and three she did not know. Lord Bellham leaned against the desk, a snifter of sherry held casually in his left hand. He had dressed up for the occasion in a black velvet cravat and charcoal suit, and his colourless eyes watched her closely. Mr. Cody and Mr. Potter, the two men who had come to inspect her before, sat on either side of the open space, and there was a mousy looking man near the window wearing tweed and toying with a pair of *pince-nez.* An unfamiliar woman in a blue dress stood beside Bellham, her hands folded neatly in front of her, and to the woman's left, a man in a navy blue tailcoat busied himself at the cart upon which Bellham kept drinks. Taryn heard the *chink* of glasses.

"Gentlemen, allow me to introduce the newly discovered Erikkson," Bellham announced. All of the buyers turned to Taryn. All save for the man in the navy coat, who continued to fix his drink with his back to her. "Come closer, 743, so we can see you."

Taryn complied with the order, though she would rather have killed herself than allow these men to leer at her the way they did. But she was trapped. There was nowhere else to go. Her fingers tightened in the folds of her skirt.

"This is the Erikkson?" The mousy man spoke up, peering at her. He fingered a gold pocket watch chain hanging from his garish red silk waistcoat.

"Yes. Quite a find, is she not?"

"She cannot be his."

"Take a look and see for yourself. His marks are there," Bellham answered, gesturing at Taryn with his glass. He seemed relaxed and authoritative, as though he controlled everything that happened in that room; obviously he had done this thousands of times.

The mousy man got up and moved toward Taryn, studying her, walking around her slowly. She did her best to imitate the hollow, glassy-eyed stare that she'd observed on other biomatons. Nothing would be worse than for Bellham to discover *now* that she was not under his control.

The mousy man studied the control panel on the back of her head, and Taryn waited, heart pounding, until he closed it again without touching any of the controls there. "She is an Erikkson, but *that*," he gestured to her arm, "is not his work."

"She was rather damaged when I purchased her. We had to rebuild her."

Taryn bit down hard on her tongue to keep from letting out a string of angry curses.

"It is too bad," the mousy man said, studying her again. Taryn forced herself to stare blankly at a spot on the floor near the window, but the man was so close she could smell him: a combination of dust and pipe tobacco. "It brings her value down considerably."

"Understood," Bellham answered. "Do I take that to mean you are not interested, Mr. Schmidt?"

"Nonsense. This is the first operational Erikkson specimen I have seen. The museum would be very pleased to add something like her to its collection."

Taryn's heart stopped. *The museum?* She suddenly knew exactly who this man was. He was Mr. Schmidt, the curator of the London Museum of Bioclockwork, the same museum she had visited with Royal and their classmates. This was the man who had torn a biomaton boy open for schoolchildren to gawk at. And here he was, peering at her, discussing her value as a *specimen*. It was both sickening and terrifying. Would he dissect her immediately, she wondered, to display all that clockwork she was told she hid inside? Or would he keep her behind glass, or in a barred cage like an animal at a zoo? Taryn wrapped her right hand around her left wrist to hide how much she was trembling.

"You do understand this is only the first of several private viewing sessions I have scheduled?" Bellham asked haughtily. "With a rare piece such as this, we must give all our loyal collectors time to respond."

"Opportunity to give you an offer, you mean," Mr. Potter scoffed from his seat.

"You have no right to scoff," Mr. Cody shot back. Taryn would not look at him, as she remembered he looked so much like Royal it stung. "You would use her for menial labour!"

"Oh, and what would you do with her?" Mr. Potter sneered.

"I should not waste her on farm labour! She is a work of art, a thing to be treasured, not destroyed!"

It was becoming more and more difficult for Taryn to remain still and silent. Shame and hatred weighed on her shoulders, and their words only added fuel to the fire.

"No biomaton is worth any more than the manual labour it can perform," Potter retorted.

A new man's voice broke in. "I believe you are at the wrong event if you think that, Mr. Potter." Taryn's breath caught in her throat. She knew that voice. The fifth man, the one who wore the navy blue tailcoat, whose face she had not seen, was someone she had truly believed she would never see again.

Ace.

CHAPTER TWENTY-FIVE

IN ONE HAND, ACE HELD A CRYSTAL TUMBLER OF WHISKEY. HIS ice blue eyes bored holes into her own and Taryn felt her throat tighten. It was his fault she was here in the first place. How *dare* he come back here! How dare he come to gloat over her when she was helpless? And what about Emmett?

Ace rose, draining his glass in a single swig before setting it on the desk. Taryn heard it land from where she stood, an audible clunk that sealed her fate. "This biomaton is, as Mr. Cody says, a collector's piece. And look at her." He strode toward her and it took all of Taryn's willpower not to balk or leap at him and attempt to strangle him; both impulses vied for her attention. "What a pretty little thing you are." He breathed the words in her face, so close that she could smell the whiskey on his breath as he grinned lopsidedly. "An excellent addition to my collection."

Taryn's blood began to boil. What was the point of all this? Did Ace really return just to rub her face in her captivity? What could possibly be his goal?

Mr. Potter snorted and stood. "I can see I am bidding in the wrong league. Lord Bellham, I should be most obliged if you would prepare a sampling of the best labourer biomatons for me. I shall return to inspect them tomorrow." He swept his dark coat to the side and left. Taryn did not feel any relief at his exit. There were still two in the room who were interested in purchasing her.

"Tell me, biomaton, do you dance?" Ace questioned, holding a hand out to her.

"A little, sir," Taryn replied mechanically. She resolved to keep up this charade until it could not go on any longer.

Ace took her right hand in his left as his right hand moved to the small of her back and hugged her tightly to him. As he did so, he muttered "play along" in her ear. So, he thought they were playing? This was all a game to him? He was so near she could hear him breathing, and she hated him so vehemently in that moment that she shook. She knew he could feel it. "Do you enjoy parties, biomaton? Balls?" He began to lead her in a simple waltz step, one she'd learned at finishing school.

"I do not understand, my lord," Taryn replied numbly. *What* was *he doing?*

"That is the life you will have with Cody. A plaything for the guests at his extravagant parties. Passed from child to child until one breaks you beyond repair and you are thrown away."

"How dare you!" Cody exclaimed.

"But if you go with Schmidt, you will spend the rest of your life as a caged animal. Now tell me, which do you prefer?"

"Master Crenshaw, I do not approve of my guests insulting one another," Lord Bellham said loudly, interrupting Ace. Crenshaw? So, he hadn't told Bellham his real name. He was posing as a buyer. But that still didn't explain what he was doing here, breathing whiskey fumes into her face.

Ace grinned, causing his ice blue eyes to flash. "I was merely explaining what is next for the biomaton."

"Then you are not interested in purchasing her?"

"Of course I am!" Ace stopped the dance and gazed at Taryn. She stared through him, her face set in stone. "How could I resist a biomaton like this? But I do not think I can afford the prices I am anticipating will be bandied about in a moment."

Taryn stared at him: bewildered, lost, and worst of all, hurt. Some tiny, pathetic place within her had hoped he was here to rescue her. But this was what she deserved for hoping. She should have learned long ago that hope was not worth the effort.

"I will give you five thousand pounds if I can take her now," Cody exclaimed, getting to his feet.

"You know that is not how this works," Lord Bellham said testily.

"It is what I am proposing. I have seen enough. I should like to take her before any other charlatans get in the way."

Ace scoffed and pushed Taryn away, turning to face Cody. Taryn noticed one hand briefly reached for a pistol he was not wearing before it landed on his hip instead. "Charlatan? I beg to differ, sir. I shall have you know my collection of rare bioclockwork is renowned the world over." He sneered at Cody.

Taryn was truly, utterly lost. Why had Ace returned after so callously leaving her to this fate? To gloat? To stall? And why would he pose as some strange aristocrat interested in purchasing her? She could not understand his presence here; once again, he had thrown a wrench into the way she understood the world worked.

"Sara, please escort the biomaton back to her quarters," Lord Bellham said calmly over the palpable tension in the room. "I see no need for her to stand there while we discuss business."

Sara nodded and beckoned Taryn, leading her from the room. The woman had remained so silent while they had discussed Taryn, she'd almost suspected she was a biomaton, too. But Taryn could see no metal plate, no clockwork enhancements. The woman was human.

She led Taryn a little way down the hall, then slowed, paused and looked back at Taryn with tears in her dusty corn-flower blue eyes. "I am so sorry," Sara said, her voice cracking. Taryn stared at her numbly, not quite understanding. "I am so sorry you had to experience that."

Taryn did not know what to do. This could be another trick, yet another test to see if they could manipulate her. She kept her face blank and did not reply.

Sara sighed. "Of course he would turn your dampers so high you cannot understand what I mean. That is how he keeps all our biomatons in the household." She shook her head.

Taryn frowned, looking over the woman standing before her in her blue dress. She still did not understand. "Who are you?" The words felt foreign on her tongue after being silent for so long. "Why would you apologize to me?"

Sara looked surprised. "So you *can* understand me! He said he'd shut you down—"

"It did not stick," Taryn answered, deciding to gamble with what seemed like a kind and understanding woman. "Who are you?"

The woman glanced away. "My name is Sara Bellham. Lord Bellham is my husband."

Astonishment turned Taryn's mind to jelly. She blinked dumbly at the woman.

"My father married me to Bellham to gain wealth and influence. I do not agree with his treatment of your kind, but he makes me join him in his private showings. He feels my presence adds a touch of femininity to the proceedings." She shuddered. "I am so sorry."

"Why do you not leave him?" Taryn asked.

Sara smiled sadly. "I am as much a prisoner here as you. My chains merely consist of this ring on my finger, rather than a number tattooed on my arm."

Taryn watched the woman warily, aware that she could still just be pretending, playacting in order to trap her. She could go and give Bellham all the information Taryn had just given her—but the sorrow in Sara's eyes begged Taryn to trust her.

"What is your name?" Sara asked.

Taryn's clockwork fingers went to the still sore numbers carved into her arm. "Taryn, though Lord Bellham has done his best to erase it."

"And what did you do before—" Sara broke off.

Taryn's face twisted.

"Before I became a *machine*?" she spat.

"That is not what I meant," Sara spluttered. "I am sorry."

Taryn shook her head, waving away the woman's apology. "I attended Grafton's School of Mechanicks in London."

Sara's expression changed, her eyes widening. A spark of bitter pride ignited in Taryn's chest at the woman's expression. "Yes. I would have a promising future if not for my deformity." She shook her head again, trying to clear it of the painful memories rising unbidden behind her eyes. "Now, were you going to take me back to my quarters?"

Sara didn't seem bothered by the dismissal. "This way."

"Miss! Wait!"

Taryn stiffened, her fists clenching into white-knuckled weapons at her sides. She recognized Ace's voice even without looking at him.

"May I have a few moments alone with the biomaton?" Ace caught up with them, smiling that fake, cocky smile.

"I am sorry, sir, but I am not allowed to do that," Sara answered pleasantly. Taryn's stomach tied itself into knots.

"Please. I shall not be long. I only want a few minutes."

Sara peered at him suspiciously. "I cannot. You need to arrange it with Lord Bellham."

Ace sighed. "Do you recognize this symbol?" He'd rolled his right sleeve rolled up, revealing the brand of clockwork and crossed cutlasses on the inside of his forearm. The blood drained from Sara Bellham's face. "Good. Then you understand I am here on royal orders. I shall accept any responsibility for what happens. I merely require a few minutes with the biomaton."

Sara Bellham nodded, still pale. "There is an empty study you may use. I will wait outside." She opened the door for them. "I apologize for my hesitancy; I did not realize who you were."

"No need to apologize, my lady. I understand." Ace nodded politely to her. He grabbed Taryn's left elbow and steered her into the room. Taryn shook him off, and he let her go to close and lock the door behind them. Fear and anger welled up within Taryn as she turned and stared at him, hands in shaking fists by her sides. She had a horrible moment of *déjà vu* as they stood there, facing off. They had done this once before, and it had started this entire, ugly mess.

Ace came toward her and she wanted to back away, wanted to get as far away from him as she could, but there was nowhere to go. The room was tiny, and the furniture was arranged so she could go nowhere.

"Taryn," he whispered. His blue eyes were fathomless pools of ice. "Taryn, what have they done to you?" He put his hands on her cheeks, and had he been anyone else, the gesture would have seemed affectionate. "Lord Bellham said—"

Taryn tore herself away from him, unable to play her role any longer. "What are you doing here?" she hissed. "Have you not done enough damage? You *washed your hands* of us! Do not taunt me by returning to gloat!"

Ace paled, taken aback by her response.

"Please," she said, her voice diminishing. "If you are here to kill me, do it swiftly. I do not think I can bear much more of this."

"What?" Ace's voice cracked, his expression bewildered. "Taryn, what are you talking about? I am not here to kill you; I am here to help you."

Anger again surged through her, hot and blinding. "It is a bit *late* for that," she spat. "If you did not notice, they are currently negotiating my bleak future. And is this not what you believe I deserve?"

He shook his head. "I—I did not understand before, and I was wrong."

"So, what? You came to apologize? Is that what this is? Your apologies are worth *nothing*. Emmett is blind now—" She felt her throat constrict, and her eyes welled with tears she did not want him to see, yet could not stop. "*Blind*. And all of this is your fault! So take your apology and go, Ace."

Ace looked stunned. "Emmett—blind?" His hands went to his face. "My God. What have I done?"

Taryn was trembling, tears streaming down her cheeks, but she had said her piece. Now she waited to see if he would abandon them again.

"This is the life you condemned us to," she muttered after minutes passed in silence. "I hope you are satisfied."

Ace's hands dropped to his sides and he stared at the tattoo on her arm, the numbers that identified her as Lord Bellham's property. "Is there anything at all I can do to help you?" he asked quietly.

A bitter, ugly laugh rose in her throat. "You can take that pistol I know you have hidden on your person and shoot me in the head. Then, you may go find Emmett and do the same to him."

Ace's face went as white as a sheet of paper. "I cannot do that, Taryn."

"Then you condemn us both to a fate worse than death!"

Ace shook his head. "Surely, we can get you both out of here."

"You do not understand, Ace! You see this mark on my arm? It means I belong to Bellham until I am sold to another. They have guards everywhere. There is no escaping this place."

Ace sat heavily on a chair, his head in his hands. "I am sorry, Taryn. I am so sorry."

Without really knowing why, Taryn sat on his left, her hands in her lap. She was still furious with him, still hated him for letting Storm sell her to these people, and even more for discovering her and taking her from her previous life in the first place. He *had* come back, in the end. It was simply too late.

Ace touched the number on her forearm gently. "Have they hurt you?"

A bitter smile twisted her lips. "No more than they believe a freak like me—half independent human, half obedient slave—deserves."

"And how much is that?"

Taryn's face crumpled, the tears returning without her permission. "Why, Ace? Why did you leave us here?"

"I did not understand what would happen to you," Ace answered quietly. "I was wrong."

"I hated you," she said through her tears.

"I know," Ace replied. "And I deserve that."

Taryn did not answer. She wiped her face with her hands,

trying hard to remove the evidence of her tears. They both sat in silence until a knock came at the door.

Ace rose, putting on the haughty voice and attitude he had put on earlier. "Yes?" he asked.

"Sir," Sara Bellham's voice came through the door. "I need the biomaton."

"I will just be a few minutes longer."

"No, I need her now. Please, sir. It is urgent."

Taryn rose as well. "I must go, Ace. They will get suspicious."

He clasped her wrist. "I will find a way to get you out of here!"

She shook her head. "Go back to the *Dauntless*. You can do nothing more for me. Although, if you truly mean to help, you may try to get Emmett out."

He nodded. "Good luck, Taryn."

"Good luck, Ace."

She pulled on her own persona, the hollow-eyed biomaton she was meant to be, and stepped from the room.

"Come quickly," Sara Bellham urged. "There is someone here to see you."

Inwardly, Taryn groaned. The last thing she wanted was to stand still and silent while someone else talked about her as they had all morning. But she followed Sara, knowing she had no other choice as she led her back to the first room, the study in which she'd faced all those scrutinizing eyes.

A single man occupied the room, and he rose as Taryn entered. He had auburn hair dusted with grey at the temples, and forest green eyes that crinkled at the corners. He wore a fine, brown suit with a copper cravat and a striped waistcoat. He was the man she'd seen so many times in her dreams. She was standing before her creator, the biomechanick Lord Anthony Erikkson.

CHAPTER TWENTY-SIX

"Sedition!" he exclaimed, coming toward her. He wrapped her in an embrace, but Taryn stood stiffly, her head spinning so fast she did not know if she could even stay on her feet. "How beautiful you have grown, little one," he said, holding her at arm's length. Taryn shifted uncomfortably and managed to extricate herself from his grasp.

"Hello, Master Erikkson," the words fell from her lips automatically, and she hated herself for saying them. She did not know this man. He had abandoned her.

"Hello, my dear," he replied, smiling. He had a nice smile, all crinkles at the corners of his eyes and lines in the stubble around his mouth. If she had to guess, she would have said it was the smile of a man who did so often. It unsettled her. "It has been a long time."

"Why are you here?" she asked, her voice flat and hard.

"I am here for you, of course."

Taryn couldn't breathe. She pressed her hand to her stomach and whispered, "You abandoned me. You wiped my memories and sent me out into the streets to die. You took my humanity, you took my love, and you left me with just enough human emotion and free will to make me abominable to every slave owner in England." Taryn could feel her voice cracking, her throat tight. "Why would you come back for me now?"

His green eyes softened and he touched her shoulder tenderly. "I never abandoned you. I was watching you, every step of the way."

Taryn scowled at him. "How could you have been watching? I suffered!" *I caused other people to suffer.* Who was this man to come soaring in, thinking he could solve everything?

"Will you allow me to explain from the beginning, little one?" he asked, leaving her question unanswered, hanging on an invisible string between them.

Taryn hesitated, wondering where all this could possibly be going. Was Erikkson here to "claim" her, to take her back as his property? Or had he agreed that Bellham could sell her in exchange for letting him see her? Eventually, Taryn nodded silently; this explanation was what she'd been seeking, whether she liked it or not. He led her to the chair most recently vacated by Mr. Cody, and together they sat. As he gazed directly into her eyes, his earnestness made him seem young, despite the touch of silver at his temples.

"When I found you in the wreckage of that fire, I truly did not know if you were going to live. You clung to me like an infant on our way home, and I knew the only way to save your life would be with bioclockwork. At the time, regulations were becoming stricter. Biomatons were ordered to be shells, rather than functional human beings with clockwork to assist them in living normal lives. They were no longer considered any better than machines." His hands fiddled with one of the buttons on his striped waistcoat. Mechanicks' hands, she realized: scarred and rough with long, slender fingers. "I never wanted that for you. But I built you with the proper dampers so you would not be taken away from me if they came looking."

Taryn sat in silence, trying so hard to understand this man and how he fit into her life as she'd known it.

"I raised you to be Sedition, to help the biomatons who could not help themselves. Your mind I left untouched, for the most part, except for those dampers which were unavoidable. It is true, you cannot love, but you are otherwise human." He paused for a moment, considering his next words. "But you were so young, and I had sheltered you from the world. You did not understand why a revolution was necessary. And though it hurt me, I knew I would have to let you experience the world outside my care, so you would understand what was at stake."

Taryn stared at him, digesting the fact that her entire life had been manipulated, directed from afar by this man she did not know, but who seemed to know all about her. "Why did you take my memories?"

"So that it would all be real to you, rather than a game to play until I returned."

"You do not understand!" she exclaimed, rising, angry now. A lock of her copper hair fell out of its pin to tickle her cheek. "I nearly starved! I was always afraid of being discovered, always afraid a bobby would catch me. The other children treated me like a pariah. Finishing school was no different, because I was an orphan! And here—" She choked on her words and had to catch her breath before continuing. "Here I have been tortured with the very controls you placed in my head. They treat me like an animal, a creature to possess as they like. And here you are saying you have been watching all this time and I do not—I *cannot* believe you. I have been alone, and I will always be alone." She made her way across the room as she spoke and stopped, gazing out the window at the grey moors while her hands twisted in the folds of her skirt.

"You were never alone, little one," he said gently. "You had

Royal, and his family. It took time, but you did find people you could trust."

Taryn turned and stared at him, heart pounding. "You know about Royal?"

"Of course I know about young Master Stokker. I was watching you, every step of the way."

The muscles in her jaw tightened. "You allowed the people here to torture me."

He frowned, his expression hardening. "You have mentioned that twice now. How did Lord Bellham hurt you?"

She wanted so badly to refuse him, to tell him she would not talk about it because she did not know him, but even as she opened her mouth the words came spilling from her lips. "He used the plate on the back of my head. The first time, he said it was to demonstrate that it was working properly. The second time," she started, but again had to pause and collect herself. "It hurt so much, I fell unconscious for a moment."

Puzzlement crossed his face. "Will you allow me to examine the plate, please?"

Taryn nodded nervously. She did not really want someone else poking around in her head, but the desire to know what was wrong with her outweighed her trepidation. She turned, clenching and unclenching her fists, and trying not to panic as she felt him open the control panel on the back of her head.

A tickle picked up in the back of her mind, and Taryn jerked away from his hands. He placed a steadying hand on her shoulder. "Keep still, little one," he murmured gently. "I will not hurt you."

Taryn wrapped her clockwork hand around her right wrist and forced herself to do as he asked.

Erikkson was silent for a long time. Too long. She stood, nervous and barely breathing, as she waited for him to say something—*anything*. Finally, she heard the *click* of the plate closing.

"The control I used to keep you from feeling the terrible violence that accompanies the removal of your love has been turned off," Erikkson said, speaking slowly and deliberately. "That is what you felt."

Taryn's stomach churned. All the violent, terrible thoughts she'd been feeling were because of a switch in her head? She shut her eyes, feeling more like a monster than she had the entire time she had been at the Black Castle. "Can you fix it?" she asked hoarsely.

"To try to turn it back on could incapacitate you, perhaps worse. I dare not risk it."

A frustrated noise sounded in her throat as anger flooded through every limb at Bellham, at Harper, and even at Erikkson. Her hands began to shake, and she could not stop them.

"Taryn, look at me," Erikkson said quietly.

She turned, but not before arranging her face in what she hoped was a venomous, defiant glare.

"This does not change anything about you. You can learn to control it, as you can learn to control anything else."

She simply stared at him. "What is it you want from me?"

"I want to take you away from this place. It is time you return to Elmhurst Manor and take up the mantle of Sedition."

"I do not want to be Sedition."

"It is what you were built to be."

"I do not remember any of it." Her voice had grown hard and cold. "You took that from me, remember?"

His emerald green eyes took on a sorrowful sheen. "You remember nothing?"

She shook her head, and he pressed his hands over his face, completely obscuring it from her view. "I am sorry, little one. You were meant to have your memories back by now. I never thought they would be locked away for good."

"So I will never remember?" she asked bitterly.

He gazed at her, eyes filled with tears. "I am afraid I do not know." He reached out and gently touched her arm. "But if you come with me, I promise I will do all I can to help you regain your memories. You shall not be a slave, as you are here. You will live freely in my home."

"I would be a different kind of slave. A slave to your cause."

Erikkson shook his head. "I will not force you to become Sedition. That is your own decision."

He was offering her an escape. It was a way out, a way to avoid the life she was otherwise destined for. So why did she hesitate? He was giving her the decision. She could choose to have no part in his war, in the terrible purpose she'd been built to fulfill. And yet… Taryn's entire life had been manipulated up to this moment, every step led to this decision, and every fiber of her being wanted to refuse, simply to defy him. But even as she stared at him, another emotion welled within her, unfamiliar and strange. She had an intense desire to please this man, to make him proud of her. It was an emotion she did not understand.

"I will go with you," she answered cautiously, "on one condition. There is a young man here who has suffered greatly on my account. He was not a biomaton before we came here, and Bellham gave him the cruelest of grafts because of me. I want you to take him from this place as well."

Erikkson nodded. "I would not dream of leaving him."

CHAPTER TWENTY-SEVEN

TARYN WAITED QUIETLY, WEARING HER SUBMISSIVE MASK ONE last time as Erikkson discussed the payment for Emmett with Bellham. Bellham was loathe to let Erikkson take Emmett, as he had not "finished with him" yet, but finally agreed to give him up, along with Taryn, for what seemed an exorbitant price. While Bellham left the room to fetch Emmett, Taryn was alone again with her creator.

She crossed to the mahogany desk in the corner of the room when the glint of metal caught her eye. There, nearly hidden by a fat, leather-bound ledger, was a small gold fob watch. Taryn lifted it slowly, almost reverently, allowing the scuffed casing to catch the light as it turned. Sure enough, it was the same pocket watch Dr. Harper took from her days ago. Taryn clutched the watch to her chest as tears welled in her eyes. Her final piece of Royal had returned to her; they hadn't used it to rebuild her arm after all.

"Did Lord Bellham replace your arm?" Erikkson asked abruptly.

Taryn glanced at the prosthetic, which still felt like a stranger's limb attached to her shoulder. "Mine was crushed aboard the *Dauntless*. Lord Bellham's mechanicks built a new one for me." She turned back toward her creator, slipping the watch into her pocket before he could notice.

Erikkson went to her and examined her arm, his expression cold. "Bellham may own the largest biomaton empire in England, but his work is of poor quality. I shall replace that arm when we get home. It does not suit you."

Uncomfortable, Taryn tried changing the subject. "Can you take whatever switch they used to control me out of my head? I do not think I could bear to feel like that again."

Erikkson looked thoughtful, a hint of a smile playing at the corners of his eyes. "Did someone turn off your programming for you?"

A crease appeared between Taryn's brows. "No. I—I cannot figure out how I managed to wake up. There was a wild biomaton in the girls' dorm last night. He attacked me, and just like that, the horrid, obedient part of me was gone. I suppose I was frightened. Or perhaps it was because he struck me." She hesitated. "I knew how to fight back, but I do not remember learning any of that."

A smile broke out on Erikkson's face. "That would be your deeper training coming into play. When you fought the other biomaton, your mind was able to break through the obedience programming Bellham activated. All your battle training will come back to you, in time."

The blood drained from Taryn's face as she considered this. It was not the fear, or even the pain that had awoken her mind the night before, but instead the terrible violence she so hated within herself. She began to feel like a monster again. "But can you get rid of it? Can you keep them from ever using it against me again?" she questioned, almost frantic in her desire to have full control of her brain.

"You broke through the programming on your own. No one can touch your mind that way again."

"You mean it has been broken?"

"In a way. It still appears to be working. If anyone were to check your control panel, it would indicate that you are still under their control. But clearly you are not. I will explain everything more fully to you later. For now, let us focus on leaving this place."

At that moment the door opened, and Taryn assumed her mask again as Bellham led Emmett into the room. Someone had taken the time to change his clothes, and he wore a simple pair of linen breeches and a white shirt. His forearms were wrapped in bandages, and his face was no longer smudged with dirt. He looked weary and submissive, his head downcast so she could not see his clockwork eyes, but Taryn noted that his hands were balled up into fists: a fighter until the end.

"744, allow me to introduce you to your new master, Lord Anthony Erikkson," Bellham said. Taryn watched Emmett's face shift ever so slightly when he heard the name.

"Hello," Erikkson answered, but he said nothing else to Emmett. "We have a long journey home, Lord Bellham, and I should like to get going now. I shall have your payment sent to you, as we agreed."

Bellham's mouth pressed into a thin line. "Take them," he said shortly. "I do not know what your plans are for the boy, but I believe I would rather *not* know. It was a pleasure doing business with you." His tone indicated he may have preferred the pleasure of doing business with a venomous snake.

Erikkson's responding grin had a sarcastic edge. "Oh, the pleasure was all mine."

Bellham's expression hardened, but he opened the door for them without another word as Erikkson touched Taryn's elbow.

"Will you please help 744 find his way? I will lead you both out."

Taryn nodded and took Emmett's hand, settling it gently

in the crook of her elbow. He pressed his fingers into her arm, as if he recognized her even though she had not spoken. Together, they left the room: the blind boy, the biomaton who believed she was human, and the creator she did not know.

As soon as they were down the hall and out of Bellham's earshot, Emmett spoke up. "*Monsieur,* what did they do to Taryn?"

"Why do you not ask her yourself?"

Emmett's grip tightened on Taryn's arm. "*Belle.*"

She touched his hand with her clockwork one. "It is all right, Emmett. I am all right now."

He leaned his head nearer to hers and whispered, "You found your maker!"

"He found me," she whispered back. *And I am still not certain that is a good thing.* But this was as close to free as she could get, now that she had been discovered, and Erikkson seemed at least to care about her. Perhaps she would regain her memories, perhaps she would not, but at least she would not be the property of someone who saw her as just an object. It was not the life she had imagined or dreamed of, but she thought she could learn to at least accept it.

There was a coach waiting for them outside, drawn by a pair of large black horses and driven by a young biomaton who had clockwork covering the right side of his neck. He smiled when he saw Taryn and Emmett, then clambered down from the box and opened the door for them. As Taryn approached, he swept into a low bow.

"My lady Sedition," he said respectfully.

Taryn's face flushed. "I am not Sedition," she stammered.

"Just Taryn for now, please, Emilio," Lord Erikkson told the driver, and the boy smiled broadly.

Taryn helped Emmett into the coach and sat beside him. The interior was fine though not extravagant; the curtains hanging over the windows were black muslin, and the cushions were comfortable, but not upholstered with velvet like the ones Lord Stokker had. Still, Taryn found a strange feeling of nostalgia wash over her as she sat in the coach. It almost felt like going home.

Erikkson clambered in and sat across from them, his forest green eyes following Taryn closely. She glanced away, swaying with the movement of the carriage as Emilio climbed back into his seat and took command of the horses. Outside, the Black Castle loomed above them, its stone towers hard and unyielding. It seemed to taunt her, to whisper that she could never truly escape its grasp. She slipped her hand into her pocket and cradled her watch, its weight in her palm anchoring her in the moment.

Erikkson leaned across the space between them and took Emmett's hands. "Allow me to introduce myself formally," he said gently. "My name is Anthony Erikkson. I am a biome-chanick and lord of Elmhurst Manor. We are on our way to my home now, where you will not be a slave, but rather a part of my ever-growing family. I want to thank you for all you sacrificed for my Taryn. I honour you as one of the noblest of men." To Taryn's surprise, Erikkson then placed Emmett's hands on his face, so that Emmett could "see" him. "*Merci beaucoup, mon ami.*"

Emmett lit up, his face becoming animated just as it had the first time Taryn spoke in his native tongue. "*Tu parles français?*"

"*Un peut,*" Erikkson laughed. "*Comment t'appelle tu, mon ami?*"

"*Je m'appelle* Emmett LeBeau," he answered. "Thank you for taking us from that place."

"You are welcome. Now, both of you rest, enjoy the coun-tryside. The journey is several hours, even with my fastest horses. There will be time enough to worry about the future when we arrive." He leaned back as Emmett settled his hands in his lap and returned his gaze to Taryn. "For now, let us focus on putting this place behind us."

Taryn turned away, watching the countryside rattle by. She fingered the small, black numbers inked on her forearm, and wondered if she could ever truly put the Black Castle behind her. She doubted it. The Black Castle had changed everything for her; her world was turned upside down because of it. Whatever the future held, it would be in part because of what she'd experienced there.

Settling in to the swaying of the carriage, Taryn wondered how her life would change. Was she truly Taryn any longer? Would she ever again be the girl she was before she boarded the *Dauntless*?

The horses pulled the coach with its silent, broken passengers ever onward into the night, and into the future.

The End

ABOUT THE AUTHOR

E. M. Wright is a writer and editor from Portland, OR. She has a Bachelor's degree in English from Warner Pacific University, and currently works at a small homeschool bookstore.

She has two cats, and a thousand imaginary friends. When not writing, she likes art, baking, and long walks with her boyfriend. She's never taken down a horde thirty of ninjas, but suspects if she had to, she would fail. She's not an award-winning author (yet), but she did win the Pulitzer prize in her sixth grade classroom for an article on the chupacabra. Her deep love of storytelling leads her to write everyday, and she firmly believes that sometimes the best way to tell the truth is through fiction.

A REQUEST...

Did you enjoy Sedition? *Reviews keep books alive . . .*

Help by leaving your review on either GoodReads or the digital storefront of your choosing.

We thank you!

www.ingramcontent.com/pod-product-compliance
Lightning Source LLC
Chambersburg PA
CBHW050840190726
48286CB00007B/2164